Illustrated for Murder

Janie Dean

ISBN: 979-8-84261-830-9

Cover designed by Melissa Woolard - m.woolard@hotmail.com

Janie Dean
Facebook@JanieDeanBooks

Independently Published in the United States of America
ISBN: 979-8-84261-830-9

Other Titles by Janie Dean

Square One

Amazon Review: *5.0 out of 5 stars* Intriguing
"A good story, well-conceived and written. Loved the characters."

Inheritance Most Deadly

"The best book I ever read! Amazing ending!"
~ Ruby S., reader

Available on Amazon.com in print and ebook!

Acknowledgements

I want to thank Melissa Woolard for my great cover and for her expertise in publishing this book. I want to thank Lee Roland, Lis'Anne Harris and all the Ink Plotters for their critiquing comments. Thanks to Abigail Sharpe and Tim McDougal for their assistance with computer problems. Thanks to Kim McDougal for pictures of her rescue dog, Millie, for the cover. And, thanks to family and friends for their support and encouragement.

Chapter One

"You put a toilet in my living room!"

"Aunt Tilly," Tori Statton uncurled her fists and extended open hands towards the white-haired tyrant ensconced in a wheelchair, "we talked about this. The rehab center wouldn't release you unless you had easy access to a bedroom and a bathroom. You agreed to converting your living room."

She exchanged glares with her great aunt. She loved Aunt Tilly. She really did, but how could such a sweet looking old lady be so stubborn and cantankerous? Though Tori had to admit, as she reminded herself why she was here, a broken leg might put anyone in a bad mood.

"That meant pushing my sofa over and putting my bed in here. There's a bathroom in the hall."

"Half bath." Tori managed to answer patiently. "And the toilet is in the bathroom I had built along with a closet." An exasperated sigh escaped with her words. "You agreed to the renovations."

Tilly waved her hand around the room. "You chopped my living room in half."

Not quite. "Your living room was huge. This *bed*room is still large." Tori emphasized the word bed and ignored her aunt's exaggeration. The New York apartment she had shared before abandoning city living was barely twice the space this one room occupied. Tori ran her hand through the tangles of her curly hair.

Her aunt muttered complaints as she tapped on the arm of the wheelchair.

"Fine." Tori grabbed the handles of the chair and wheeled it across the carpeted floor and into the wide hall, steering it toward the front door.

"Stop! What are you doing?"

She ignored her aunt's strident voice and jerked open the door. "I'm taking you back to rehab. When you are able to climb those stairs, they can bring you home. In the meantime, I'll have them tear out the wall."

"Don't be so snippy, girl. It's done and I may as well make use of it."

Tori hesitated long enough to give her aunt something to think about then pushed the door shut. Thankfully Aunt Tilly didn't notice Tori hadn't grabbed her car keys and that the wheelchair access ramp was out the kitchen door, not the front. She remembered those 'eyes in the back of her aunt's head' when she was a child and erased her smile before turning around.

"Lock it!" Tilly commanded, pointing toward the door. "You did change all the locks like I said, didn't you?"

Yes, she had, but with that tone from her aunt, she would have happily lied about it.

Tori turned the dead bolt. Pleased that her bluff worked, she pivoted the chair and headed back to the bedroom. "I put keys to the new locks in the top drawer of your nightstand for whenever you're ready to leave the house on your own." A frown replaced her suppressed smile. "What's so important about changing the locks?" Aunt Tilly had insisted she get them replaced and to do it before Tori spent a night in her aunt's Victorian home.

"I'm not clumsy enough to fall down those stairs by myself." Her indignant voice held a tinge of bitterness as her eyes traveled over the worn, faded blue runner covering the steps to the second floor. "Someone was in my house. I heard a noise and was partway down the stairs when they snuck up behind and pushed me."

"What!" Tori stopped so quickly she felt her passenger jerk forward and put a hand on her aunt's shoulder to steady her.

"I'm supposed to be the deaf one here. I said someone pushed me."

Tori moved around the wheelchair to face her aunt. Truth and determination reflected from her aunt's sharp blue eyes. Tori's body tingled at the thought that someone had actually broken into her aunt's home and tried to harm her.

"I've been here for over three weeks. I've seen you every day. Why didn't you tell me something sooner? Did you report this to the police?" Tori folded her arms over her quivering stomach.

Tilly waved her hand in dismissal. "Those know-it-all nurses thought I was delirious and ignored me. A broken leg doesn't make you delirious."

"No, but sometimes the medicine they give you for pain can make you hallucinate. You should tell someone again. Call the police and report it now that you are not so medicated."

"I'm telling you." Aunt Tilly jabbed a finger in Tori's direction. "They had their chance. Those EMTs wouldn't listen when I told them to call the police. It's up to us to find out who pushed me." She leaned back in her wheelchair.

"Us?" Whoa. Tori had agreed to take care of her aunt until she was back on her feet, literally, not play detective.

Tori rubbed her forehead as she remembered the mussed drawers she had straightened when Aunt Tilly's antique furniture was moved downstairs. She had thought the messiness was due to age. Was there any truth to the claims? Had an intruder reentered the house while her aunt was hospitalized before Tori arrived and changed the locks? Or had they rummaged through things while she lay injured and unconscious at the bottom of the stairs? A shiver ran through her. She had been sleeping alone in this big house for three weeks.

No. Maybe Aunt Tilly hit her back as she fell and remembered it as a shove. She studied the certainty on her aunt's lightly lined face. Though she was in her early seventies, she looked ten years younger.

Or maybe Tilly wasn't mistaken. Tori's shoulders slumped and she asked, "Who has a key besides Alice Clayton?" The next-door neighbor had been the one to find her aunt moaning at the bottom of the staircase and called 911 for help.

"You didn't give her a new one, did you?" Tilly sat up straighter in the wheelchair and speared Tori with a challenging look.

"No. She asked though. I told her when I left, I was sure you would give her a new key." Tori hesitated then asked, "You don't think she had anything to do with your fall, do you?"

Tilly shook her head. “No, but she has my key hanging by her back door and half the time she doesn’t lock up her house. Anyone could have taken it.”

“If someone did, they returned it. She ran home to get it when you didn’t answer the phone or her knocking at the back door.”

“Humph. She just wanted to borrow sugar for her morning coffee. Too much trouble to make a grocery list so she doesn’t forget things she needs. And I haven’t given anyone else a key,” Tilly grumbled. “Except,” Tilly’s shoulders rose and fell in a deep sigh. “Talbert Hatchett probably has one somewhere.” Disgust twisted her mouth as she said the man’s name. “I gave one to his wife Mary, but she died months back in a bad car accident. Don’t know what she was doing out in that storm. She didn’t drive at night and certainly not when it was raining.

“Didn’t want to bother asking him for it. I doubt if he knows it’s lying around in his house somewhere. He might have even thrown it out when he got rid of a lot of Mary’s things.” The corners of her mouth turned down as she tilted her head. “Talbert did that pretty quick. Guess he couldn’t stand all the reminders.” Her biting remark did not reflect sympathy.

Tori swallowed hard. She moved behind the wheelchair to grip the handles. She had agreed to take care of an injured aunt, not deal with real or imagined criminals. Her voice was a little high as she attempted to change the subject. “Would you like to go back and watch some television or would you like to...” Oops, she almost said *nap*. “Rest awhile?”

“I’ll watch TV while you fix us something to eat. Maybe after lunch, I’ll lie down for a bit.” Tori’s stomach still quivered, but Aunt Tilly seemed to relax as she was wheeled into the room that would now be used as the living room. It was like a family room with a well-worn hunter green sofa and a recliner facing the television, but Aunt Tilly called it the sunroom. It had been remodeled years ago by combining two rooms. A rear wall of windows overlooked the backyard with its rose garden and birdbath.

Tori had spent several afternoons in one of the Adirondack chairs placed in the shade of the large oak that used to hold a rope swing. Sketching the garden and adding fairies hiding among the colorful flowers helped her recoup from a morning spent with Aunt Tilly's complaints about her forced stay at the rehabilitation center.

"I have to warn you. After a few of my meals, you'll be thinking how good that food was at the rehab place." She had listened to plenty complaints about the food and had even brought a few takeout meals to her aunt.

Tori handed Aunt Tilly the crutches she had learned to use at rehab and helped her move into the recliner. Her slender frame was only three inches taller than her aunt's shrunken five-one, but she was strong enough to manage if her aunt needed more help. Tori raised the footrest and handed her aunt the remote.

"Those meals were worse than the mud pies you used to make. A person could starve to death before they get well."

"I thought you liked my pies." Tori smiled at the memory of those childhood mud pies. Aunt Tilly had raved over her culinary skills. Her mother had raved about the mess and dirty clothes. Her real food didn't taste much better than those pies.

Her comment was answered with a laugh. As Tori escaped down the hall toward the kitchen, Aunt Tilly called after her, "You be thinking who could have broken into my house and pushed me down the stairs."

How was Tori supposed to guess who might have broken into the house? She hadn't seen her aunt since she was a child. Some quarrel between Tori's mother and her dad's aunt had ended visits. She was here because her mother had manipulated Tori, pointing out that she was Tilly's only living relative and Tori could write her children's stories anywhere, but her mother would have to cancel a scheduled cruise.

Mud pies. Tori smiled. It was good to get a glimpse of the aunt she remembered.

Between de-stressing after visits with Aunt Tilly and supervising the addition of the bathroom and closet, Tori hadn't gotten much writing done. She had set up her computer in what her aunt called the library but so far it was just collecting dust.

Tori rummaged through the junk drawer until she found a rubber band. She brushed her curly, shoulder length hair back from her forehead with her hand and secured it in a makeshift ponytail then jerked open the fridge. She half suspected her mother had scheduled that cruise after she had gotten the call from the rehab center so she could coerce Tori into coming instead.

Her shoulders heaved with a sigh as she studied the contents of the fridge. She'd bought groceries earlier in the week, passing up the quickie microwave meals she usually ate. She'd fix soup and sandwiches for lunch and save the casserole Alice had brought over for supper. Maybe a few hints to the neighbor would elicit more food and Tori wouldn't have to tackle creating a meal from those groceries.

Tori added water to the tomato soup she had poured into a saucepan and turned the burner on low to heat while she made turkey sandwiches. The handyman Alice had recommended hadn't commented about any evidence of forced entry when he changed the locks, and she certainly hadn't snooped around to notice anything out of place. She wouldn't know what was out of place anyway. But she would examine the doors for scratches or whatever when Aunt Tilly napped—uh rested.

In the meantime, she'd talk to Aunt Tilly about why someone would push her down the stairs, not that she was going to investigate. She looked around the kitchen and thought of the rest of her aunt's home with its dated wallpaper and worn furniture. If someone broke in, they had to be sorely disappointed in finding anything worth stealing. She grinned. Unless Aunt Tilly had a mattress or a shoe box full of money tucked away somewhere. And why push her down the stairs? There were plenty of closets and corners to hide in or behind. They just needed to wait until she went back to bed to make their escape.

Tori loaded everything on a tray and headed back to the sunroom-cum-living room. It had been too long since she had spent time with Aunt Tilly. She didn't know her well enough to determine if this wild idea was a stubborn mistaken belief or due to the mental sharpness she glimpsed when she and her aunt locked glares.

She needed to think of this time as a chance to become reacquainted with her dad's aunt instead of being a caregiver for a needy relative.

When Tori finished rinsing lunch dishes and stacking them in the dishwasher, she returned to the sunroom intent on questioning her aunt more about her 'push' down the stairs and why or what someone would want to steal, but Aunt Tilly was quietly snoring. Her frown was gone and laugh lines marked her relaxed face. The trip home and settling in must have tired her aunt or she was rebelling against using her new first floor bedroom.

Tori turned away and looked out the windows into the backyard. The roses were starting to bud. There were a few full blossoms of red, pink and yellow spotting the bushes with color. She'd cut some while her aunt slept and put a vase of them in her new bedroom.

She shifted her gaze to the oak tree where her swing used to hang. She smiled at the memory of sitting on the wooden seat and hanging on the side ropes while her legs pumped back and forth to make the swing go higher. A smile still on her face, Tori tiptoed out, leaving her snoozing aunt. If only her Aunt Tilly's attitude could match her sleeping demeanor.

Chapter Two

Tori sat in the library. Her mind was as blank as the computer screen in front of her. Blank as far as the plot for her new project. Her brain buzzed with thoughts of a break-in and deliberate attempt to harm an old lady. She sighed. An old lady from Tori's point of view. It certainly didn't seem to be her feisty aunt's opinion of herself.

After finding Aunt Tilly quietly snoring, she had taken time to check the wood frames of the front and back doors for any signs of fresh dents or splinters. She had even called the repair man who had changed the locks before settling at the desk. He didn't remember seeing anything questionable but offered to install alarms and outdoor motion lights. She passed on those. Yeah. Maybe they'd consider his suggestion of an extra deadbolt to lock at night. She'd let him know.

After Aunt Tilly's adamant insistence that she change locks before she spent a night in the house, Tori had wandered through the house, checking the windows while the door locks were replaced. They had all been locked.

Tori returned her attention to the computer and typed a few words which she immediately deleted. She was successful enough with her picture books for young children to quit her day job if she sublet her New York apartment and moved to cheaper digs, a.k.a. her old room in her mother's house. Tori hadn't even unpacked before her mother had convinced her to come take care of her aunt who was recouping from a broken femur.

She put her fingers on the keyboard and forced her wandering mind to focus on her current story, a tale of magic and adventure for middle grade readers. More plotting, fewer pictures than the fantasy fairy stories she usually wrote and illustrated. Half hour later the words were finally flowing when she was jerked out of the story by uneven thuds of Aunt Tilly's crutches coming down the hall. Tori's shoulders tensed in anticipation of dealing with her aunt. She jumped up to go help then sat back down. The time in rehab had been spent making her aunt mobile and independent. Tori's job was to help, not take over.

The thumping stopped in the library doorway. "There you are. I was wondering if you'd decided I was too much trouble and taken off."

"Aunt Tilly, getting you walking again and back to living your life is not too much trouble." Dealing with your attitude might be. "And if I leave, I won't sneak off. You'll see me going with suitcases in tow." Tori shifted in her chair and grinned. Her aunt raised an eyebrow then continued through the double doors into the library with a repressed smile puckering her lips. She dropped clumsily into a chair near the desk. A crutch slipped from under her arm and clattered to floor. Her mouth twisted as she glanced down at the offending object then looked up at Tori, her eyes sharp. She nodded at the computer. "You looking up stuff on the internet thing about breaking into houses?"

Tori sighed and clicked on save. "No. I was trying to work." She didn't say write. Too many people took that to mean she wasn't busy and it was alright to interrupt. She looked over the top of her screen. But that's exactly what happened anyway. Aunt Tilly's expression said deal with it. The sooner we do, the sooner we can dismiss it or call the police. At least that's what Tori wished it said. Aunt Tilly expected her to play sleuth and solve some mythical or maybe not so mythical crime.

As if to prove her point, her aunt said, "I'm counting on you to find out why someone broke into my house. You're a writer. You know all about researching and using that computer to find out things." She pointed at Tori's laptop.

If only she could click on Google and type in 'who broke into Aunt Tilly's house.' She almost grinned at the thought. "I write stories for children about fairies. It's imagination made up in my head."

Aunt Tilly leaned forward. "Your Uncle Hank was a smart man. Your dad was a smart man. Your mother diluted the strain, but I bet you still have plenty of smarts."

Tori set the mouse aside and folded her hands on the desk. Her shoulders dropped in capitulation. "Let's start with why you think you were pushed."

Aunt Tilly banged the crutch she still held on the faded Turkish rug covering the floor and answered, "I know someone pushed me because I was hanging on the rail, moving slow so I could listen for the noise that woke me up. A big hand shoved me right smack in the middle of my back." Her body shook. "I twisted and grabbed the banister with both hands, and he hit me again on my shoulder. Hard enough to knock my hands loose," she ended emphatically. "I guess I got knocked unconscious, too. Next thing I remember was my neighbor wailing and them hauling me off to the hospital. I tried to tell them what happened, but they just poked a needle in my arm and things blacked out again."

Tori felt her eyes widen. Knots gripped her stomach as she listened to her aunt speak with conviction. "You didn't ask to speak to the police when you were in the hospital?"

"Humph. Those nurses treated me like I was some dimwit. Talked to me real loud and real slow like I was senile. Bad enough being in the hospital, I didn't want them sending me to some loony bin."

Tori stood and paced. Her aunt absolutely believed someone broke into her house and pushed her down the stairs. Tori was starting to believe it also. "Why didn't you say something to me?" She stopped and faced her aunt, hands on her hips.

"I heard the nurses tell you I was delusional, out of my head. Didn't think you would believe me either."

Tori looked out through the library door. She probably wouldn't have believed this story coming from her elderly aunt ensconced in a hospital bed, dosed with pain meds.

She shook her head and frowned. "I hired workers. Paid them extra to do a rush job on your bathroom. They made a big mess. There was dust everywhere. I've wiped and cleaned everything. If there were any fingerprints, I've polished them away." She sat and placed her elbows on the desktop, fingertips rubbing her temples. "Do you have any idea what the burglar was looking for? Do you have money or jewelry hidden?"

"What I have hidden no one's going to find," Tilly announced cryptically.

"But if they thought..." Tori stopped as Aunt Tilly waved her words away. She gripped her hands together then continued,

"Well, we have to talk to the police, even if I've destroyed any evidence the intruder might have left."

"They aren't going to do anything," Aunt Tilly objected.

"Probably not, but they'll have to write a report." Tori thought about how she had straightened her aunt's drawers after she'd had movers carry her aunt's bed, dresser and nightstands downstairs. They had removed the drawers to make the furniture lighter, so the messiness of the drawer contents wasn't a result of them being moved.

"Aunt Tilly, do you keep your drawers and closet real neat?" Her aunt sat up straighter and both eyebrows shot up. Tori rushed to clarify, "Do you fold things and put them in neat stacks, or do you just toss them into a drawer, like socks in one drawer, underwear in another?"

"I'm not natty about it, but I fold and pile things when I put them away. Why?" Her aunt answered, voice a little stilted.

Tori rubbed the chill that snaked down the back of her neck. She definitely believed someone had been in her aunt's house and had rummaged through drawers the night her aunt had tumbled down the stairs. Or maybe they'd come back while she was in the hospital. Her brow furrowed. "I wasn't going through your stuff. I just straightened the clothes in your drawers when I was arranging your new bedroom. Things were definitely not in piles. If you're up to it tomorrow, maybe you can check to see if anything is missing.

"The kitchen wasn't bad, but..." Tori waved her hand and looked over her shoulder toward the built-in book shelves that covered the far wall which had no windows or doors, "I straightened books and organized this desk." She dropped her arm to her side, hand curled into a fist.

Aunt Tilly pursed her lips. "The books might get dusty, but they are neat on the shelves just like your late Uncle Hank kept them." She pressed on the arms on her chair and struggled to stand. "If you hand me that dang crutch, I'll go start checking right now." She pointed to the needed support on the floor near her feet.

Tori hurried to hand her aunt the crutch, then helped her balance while she adjusted both under her arms.

Aunt Tilly thumped awkwardly across the room. She turned

to head down the hall and called over her shoulder. "Well, come on, girl. I can't balance on these sticks and dig through drawers. Get my wheelchair and come help."

Tori gave her computer a longing glance and sighed. She hoped she could remember where she was heading with the current scene. At least she wasn't facing a deadline. She clicked save again and went to retrieve the wheelchair from the sunroom.

When Tori entered the bedroom, her aunt was already sifting through a drawer.

"Can't see why anybody'd want to steal my old lady underwear. And I didn't hide anything in here."

Tori pushed the chair closer to her aunt and said, "Why don't you sit. I'll put the drawers on the bed so you can go through them."

Aunt Tilly grumbled but settled in the chair and handed the crutches to Tori. "Put these where I can get at them when I need them later. Did you wash my clothes when you hauled everything down here?"

"Uh, no. I didn't know it had been someone besides you messing up your clothes." Tori put a drawer on the bed. She hesitated a minute then pivoted on her heel and headed to the laundry room for a basket. Dang, it would mean a lot of washing, but she wouldn't want to wear clothes some creep had been pawing through either.

She put the basket beside her aunt. "We'll start with light colored clothes and make a separate pile of dark. Put what you'll need most in this first load. Underwear, night gowns, whatever you want to wear tomorrow."

They worked methodically through the drawers. Tori carried the overflowing basket out and started the first wash load. She returned carrying a can of disinfectant spray. "I'm going to spray the inside of each drawer," she said as she dropped the empty basket beside her aunt." If the smell is going to bother you, I can do it in the hall."

Aunt Tilly gave a distracted wave and muttered something which Tori interpreted to mean 'go ahead.' Buried in the low sounds, she thought she caught an actual 'thank you.'

Three washer loads later Tori stuck the casserole in the oven to warm. She'd tried several times to get Aunt Tilly to take a break and save the rest until the next day, but her aunt was like a runaway horse with the bit in its mouth. She'd have to stop for dinner. Tori chopped greens, tomatoes and cucumber for a salad and set the oak table in the kitchen. She didn't remember her aunt being an eat-in-the-dining room person. That was Tori's mother. When the timer dinged, she lifted the casserole out of the oven and put it on the stove top. The aroma of chicken and vegetables had her mouth watering. Brushing a curly strand of brown hair out of her eyes, she went to pry her detective aunt from her clue-finding mission.

As she entered the disheveled bedroom, her aunt was digging through her jewelry, most of which seemed inexpensive. "Find anything missing?"

"This is all cheap stuff, but in the dark the thief might have thought differently. As far as I can tell, nothing's been stolen. I don't know what he could have been looking for. If it was vandalism, seems like he would have thrown stuff out onto the floor." Aunt Tilly shook her head, a puzzled look on her face.

"Well, you have to stop now. Dinner's ready." Tori lifted the jewelry drawer and slid it back into the dresser. Grabbing the chair handles, she wheeled around and headed for the kitchen. She parked the chair at the round table tucked into a bay window area.

A blue padded seat where two could sit curved under the glass panes of the window that overlooked the side yard. Chairs were usually arranged around the table, but Tori had pulled all but one away to make room for the wheelchair. She moved the casserole to the hot pad on the table beside the salad and poured two glasses of ice tea. She settled across from Aunt Tilly and waited while her aunt piled food on her plate. Her busy afternoon must have given her an appetite. Or this was better than a turkey sandwich.

They ate in awkward silence both taking second helpings of the creamy mixture. Alice was a good cook. Tori was going to follow her plan to drop hints in hopes it would have Alice dropping off more casseroles. A buzzing sound from the laundry room momentarily interrupted the clink of forks against plates. Another load of clothes was ready to be folded and returned to proper places.

Tori sighed and put down her fork. She took a sip of tea and focused on her aunt. She stumbled over the question that had been bothering her all afternoon since, drawer after drawer, nothing seemed to be missing. "Is anyone angry enough or hate you enough to want to seriously hurt you?" She couldn't bring herself to say someone might have meant to kill her relative.

"This is a small town, Victoria. I've quarreled and made up with most people living here. Nothing serious enough to make me want to kill them or them kill me. Thought about putting Ex-lax in brownies I took over as a make-up gift once, but your Uncle Hank talked some sense into me."

The use of Tori's given name emphasized the fact that her aunt had not addressed Tori by name since she had arrived and faced the quarrelsome lady in a rehab bed. Was it finally acceptance that Tori was here to help, or a warning not to eat brownies? Aunt Tilly didn't pussyfoot about using the word kill.

Tori spread her hands in front of her. "Then what? Someone was in your house and pushed you down the stairs. Why?"

"Danged if I know. I don't have that shoe box of money you asked about and I'm not about to replace comfortable padding with crinkly money that's going to make noise every time I roll over in my sleep. And I don't know anything about anybody that everyone else in town doesn't know too so I'm not likely to blackmail anyone." She pushed herself back from the table and started propelling the chair toward her room.

"I'll get a glass of water for your nightstand and come clear the floor in case you need to get up during the night," Tori called after her aunt as she removed food and dishes from the table. She grabbed the piece of foil that had covered the casserole and pressed it around the top of the dish.

Aunt Tilly wheeled back into the doorway. She gave a snort of laughter. "You telling me I got to go to bed now?"

Tori rolled her eyes toward the ceiling and blew out a heavy breath. She turned toward her aunt. "No. You can stay up as late as you want and you can get up early or sleep late in the morning. When you wake up, we'll eat breakfast and go talk to the police. I'm through detecting today." Actually, she'd been the female lackey. Her aunt had done all the detecting.

Aunt Tilly rolled away muttering something about snippy people.

"Yeah, wonder where I got that from. Must be hereditary," Tori replied in a voice too quiet to be heard by her departing aunt, who didn't seem to be hard of hearing at all.

She finished putting food away and cleaned the kitchen. Dropping ice cubes in a glass, she filled it with water and grabbed the empty laundry basket. Her aunt was in the bathroom. Tori could hear water splashing. She quickly gathered clothing that had been dropped on the floor by the bed when the basket had been in use elsewhere and escaped before Aunt Tilly emerged.

She put the basket down beside the washer to be dealt with the next day and headed toward the library. Maybe she could get a few pages written before climbing the stairs to her own bedroom. She settled at the desk and read the last words she had typed.

It was as if the eyes in the back of her own head were working overtime. Tori kept picturing the books stacked at angles and toppled on the floor. She pivoted her chair and studied the shelves. She had straightened the books but hadn't examined them. She didn't know that she should have. She could leave them until morning but the thought that something might be hidden between them or tucked inside would keep her awake. Or not. She hadn't dusted the books, just straightened them. Could she talk the police into dusting for fingerprints?

Chapter Three

It had been that kind of day. Tori pulled her small Honda into a handicap parking space in front of the police station, relieved to finally be here. The small lot was almost filled. Trucks and cars were scattered among official law enforcement vehicles. She dug in her purse for the handicap tag the rehab center had suggested she get and hung it from her rearview mirror.

Aunt Tilly sat rigidly in the passenger seat. "What if they don't believe me? Maybe we should just skip this reporting business."

So that was it. Her aunt was afraid the police would react the same way as the hospital staff. "These people are in charge of protecting us. Let's hope they are more discriminating than those nurses. At least we're starting a paper trail."

"Paper. Humph. It'll take a lot of trees to get them stirred up," Aunt Tilly muttered loud enough for Tori to hear.

Tori pushed her door open and slid out. "I'll get your crutches and then I'll get your car door," Tori said. Why did she think her aunt would be patient enough to let her do that? All she needed was to have to pick her aunt up from the pavement, though there were plenty of men in blue around to help.

Aunt Tilly woke up impatient and snapping this morning and Tori didn't want her attitude to antagonize anyone until they had a chance to report the break-in.

Of course, Aunt Tilly had unfastened her seat belt and opened the door before Tori could get there. At least her aunt had waited. More likely, she hadn't had time to exit the car. Aunt Tilly swung her right leg out first. As the toe touched the pavement, she tugged the hem of her navy culottes over her knee. Tori reached in to lift the casted leg.

Her aunt shook off Tori's attempts to help. "Gotta learn to do this myself. You aren't going to be around every time I want to get off my butt." She grabbed under her cast and lifted it out of the car. She wobbled for a moment but managed to stay upright and get the crutches tucked under her arms.

Tori's patience was starting to wear with her aunt's defensive attitude, or was Aunt Tilly being offensive? The word belligerent belonged somewhere in that description. Tori slammed the door with more force than necessary and hurried after her aunt, who had taken off like a pro. Aunt Tilly stopped at the steps leading into the building. There was a handicap ramp off to the side but that was ignored.

Uniformed officers stood on either side of her smiling aunt. Tori blinked. Did Aunt Tilly actually wink at the man on her left? Nope, it had to be the sunlight making her squint when she turned her head.

Both men grinned at whatever her aunt had said before Tori caught up and each grasped an elbow. The two officers helped her aunt hobble up the steps and through the door.

Shaking her head, Tori stepped aside to let a couple exit then followed her aunt's path and entered the building. A few people sat in chairs pushed against the wall, their expressions bored, impatient or scared. A man with a teenager in tow argued with the officer at the check-in desk. An overhead fan stirred the musty odor of humanity.

Tori spied her aunt across the room. Her escorts had vanished and she had the attention of two different men. Both wore suits but had the demeaner of police officers. The older one was bulky with a slight paunch, like an athlete that hadn't continued an exercise regimen. His thinning brown hair showed wisps of grey at the sides. The younger officer earned a second look. His dark hair was longer than the buzz that many of the officers wore and he definitely had continued to exercise. He had broad shoulders that made you want to dump your troubles which was what she was about to do.

Tori looked down at her white sandals, a little self-conscious as his eyes swept her from head to toe. As if assessing her like he would a suspect. At least her pink toenails were freshly painted and perfectly matched her pink blouse. Too bad he couldn't see them from across the room.

Aunt Tilly was beaming. Her shoulders looked more relaxed in spite of being pushed up with the use of crutches. She nodded Tori toward them. As she neared the threesome, her aunt began introductions. "This is my niece Tori Statton, Jim's daughter. Tori, this is Sam Lauris. He and your dad went to school together. Stars of the football team. Sam knocked the other players out of the way so your dad could score touchdowns."

Sam Lauris shifted his weight, his ears tinged pink. "Now, Miss Tilly, that's a bit of an exaggeration." He turned his attention to Tori. "Nice to see you again. You were just a toddler last time." He smiled his greeting. "Truth is your dad could catch even the worst pass and he was fast."

Tori returned his smile. She didn't remember Sam, but meeting someone who had known her dad gave her a warm feeling.

"Don't be modest, Sammy," Aunt Tilly said and patted his arm. "What's your rank now? I've been reading about all your brave deeds."

The pat and words deepened the red tinge to Sam's ears. "Captain, ma'am." Sam stepped back and nodded toward the officer beside him. "This man grinning like a coon is Detective Derrick Stone."

Tori looked up at Derrick. He was slightly taller than Sam who was five-ten, maybe five-eleven. His smile and the humor in his blue-gray eyes softened the strong lines of his face, but the smile lines accented the tiny scar at the corner of his left eye.

"Happy to meet you ladies."

Sam interrupted Derrick's greeting and asked, "What brings you down to the station?"

Tilly straightened on her crutches. "I want to report a burglary at my house."

Sam frowned. "You should have called and let the police come to you."

"Except the EMTs thought I had just fallen down the stairs and hauled me off to the hospital. Wouldn't pay any attention to the fact that someone broke in." Aunt Tilly's voice grew more indignant as she talked.

"Perhaps we can go somewhere and explain what happened." Tori suggested.

"Of course," Sam agreed. He looked around the room and ran is hands down the lapels of his tan suit jacket. "I'm sorry I have a meeting and can't handle this myself, but Detective Stone will be glad to assist you. It was nice seeing you again, Ms. Tilly and you, too, Tori." He shook his head. "You sure remind me of Jim with that curly brown hair. He was always complaining about it, but the girls loved it. Got his blue eyes, too." He glanced at his watch.

"I hate to leave but the job's calling." He clapped Derrick Stone on the shoulder. "Take good care of these ladies."

Aunt Tilly slumped as Sam turned on his heel. She heaved a heavy sigh as her attention followed him out the door.

Sam's words managed to erase the smile from Officer Stone's face as well. The blank cop face that replaced it gave Tori a sinking feeling. Did it mean he wasn't going to give any credit to what had happened to Aunt Tilly?

So much for dumping on his shoulders.

Accepting his new assignment, Derrick Stone gestured toward the doorway behind him. "Let's go back to my desk and discuss this break-in." The smile he gave Tori and her aunt was a pale version of the one he wore when he was enjoying the earlier conversation and Sam's discomfort. He walked slowly into another room filled with desks, some occupied, most cluttered with papers and folders. The buzz of conversations competed with a phone ringing across the room until the caller hung up or it went to voice mail.

Tori followed the determined pace of her aunt. Derrick paused at a desk near the back of the room and helped Aunt Tilly have a seat. He pulled a chair over from another desk for Tori. She shifted uncomfortably on the hard metal and glanced over at her relative. Aunt Tilly's chin was thrust forward, and she had a white-knuckle grip on her crutches.

Detective Stone took off his gray suit jacket and draped it around the back of his seat before he settled in. Tori could actually see the metal top of his desk. Papers and folders were stacked neatly in a pile. He tapped a few keys on his computer. "If you told the responding team about a break-in, they will have notified the police. What is your address?" As Tilly told him, he typed it in. "Yes, an emergency responder called and reported the patient claimed a break-in. There was no evidence of that, but he was following procedure. No one was home when an officer went to the scene."

"Of course not. They had hauled me off to the hospital," interrupted Tilly.

"When he questioned neighbors, one of them, Alice Clayton, had a key and after checking with the victim in the hospital, accompanied the officer as he inspected the premises.

"So that's what she was yammering about. I couldn't understand what she was wanting, finally told her to do whatever." Tilly shrugged.

Officer Stone glanced at Tilly then continued to read. "There were no visible signs of forced entry or interrupted burglary. He concluded the incident was an accidental fall." He turned from his computer and looked at the women seated in front of his desk.

"That's not true." Tori leaned forward. "Drawers had been rifled through and books knocked from shelves. No one talked to my aunt about what happened. It's just too convenient to call the whole thing an accident."

The officer held up his hand, stopping Tori's angry words. "We don't close cases just because it is convenient." The blank face remained but the clipped reply was tinged with a bit of his own anger.

Detective Stone opened a drawer and pulled out a recorder. "It's standard procedure to record a statement if that's okay with you." He focused his attention on Tilly.

She nodded her permission.

He turned to Tori. "Were you in the house when the break-in occurred?"

Tori gave a negative shake of her head. "I came to take care of Aunt Tilly when she got out of rehab. I'm afraid I dusted and cleaned any evidence or fingerprints."

Derrick Stone hesitated, then continued, "You can explain that after Ms. Statton tells us what happened." He turned on the recorder, stated the date, named people present and the purpose of the report. Then he pushed the microphone closer to Tilly and asked her to tell what happened and when.

Aunt Tilly repeated the story she had told Tori, speaking slowly and distinctly as if the police officer might not be able piece together the facts or the recorder might not catch all her words.

Derrick Stone picked up a pen and made a few notes on the pad in front of him as she talked. Tori wondered if he actually believed her aunt or if his actions were for show.

When Tilly finished, he frowned and asked, "When no one talked to you, why didn't you report this sooner? It's been over five weeks since this happened."

"I tried to," Tilly huffed indignantly. "When the emergency people came to my house, I told them to call the police, but they ignored me. At the hospital, they thought I was delusional. One nurse even said something to my niece about my having dementia."

Derrick directed his attention toward Tori. "Do you believe your aunt's story?"

"Absolutely," Tori declared.

At her words, Aunt Tilly relaxed against the back of the chair and gave a satisfied smile.

"You don't think she may have experienced some confusion from her fall or be suffering from dementia?" he asked, tapping his pen on his desk.

Tori sensed her aunt stiffen beside her. Anger heated Tori's cheeks. She stared at Detective Stone. "She may be cantankerous and a pain in the...a pain, but her mind is clear and sharp."

Tori saw the officer grin at her near blunder before he ducked his head and scribbled more notes. She had noted a sharpness in his eyes. Too bad he was just going through the motions. Probably spending more time because Aunt Tilly knew Captain Sam Lauris.

Derrick Stone's next few questions had Tori rethinking his seriousness.

"Miss Statton, you said you wiped away any possible evidence. What did you mean?"

"It's kind of confusing calling my aunt Ms. Statton and me Miss Statton. Please call me Tori." She took a deep breath. "My aunt is unable to climb the stairs. We converted half the living room into a bedroom and added a bathroom. Rehab wouldn't release her unless she had access to facilities. There was a lot of dust from the construction. I cleaned the whole downstairs, except I haven't dusted the library yet. Only straightened the books.

"I hired men to move her bedroom furniture to her new room." She leaned forward to emphasize her observations. "They removed drawers to make things lighter. Her clothes were all jumbled in the drawers. I just assumed she threw her clothes into the correct drawer without bothering to fold them. My college roommate did that.

"But, after Aunt Tilly told me someone had broken into her house, I was trying to get facts from her and she said she always folded her clothes. Also, a lot of clothes in her closet were half off hangers, a few on the floor."

"Did you clean her upstairs bedroom, too?"

"I... No. I ran out of time and needed to pick up Aunt Tilly from rehab."

"So there might be something in her old bedroom that would help the investigation?" he asked.

Tori's hopes rose for a minute then her shoulders sagged. "The movers were all over the room carrying furniture downstairs. Their prints will be everywhere."

"What about the closet? Did they move clothes down?"

Tori answered, "I moved some down, but they didn't go into the closet."

"Don't clean or touch anything in that room. I'll send a tech out to dust for prints. It'll be a day or two because it is no longer a critical crime scene. We'll take Ms. Statton's and your fingerprints before you leave today so we can eliminate them."

Aunt Tilly smiled and thumped a crutch. "I knew you had character and smarts. If you'd played football against Sam, he wouldn't have been able to block you out of the way."

"Thank you, ma'am." Detective Stone scribbled on the pad. "I don't think we'll be able to find whoever broke into your house, but we'll check things out. Doubt if your neighbors will remember seeing anyone who didn't normally belong."

"It was the middle of the night. Everyone was sleeping, unless Alice Clayton was having one of her can't sleep nights she keeps carrying on about," Tilly commented.

"We'll talk to all the residents on your street. The burglar might have been seen casing the neighborhood or watching your house. We try to educate people to report suspicious strangers." He shook his head. "Most don't want to get involved or assume the stranger has a legitimate reason for being there." He snapped off the recorder and stood.

Their interview was over.

"Thank you for believing my aunt."

"And just why wouldn't he believe me?" Aunt Tilly asked

indignantly.

Derrick Stone addressed Tori with a grin. "I agree she has a clear mind and is intelligent. I'll let you know if we find any evidence."

Aunt Tilly shrugged off Tori's attempt to help her and headed toward the door. "We'll let you know what we find out, too."

Tori noted the policeman's raised eyebrow but followed her aunt without explaining. So much for turning the matter over to the police. Aunt Tilly still had her cast in the role of finding the culprit who pushed her down the stairs.

It took a while to get their fingerprints taken. The technician was busy processing three uncooperative suspects of a car theft. Finally, the wait was over. A tired and frustrated Aunt Tilly admonished the harried tech, "Don't you go mixing our prints with the fingerprints of those crooks."

Chapter Four

Aunt Tilly wobbled out of the police station at a much slower pace than the one she had when she entered. She didn't even glance at the steps but headed down the handicap ramp. Tori started to grasp her aunt's arm but received a forbidding scowl. Instead, she moved slightly ahead of her aunt, ready to catch her if she faltered.

Aunt Tilly surrendered her crutches and settled into the passenger seat. Tori looked over at the slumped shoulders of her aunt. Was she just tired or was she discouraged that the police hadn't given her any hope of catching the guy? She turned the ignition and backed out. Well, nothing may come of it, but they had started a paper trail. If the police did a little investigating like Detective Stone promised, maybe her aunt would be satisfied and forget about the amateur sleuthing.

Tori flicked on the right blinker before pulling out into the street.

"No. Turn left." Her aunt pointed. "Let's go to Ed's Eating Place for lunch and then we can stop by the grocery store."

"Are you up to all that?" Tori cast a doubtful glance at her aunt slumped in the seat beside her but signaled for a left turn. Eating out meant she didn't have to cook.

Aunt Tilly sat up straighter. "I'll be sitting down resting while we're eating, and I can ride around in one of those scooter things while we're shopping."

"You don't just ride around. You have to steer and not run into people or shelves." Tori didn't know how Aunt Tilly was behind the wheel of a car, but she'd exhibited wall and furniture bumping with her wheelchair.

"I got a feeling if I don't take over some of the cooking, I'm going to be eating a lot of sandwiches and canned soup," Aunt Tilly grumbled.

"I can still make a tasty mud pie," Tori said.

"Don't get sassy, girl. They didn't just have us exercising. We had to do stuff in the make-believe kitchen. Mostly reaching up on shelves or into the refrigerator, but we had to stand at the stove and stir a pot, too."

"I'll try to be more creative with my cooking. Maybe I can cut the sandwiches in triangles."

Aunt Tilly turned her head to look out the window, but Tori caught a glimpse of a smile before she did so. They rode the rest of the way in silence.

Tori pulled into a just-vacated space a few shops down from the restaurant. As they neared the entrance of Ed's, the aroma of home cooking wafted out as a family exited. Tori's stomach rumbled in appreciation.

The place was packed. Several groups waited their turn near the door. Mae, Ed's wife, rushed over to greet them. From her size, she obviously enjoyed her husband's cooking. Her salt and pepper hair wisped out in odd directions from a bun on top of her head. Blue eyes twinkled above rosy cheeks. Mae wiped her hands on her stained white apron and hugged Tilly, crutches and all. "Tilly, it's so great to see you up and about."

"This is our first outing. Tori's not much in the kitchen. I thought we should come by and fortify ourselves on Ed's cooking. And get something to go, too." Tilly looked up at Mae.

Tori rolled her eyes upward. If her aunt was going to start proclaiming her non-existent culinary skills, maybe it was time she looked at some of those cookbooks in Aunt Tilly's kitchen.

"We'll make sure you get plenty. Janet just about has a table cleared." Mae squeezed Tilly's arm and led them past the frowns of the waiting crowd toward a booth near the back.

Tori's cheeks warmed. She avoided looking at anyone as she brushed past the waiting people and followed Mae. Several customers waved or called out greetings to her aunt.

Aunt Tilly maneuvered into the booth and Tori slid in opposite her.

Mae kept up her chatter. "It sure is good to have you back even if it is on two sticks. Our special today is beef stew with rice and a side of green beans. That's easy to warm up. I'll have them pack up two to go." She didn't even pause for a breath as she placed two menus on the table.

"We've made a few changes to the menu since you were last in, Tilly. You might want to try one of our new items. And Ed made banana pudding. I'll have them box that up for you, too. You both want ice tea?" She pulled two straws from her apron pocket and set them on the solid wood table, scarred with years of use. "Janet'll be over in a minute to take your order. I gotta get back and help Ed. He's short-handed today. So glad I was out front to see you when you came in." She bustled away, dodging tables, and disappeared through swinging doors.

"Mae's exuberance is enough to wear one out, but she'll see we have plenty of that stew and pudding to take home," said Tilly

Tori silently hoped the takeout would be enough for several meals in case her planned cooking debut flubbed big time. Her mother hadn't been patient with Tori's cooking attempts. As a consequence, Tori had given up. Even living on her own, she had relied on sandwiches and takeout. She picked up the glossy menu and flipped it open. She had stopped in and gotten takeout often enough while Aunt Tilly was in rehab that she should have it memorized.

"Oh, Tilly. I thought it was you. So glad you are out of that rehab place. This must be your niece."

Tori winced at the shrill voice of the lady standing beside their table. Not as old as her aunt, but certainly a senior citizen. The purple dress hung loosely on a thin body, but alert brown eyes studied Tori from under the bangs of a brown wig. Bangles jingled on her wrist as she thrust a hand forward and grabbed Tori's. She gave a vigorous shake before releasing it. "I'm Linda Carmichael."

"Hello, Linda." Tilly greeted her friend. "It was real nice of you to come visit me in the hospital, especially since I know how you hate being in that place."

Linda's interruption was the first of many as friends came over to speak to her aunt and meet the niece. Tori shook hands and smiled with closed lips. Unable to talk with her mouth full of food, she nodded a lot. She finally gave up eating and asked the waitress to box up what she had left. She was glad so many people cared about Aunt Tilly, but she wanted to get home and work on her middle school book before the deadlines for her fairy stories halted her progress. Especially now that she didn't have to face cooking an evening meal.

They left amid farewell waves and 'good-to-see-yous.' The grumpy lady Tori knew seemed well liked by everyone they had met. Why would someone come into Aunt Tilly's home and push her down a flight of stairs?

Armed with two boxes of leftovers and two take away dinners plus pudding, Tori hoped Aunt Tilly would be willing to skip grocery shopping and go home. No luck.

In the store, Tori stood back, ready to jump even farther, as the teenage clerk explained again how to operate the scooter. His fingers pulled the left lever back on the handlebar and the scooter instantly whipped backward a foot. He more gently squeezed the right lever and the machine rolled forward at a more sedate pace. Aunt Tilly perched on the edge of the scooter seat, a smile beaming, ready to be graduated from his lessons and take down the store – uh, take off and shop. She was gone in a flash with the freckle-faced teen scurrying to keep up beside her.

Tori hurried after them. "Aunt Tilly, did you hear him say drive slow? Ease up on the lever!"

"Of course I heard him, but I have to go before I can go slow."

"Great. Then let go of the power and give me half the list."

The teenager looked relieved when his student complied. Aunt Tilly fished a piece of paper from her purse and Tori cautiously moved closer. Stretching out her hand, she took the list and tore it.

"I'll take the bottom half. You get the things on the top." She thrust the torn paper back at her aunt. "This young man," she read his name tag, "Jeff, is going to accompany you while you shop so he can help you control that thing." She spoke to her aunt, but looked at the teenager.

His Adam's Apple bobbed as he swallowed, and his face paled causing his freckles to stand out. Tori felt guilty for abandoning them. The poor guy's orange hair would probably be white by the time they checked out. The smile she gave him was weak.

Tori grabbed a cart and headed to the opposite side of the store. When the crash came, she would hear it but could act oblivious to its cause. She paused halfway down the aisle and looked back. Maybe she could recommend to the manager that he also provide helmets and seatbelts with the scooters.

The young man hopped back as Aunt Tilly slowly backed up. And suggest shin guards for the helpers. They started forward, maniac driving and brave teen running after her. They must have both survived without incident. They arrived forty minutes later at the checkout, scooter basket loaded.

Tori thanked the teen and slipped him a twenty-dollar bill. He grinned and stuffed it in his pocket. "Uh, maybe next time y'all could shop someplace else." His face turned red. "Uh, you know, so she gets to practice on different kinds of scooters." He started backing away. "Uh, bye Miss Tilly. I gotta go shelve stuff now." He spun around and hurried away.

"Bye, Jeff. I'll ask for you next time I come in."

Tori suppressed a grin. Jeff must have heard Aunt Tilly. His speed increased as he headed toward the back of the store.

Chapter Five

The persistent ringing of the doorbell finally aroused Tori from the plot of her current story. This one for middle graders had a more complex plot. She ran her fingers through her hair in frustration. Aunt Tilly was back watching television or snoozing in her recliner, but Tori really didn't want her swinging down the hall on crutches to answer the door.

Word must have spread from the friends they saw at the restaurant yesterday. Would there now be a parade of people checking to see how Aunt Tilly was doing? At least, at rehab there were visiting hours, not to mention someone to admit the visitors.

She pushed her chair back from the desk and went to answer the door. She tugged her yellow t-shirt down and tried to smooth her hair. The curls tended to get wild as she ran her hands through them when she plotted. Or maybe it was when she was stuck with where to go next.

The bell rang again as she reached for the doorknob. The door swung open to reveal Detective Stone accompanied by a young, uniformed policeman. Derrick Stone's worried expression switched to one of relief when he saw her.

Tori opened the screen door. She stepped back and gestured for them to enter.

"I was beginning to worry that something else had happened." A lopsided smile accompanied his words.

"Sorry. I was working and sometimes it takes an earthquake to jar me back into the real world."

The detective raised a questioning brow. When Tori didn't explain her working comment, he nodded toward the other officer. "This is Officer Frank O'Meara, one of our technicians. He's going to check for latent fingerprints and look for any other evidence that might have survived your cleaning."

A lock of dark hair flopped onto his forehead as the officer nodded a greeting and shifted the bag he carried to his opposite hand. His sagging shoulder indicated it was heavy.

"Sorry we didn't call first. You said you'd be home because of your aunt's limited mobility. I hope our timing is all right."

"Oh, of course." Tori finally shook off the remnants of her interrupted writer's daze. "Where would you like to start?"

The clacking noise coming down the hall indicated Aunt Tilly's approach. "Good morning, Detective Stone and...Frank? Is that you? My, you've grown. An officer of the law. Bet your grandma's proud of you."

Frank shifted his weight and grabbed his bag with both hands. "Yes, ma'am. How you doin', Miss Tilly? Sorry you got hurt, but I'm gonna check to see if there's any fingerprints or anything so maybe Detective Stone can catch the guy that broke into your house."

Tori's attention moved between her aunt and the young officer. Small town syndrome? Aunt Tilly seemed to know everyone and who they were related to.

Detective Stone interrupted her thoughts. "Tori, why don't you show Officer O'Meara your aunt's upstairs bedroom so he can get started, and Ms. Statton, you can show me where you fell and go over what happened again."

Tori nodded and led the way up the stairs. At the top, she paused and glanced down. Aunt Tilly was pointing to a place near the top of the steps. Derrick Stone had pulled out his cell phone and was taking pictures.

Officer O'Meara nearly bumped into her. "Sorry, Miss Tori."

She turned quickly and opened the door to her aunt's former bedroom. "My fault and it's just Tori. No Miss please."

"Yes, ma'am." He was making her feel old.

She stepped inside and waved her hand. "We moved all the furniture downstairs. There's nothing left." Except faded peach wallpaper and a light green carpet marked where furniture had been. And a few dust bunnies. She scanned the room and added, "The men were all over touching things and bracing against the walls to shove the heavy stuff."

Frank nodded. "I'll get what I can. Detective Stone mentioned the closet."

Tori pointed to the open doorway of the walk-in closet and then nodded toward a second door. "That's the bathroom. They didn't move anything from there either. I did that. They took my prints at the police station so you can eliminate them."

"Yes, ma'am." Officer O'Meara put down his bag and pulled on gloves.

She opened her mouth to reply then shut it without saying anything. Stop babbling, she told herself. He knows what he's doing. She backed out of the room.

She glanced into the bedroom she was using across the hall. Tori took a quick breath. She had combined the contents of several drawers to make room for her things. The contents had been messy and she'd had to refold things. Maybe? She moved into her room.

Her hopes dashed. There would be no prints. She had changed the sheets and dusted in here, too. She pivoted on her heel and headed down the stairs where Detective Stone was still listening intently to her aunt recounting what she remembered.

But she hadn't even checked the other rooms. If the intruder searched in those rooms, Officer O'Meara needed to dust them. She backtracked and went into her aunt's former bedroom. "Officer O'Meara, she called into the empty room."

"Yes, ma'am." A muffled voice came from the closet. "Just a minute, ma'am." Tori waited a couple of minutes then started across the room. A head popped out of the closet.

Tori had had enough. "I tell you what. I'll call you Frank and you call me Tori. No miss. No ma'am.

"Yes, Miss..., Ma'am... okay." He grinned at her.

"I just remembered things were messed up in my bedroom, too." She pointed across the hall. "I've dusted and cleaned in there, but if the intruder looked in there, he probably went through things in the other rooms. I've opened the doors and peeked in, but that's all."

Frank nodded. "I'll check them out and dust them. Why don't you tell Detective Stone. He'll want to check them out, too." He ducked back into the closet.

She brushed a curl back from her face and headed down. She found Derrick Stone on the bench seat and Aunt Tilly seated on the lone chair at the kitchen table drinking coffee. The detective's notebook and pen lay beside his elbow.

"Tori, get a cup and join us. I was going to have you bring Frank some hot chocolate, but Derrick says he can get some later. There's extra hot chocolate if you want it." Tori glanced at the officer. So it was Derrick now.

"Coffee sounds good." Tori carried a chair from the dining room where she'd stored the extra kitchen chairs then grabbed a mug and poured herself a cup. She slipped into the chair and sipped the black brew. "Frank might prefer coffee, too."

"He always liked my hot chocolate when he came over with his grandma." Tilly smiled at the memory.

Tori glanced at the notebook and took a few more sips before repeating what she had told Frank.

"Might mean we'll get a break after all." Derrick pushed his chair back and headed up to the second floor.

Both officers spent a long time upstairs in the unused bedrooms. When questioned about whether they had found anything, Derrick's answer was non-committal. They needed to eliminate Tilly's and Tori's prints from their findings. Derrick pulled out his notebook again and questioned Tilly about who else might have been in the rooms. Guests? Workmen? Someone else cleaning?

Tilly shook her head. "No one since my fall. Martha comes in to clean. But I don't have her bother with those rooms except to wave a dust rag every month or so and maybe vacuum. She's away right now."

Frank drank the hot chocolate with only a glance at the coffee pot, but he had been rewarded with cookies that hadn't been offered to Tori or Derrick. The detective kept eyeing the plate of cookies near Frank. Unable to resist, he reached over and picked up a couple from the plate near Frank. "Hope you don't mind sharing. These smell so good." When he finished eating his first one, he grinned at Tilly. "There are really delicious."

The young tech apologized about the black dust mess as the questioning was wrapped up and the men headed toward the front door. "We'll let you know if we found anything." Derrick nodded as he followed Frank out.

"Thank you, Detective," Tori said as she shut the door behind him and locked it.

Chapter Six

Tori entered the front door. She'd gotten Aunt Tilly happily settled with her bridge group at Isabelle Thornton's. Or maybe Tori was the happy one. She had several hours of peace to write. Aunt Tilly had insisted she leave the fingerprinting mess for Martha to clean. She was due back in two days. Who knew Aunt Tilly had someone coming in twice a week to help? Martha had gone to Tennessee to help with her new grandbaby and spend time with family. Aunt Tilly had sent her on her way when she wound up in the hospital. She had told Martha she wasn't home to mess up so no need to clean. There'd be plenty of dust when she got back.

Tori went into the kitchen to microwave a cup of leftover coffee before getting started writing. She stopped mid-stride.

Glass littered the floor near the back door. It stood ajar. Her heart raced. It took a minute for her to shake herself enough to dig her cell phone from her purse. She hit 911 and rattled off her aunt's address. What if the person was still here? She had to get out of the house. Front door or back? Pain and blackness ended the need for a decision.

Tori opened her eyes and fought back a scream as a blurry figure hovered over her.

"Get out of my way young man."

Her aunt's voice penetrated her fog. Had she picked her up already? No. No, that wasn't right. Someone had broken in! Tori struggled to sit up. Pain radiated through her body. Blackness tried to grab her again.

"Take it easy, Miss Statton." A hand gently pushed her down. "You're safe now." A female voice tried to reassure her.

Her vision cleared a little. She blinked at the woman hovering above her. Her features were still indistinct. A stethoscope dangled in front of a white shirt. But she'd heard... "Aunt Tilly?" Her voice came out garbled.

"There. She's calling for me." Her aunt's strident voice sent more pain shooting through her head.

"Miss Tilly, let them take care of her."

She knew that voice, too. She relaxed but fought the darkness.

Derrick was here. After a few more pokes she felt herself being lifted and settled on what must be a stretcher.

"I'm going. You'll have to boost me up into the ambulance." Tori heard her aunt proclaim.

"Miss Tilly, I'll have someone drive you to the hospital." Derrick's voice remained calm, but there was a tinge of anger in it.

Was he mad at her? Tori didn't want to go anywhere. "No. I'm fine." They evidently didn't hear her. More likely ignored her protests.

***

Tori woke feeling like she was finally coming out of a daze. Some of that daze was probably due to the medicine they had been giving her until she refused and said she was fine. Her head still felt like someone was beating a base drum and clanging symbols in there. She'd take an aspirin if she ever got out of the hospital.

She turned her head and saw Aunt Tilly dozing in a chair near the window. Her aunt woke and pulled herself up as voices sounded outside the door.

"You weren't here all night, were you?" Tori asked.

"No. They chased me out at nine o'clock. I stayed at Creek View Hotel." She shifted in the chair and stretched her good leg in front of her. Her casted leg was resting on a small footstool. "I wanted to stay at Marian's bed and breakfast, but she doesn't have an elevator. Isabelle offered, too, but I wasn't in a mood to sleep on her fold out sofa even if it meant I would have company. I've booked us a suite until we can go home."

"I'm good. We can go home as soon as they let me out of here." Tori pushed the control to raise the head of the bed. She tried not to grimace as the bed jerked to an upright position.

Aunt Tilly shook her head. "My house is a crime scene. Derrick said he would release it as soon as he could. He's pretty ticked off that my neighbor and the EMTs didn't call the police right away when I was hurt."

"You. Me. Him. I guess that makes three of us. Did he say if Frank found any prints?"

"I was too upset about you to ask. What happened? Did you see who it was?"

"Those are my questions, Miss Tilly." With a tap on the door frame, Derrick Stone walked into the room. It must have been him talking outside her room. "How are you, Tori? Are you up to telling me what happened?"

Tori started to shake her head. Pain made her answer vocally instead.

"Miss Tilly, I should ask you to move out into the hall, but if you can sit real quiet, I'll let you stay."

Tilly pressed her lips together and nodded.

Derrick pulled the remaining chair over close to the bed and pulled out the inevitable notebook. He looked Tori in the eyes. "Miss Tilly said you had taken her to play bridge with friends about one o'clock. Did you go straight home or run errands on the way?"

"I went straight home. I was looking forward to having a couple of hours to write."

"What do you write?"

Tori wasn't sure what that had to do with being hit on the head but she answered. "I usually write and illustrate stories about fairies for young children, but I'm trying to branch out and write for middle graders. I'm working on an adventure story." She couldn't help asking what her writing had to do with someone breaking into the house a second time.

"We think this break in is related to what happened to your aunt, but we need to make sure this one wasn't directed at you." He paused and glanced at his notes. Your car was in the driveway. Did you notice any cars parked in the area or anyone walking nearby?"

"I wasn't paying attention to the neighborhood. I parked the car and went in the front door. If Aunt Tilly had been with me, we would have gone in the back because there's a ramp for her." Tori pursed her lips in regret. "If I'd gone in the back door, I'd have seen the broken glass and never entered the house."

"Was the front door locked?"

Tori started to nod her head but stopped and pressed her fingers to her temples. She needed to stop moving her head. "Yes. We keep it locked, but I checked it anyway before we left out the back and I used my key to get in."

"Did you notice anything unusual when you entered?" Derrick asked.

"No." she was starting to feel stupid. What should she have noticed?

Derrick scribbled in his notebook. "What did you do after you entered?"

"I decided to grab a cup of coffee to drink while I worked. I went into the kitchen and saw the back door." Tori gave a half shrug. "I called 911. I thought maybe someone was still in the house. I didn't know if I should go back out the front door. The backdoor was closer. But I was hit on the head before I could leave and that's all I remember. Well, until the emergency people were there, but I don't really remember that either. You were there and I think I heard Aunt Tilly." Her aunt give a grunt of satisfaction.

Derrick frowned when she mentioned her 911 call. After scribbling something in his notebook, he asked, "You didn't see who hit you?"

Again, Tori answered, "No."

"Did you get a feeling it was a man or a woman?"

Tori reached up and gently touched the bandage on the back of her head. A compassionate nurse had wrapped gauze around her head to hold it in place instead of shaving away hair and applying tape. The effect made her injury look worse than it actually was. "It must have been a man." She shrugged with a second thought. "I guess it could have been a strong woman." Her voice trailed off.

"Did you catch a glimpse of clothing or a shoe?"

"No."

"You didn't go into the library or any of the other rooms?"

"No." She wasn't being any help.

"Referring back to the 911 call, what did the 911 operator direct you to do?"

"I just dialed and gave my address. I don't remember any directions."

Derrick frowned. He tucked his notebook back inside his jacket.

"Did Frank find any prints? From before?" Tori reached for

the plastic cup on her bedside table. It was just out of reach.

Derrick stood and picked up the cup. His fingers brushed hers as he handed it to her with a smile. He opened his mouth to speak then hesitated. He stuck his hand in his pocket. "Whoever it was wore gloves. He or she must have snagged them without knowing. We got a partial print from the hole in one finger."

The fear and worry in Aunt Tilly's blue eyes was mirrored in Tori's chest. Whoever the person was, they weren't above injuring or possibly murdering people who might be in their way.

***

Tori sank down onto the plush sofa in the suite Aunt Tilly had reserved for the next several days. The doctor had come in shortly after Derrick left and released her.

She leaned back and relaxed. This was the perfect place to recoup. Derrick had allowed a woman police officer to pack clothes for Aunt Tilly and herself. The hotel supplied the other necessities. Could she talk the detective into releasing her laptop and a sketch pad?

She looked around at the luxurious decor. "Aunt Tilly," Tori's gesture swept around the room. "are you sure you don't have a shoe box full of money?"

Aunt Tilly sniffed. "My money is securely in the bank or invested so it's putting more money in the bank. If I can't be comfortable in my own home, I'm going to be comfortable in this hotel."

Tori raised a questioning brow.

"I've got enough to pay for this suite and enough to buy a new sofa. The police don't know if that confounded criminal came back to look some more for whatever or if he was plain old set on destruction. They think you came home and interrupted his plans. Thank goodness he just hit you on the head and didn't stab you with whatever he used to slash up my sofa."

Tori felt deep cold grip her. Suddenly, the headache was a good thing. She could be dead. Dizziness vied with the chill. She felt a blanket being awkwardly shoved around her.

"Here I am not taking care of you." Her aunt fussed with

tucking the edges under her. "You should be in bed. You just seemed so rambunctious in the hospital. I guess the trip here took a lot out of you."

"Aunt Tilly, I'm supposed to be taking care of you." Tori argued weakly.

"I guess we'll have to take care of each other," her aunt retorted. "I'll have them send up some soup for you." She grinned as she added, "Maybe a sandwich cut in triangles, too. Then you can take a nap."

Tori struggled against the blanket. Her aunt didn't have trouble using the word nap. "I'm okay. It just hit me, what could have happened to you if you had been with me. Let's go down to the hotel restaurant. I need to move and do something As nice as these rooms are, we are probably going to be tired of them before we can go back home."

"If you're up to it." Aunt Tilly frowned as she watched Tori get to her feet. "You didn't eat much of the breakfast the hospital gave you. Can't say as I blame you having to eat that stuff for weeks myself."

"We'll both take it slow." Tori headed toward the door.

"I'll catch you if you fall." Aunt Tilly grinned and thumped after her toward the elevator.

It was after the lunch rush and the dining room was nearly empty when they entered. A family was finishing their meal and an elderly couple lingered over coffee, their empty dessert plates pushed aside.

They settled at a table and Tori leaned back in her chair. A waitress appeared with water and menus. Their orders were quickly filled and they ate in silence, trying to forget for a little while why they were at the hotel. Feeling stuffed, Tori pushed her half empty plate away. Aunt Tilly had no problem finishing her lunch and signed the tab. They headed back to the suite and collapsed onto sofa and chair. If Tori closed her eyes, they would probably both drift into sleep. Her aunt had been at the hospital late and returned early.

But Tori needed to find out what had happened at the house. She had dropped Aunt Tilly off to play bridge, so that means whoever had broken in was watching and waiting for them to leave. That thought brought another shiver of fear. She'd only been gone for about fifteen or twenty minutes. Not much time for the bad guy to search the house again. He'd heard her call 911 so most likely he hadn't finished ransacking the place. That means he'd no doubt be back. Tori was thankful to be safely in the hotel room.

Derrick must have heard the address over the police scanner. That explained his voice swimming in Tori's semi-consciousness with the EMT's. But how had Aunt Tilly gotten back to the house? How had she even known to rush home?

Tori shifted on the sofa and turned to ask her questions, but Aunt Tilly had closed her eyes and was snoring softly. Real or pretend, it ended any attempt Tori had to get information.

She needed to call Gary, the repairman, about the alarm system and motion lights he had suggested.

Chapter Seven

Streetlights were flickering on when the cab deposited them at the door of Ed's Eating Place. Aunt Tilly had decided they needed nourishing and friendly faces. The noise of the diner quieted to whispers and low mummers when they entered. Mae hurried over and gave them both a gentle hug before leading Tori and Tilly over to a booth.

"We heard what happened." She studied Tori with an assessing gaze. "I'd ask how you're doing, but I can see for myself. Not even going to ask what you want. Ed'll fix you something special." She put her hand on Tori's shoulder. "Glad to see you up and about." She gave her a gentle squeeze and hurried toward the kitchen.

A waitress appeared carrying a pot and balancing two cups.

"I don't think we care for any coffee tonight, Wanda," Tilly said.

"This is hot tea. Mae's special mixture. And she'll be upset if you don't drink up." She filled the two cups and put the pot in the center of the table then hurried over to answer the summons of diners at another table.

"Don't know what things are coming to." A gruff voice startled Tori as she stared at the steaming cup. "Person's not safe in their own home." The overall-clad man standing beside their booth was built like a linebacker. Brown bushy brows emphasized his frown.

"Hi, Carl," Tilly smiled up at the man. She nodded toward Tori. "This is my niece. Jim's girl. Tori, this is Carl Wilson, another one of your dad's friends."

Carl cast a nod in Tori's direction and turned his attention back to Tilly. "What you need is a dog. A shepherd would be good, but for two women something smaller might be better. My daughter got one of those fancy name breeds. Daisy got out of the fenced yard and now she's got a mixed litter. My daughter dumped the whole lot at my place. My wife's a bit ticked. Well, more'n a bit. One of those pups would make a good guard dog. They're not yappers. Got a healthy bark though."

"Thanks Mr. Wilson, but..."

"Now, Tori, maybe that's what we need." Aunt Tilly spoke up, sounding enthused. "A barking dog will scare off anyone trying to break in again and when you leave, I'll have a companion and won't get so lonely."

Wow. Guilt trip. Tori vowed to be better about phone calls and visits in the future. Well, even one would be better than her past performance. Some argument between her mother and aunt had abruptly ended their last visit. All Tori remembered was her own crying, wailing more like it, as they drove away.

"We need to talk about this, Aunt Tilly." They could talk but her aunt looked like she was ready to head to the pet store for a dog bed, collar and whatever else some enterprising salesperson could talk her into.

Tori tried again. "I don't think either of us is ready to train a pet, Mr. Wilson."

"Call me Carl. These pups are housebroke and they been raised around my grandkids so they're good tempered." He paused, then quickly added, "They'd make good guard dogs though." Carl smiled at Tilly. "They're real lovable and would be a perfect companion." He knew who the softy was. "Y'all come out to the farm tomorrow and just take a look."

Again, Tori tried to head off the adoption. "We're staying at the hotel right now. Aunt Tilly's house is a crime scene. We don't know when the police will let us go home and there are some repairs that need to be done."

"Anything I can help you with, Miss Tilly?"

"Thank you, Carl. I've already called someone to do the repairs. If we decide we need a dog, we'll give you a call."

Carl didn't try to hide his disappointment. He nodded to Tilly. "Good to see you and good to meet Jim's daughter. You ladies be careful." He walked over and joined three men sitting at a corner table.

Tilly stared after him. "Maybe that's just what we need. If I'd had a dog, it would have barked and growled at anyone trying to get into my house."

That part was true, but what about chewed up shoes and holes dug in the backyard. Before Tori could comment, their food arrived. Mmm. It smelled delicious. Pan fried chicken, mashed potatoes and shoepeg corn. She followed Aunt Tilly's example and dug in.

***

The next morning, when they returned to their suite after feasting on the hotel's breakfast buffet, Tori punched Detective Derrick Stone's number into her phone. She looked out the window at the overcast sky as she listened to the phone ring.

He sounded distracted when he finally answered on the fourth ring. "Good morning, Tori. How are you feeling today?" She had evidently showed up on his caller ID.

"Much better." She was still careful not to shake her head. "Any more information on the break-ins?"

"We're still talking to neighbors, but so far no one noticed anything. Most were at work." She could hear him tapping something. His computer? A pencil?

She leaned back in the soft chair. "He wasn't invisible. It was daylight. He had to leave some trace."

Tilly stood nearby, her head tilted and brow raised. Tori shrugged at the unasked question and mouthed, "nothing." Into the phone she said, "I'd like to get my laptop from the house and pick up my car."

"The car you can pick up. It wasn't there when the intruder broke in. I'll have to check with the techs about the computer, but we hope to wind up things at the house today. The scene should be released tomorrow but you may want to stay at the hotel another day or two and hire someone to clean up the place. It's worse than messy drawers this time."

"Aunt Tilly told me about her sofa." She heard deep voices in the background. Someone must have entered Derrick's workspace.

"I have to go. I'll send an officer to give you a lift to get your car."

Forty minutes later they were in the back seat of a police cruiser. The driver introduced herself as Officer Evans. Hopefully no one would recognize who was in the back seat. Maybe it would have been better to take a taxi. Tilly had suggested they go look at Carl's puppies once they had transportation, but when Tori repeated Derrick's warning that it might be days before they could move back, she decided furniture shopping would be a good alternative.

Tori peered out the side window of the cruiser as it pulled into Aunt Tilly's driveway and stopped behind her red Honda. A white van, police technician logo on the side, was angled in front of the house. The black and yellow crime scene tape stretching across the front porch fluttered in the breeze. A picture of the open kitchen door and broken glass flashed through her thoughts. The last thing she'd seen before being hit on the head.

The cruiser crunched to a stop. She sat a minute and then forced herself to climb out. Aunt Tilly slid out behind her, balanced on her crutches and stared at her home. "We've got to get a dog."

Tori didn't even argue. "Soon as we can move back, but we may want a Doberman instead of a puppy." She fished in her purse for her keys. They weren't in the compartment where she usually kept them. She set her purse on the hood of the cruiser and dug deeper. Her fingers felt the rough edges and she pulled them out. The smile at finding them quickly changed to a scowl.

The officer who had driven them stepped out of the cruiser and moved toward her. "Something wrong, ma'am?"

Tori's gaze met Officer Evans' quizzical eyes. "Did Detective Stone take my house key?"

"No," Tilly responded. "I gave him the keys that were in the drawer of my nightstand."

Tori shifted her attention to her aunt and then back to the female officer. "My house key is missing." Tori extended her hand, displaying the key ring.

The officer raised a brow and pulled out her phone. "I'll check on that for you." Tori listened as she asked for Detective Stone and then explained the situation. The officer ended the call. "We're to wait here until Detective Stone arrives." Deputy Evans retrieved an evidence bag and motioned for Tori to drop her keys in it.

"I need my keys to drive my car," Tori argued, but the officer just shrugged and continued to hold out the bag. She almost missed the bag as she threw her key ring into it.

"You ladies want to wait in the back seat?" She nodded in the direction of her vehicle. Tori eyed the Adirondack chairs under the oak tree in the backyard, but the ground was soft from last night's rain and it would be difficult for her aunt to negotiate the distance with crutches. Clouds were keeping the sun at bay. It might get too cold if Derrick kept them waiting long. She helped Aunt Tilly into the cruiser and leaned against the back fender. She zipped up her denim jacket and crossed her arms in front of her.

Derrick arrived and confiscated her keys to check for fingerprints. His gray suit matched the day and Tori's mood. He wanted to take her purse but after Tori pointed out how many people had handled it over the past days, he let her keep it. Derrick finished his questions by asking if she had another set of keys. Fortunately, she did and he sent the officer to retrieve them from her bedroom.

Tori still fumed as she paced back and forth the length of the police car. She stopped in front of Derrick and looked up into his frowning eyes. "We need to get our locks changed again. Today. Once your people leave, it's open season on my aunt's house."

Derrick reached out and brushed her arm with his hand. "Could you wait a day or two? I'd like to have officers inside for a couple of nights to see if our perpetrator does show up when we remove the crime scene tape."

The tape wasn't going to stop their intruder. Even though the back door had been boarded up, he now had the help of her house key to enter whenever he wanted. Tori wasn't going to voice that concern. From Derrick's expression and the twist of his mouth when he spoke, he had the same thoughts.

Tilly joined the discussion before Tori could answer. She glanced at her house and muttered, "I'm ready to get back home and I'm loading up Hank's shotgun." Before Derrick could say anything, she looked at him and added, "I know how to handle a gun. It's like riding a bicycle. Once you learn, you don't forget."

Derrick ran his hand through his hair. The officer who had given them a ride stood behind the detective. Her lips twitched as she tried not to smile. After a short discussion and a threat to keep the crime tape up, Tilly reluctantly agreed to wait two more days before returning home, but she was sending in a cleaning crew tomorrow. She'd leave Hank's gun in the closet, too. For the time being anyway.

Tori watched the taillights of Derrick's car and the cruiser depart down the street and disappear around a corner. She helped Aunt Tilly into the passenger side and then slipped into the driver's seat, happy to be in her own car. "At least we don't have to ride in the backseat of a police car or rely on taxis." Tori could see the grim line of Aunt Tilly's mouth reflected in the car's side window as she stared at her home. The dreary morning added to the chills sliding down her spine as she glanced at the crime scene tape before backing out of the driveway.

"You still want to shop for a sofa?" Tori asked.

"It's way past lunch time. Let's get a bite to eat at Ed's Place. If the rain holds off, we can head over to Henderson and shop at Riley's. They deliver to Cotton Creek."

"How'd this town get the name of Cotton Creek? It's certainly not cotton growing country." Tori was ready to talk about anything but recent events.

It was good to hear her aunt chuckle as she answered. "Some folks came up from the south to settle. It was spring thaw a little further north and the chunks of ice floating downstream reminded them of the cotton fields they had left behind."

Tori found a parking spot near Ed's. As they entered the restaurant, the drizzle of rain changed to a downpour. "That was good timing," Aunt Tilly said, looking out the large front window. She settled in a chair and leaned her crutches against the table. "Maybe it'll stop and we can still go to Riley's."

The lunch crowd was gone, but the lingering smell of Ed's homestyle cooking teased their appetites. It was easy to get tired of hotel food and the same menu every day, but Ed's was always good and he changed the daily specials. Only a few customers remained. A couple chatted in a booth, remains of their sandwiches in front of them. A young man in jeans and T-shirt hunched over his laptop at a table near the window. His fingers flew over the keyboard making Tori long to do the same. A waitress carried a tray of clean glasses through the swinging doors of the kitchen. She called out, "I'll be right with you."

The rain had almost stopped when they finished eating and left the restaurant. Tori followed Aunt Tilly's directions to Henderson. Once they left the hills surrounding Cotton Creek, they wound through flat farmland. The planted fields were edged by trees in full leaf. A lone windmill leaned precariously in a pasture of black and white cows. The zigzag road was designed at a time when laws dictated you didn't cut across someone's land. You followed the property lines. Tori drove carefully on the rain slick road. The less cautious drivers, familiar with the road, roared past in their trucks and SUVs.

Tori glanced in her rearview mirror. She wasn't the only cautious one. The dark vehicle that had been following since they left Cotton Creek still trailed, traveling at her own sedate pace. At the next long straight stretch, she'd slow down and let him pass. But when the road straightened out and Tori slowed, the driver of the dark vehicle slowed, too. Tori shrugged and sped up. So much for being polite. She frowned as the other vehicle increased its speed to keep pace. Was it following them? No. Why would someone be following them to Henderson? It had to be someone who wanted a set of taillights to follow in this weather.

Riley's Furniture store was located just inside the town limits of Henderson. Windows across the front displayed merchandise, but the rest of the building was like a large warehouse. Aunt Tilly almost danced on her crutches as she headed toward the front door.

Tori dashed after her. "Don't act so excited. We don't want to lose our negotiating power."

"We can't do much negotiating on one sofa except maybe for free delivery. I was stuck in a rut with all my old furniture. That vandal did me a favor." Tilly hurried through the door as Tori pulled it open for her.

The building was filled with furniture, most staged as individual rooms. It didn't have all the sofas grouped in one convenient place. Aunt Tilly was going to have a hard time making her way through the place on crutches.

"You ladies look eager to shop." A salesman separated from his cohorts and greeted them.

"Just eager to get out of that drizzle before it starts pouring down. We're heading to the pet store to get things for our new dog, but my niece wanted to look around while we're over this way." She headed down a path between recliners and dining room displays. "We'll just wander around. If we have any questions, we'll holler."

Tori smiled at the disappointed man and followed her aunt.

Living room groupings were arranged against the side wall. Tilly slowed her pace. "Don't want leather. Poke a hole in it and it's ruined. And unless we lock our dog outside, it's going to be up on the furniture with sharp toenails when we're gone."

Tori held her breath when her aunt slowed then paused near an overstuffed sofa with a large floral print in bright pink and lime. She let out a relieved breath when Aunt Tilly pointed to a burgundy one in the next display. "That color looks smart in our hotel room."

"Or you could get a neutral taupe or beige and add colorful pillows that you could change with the seasons," Tori said. She lifted color samples attached to the sofa. "Why don't you choose a style you like and we can check the color choices."

A decision was finally made on a small sofa in taupe and two complimenting chairs in navy and taupe stripe. Tilly added two end tables but allowed Tori to talk her out of a coffee table until they had their selections arranged in the sunroom. Two lamps were added to the list. Still in a shopping mode, Aunt Tilly included an electric-operated recliner that matched the dark blue of the chairs. Then added a second one in case Tori wanted to join her in watching TV.

A happy salesman opened the door when they were ready to leave. "Aunt Tilly, wait here. I'll pull the car close."

Tilly opened her mouth to protest, but the cold rain sent her backing into the store.

The salesman had disappeared but hurried back with a golf umbrella as Tori parked near the door. He held it over Tilly and helped her into the passenger seat.

"Hey, is that guy with you ladies." He pointed to the dark SUV, so close to the edge of the parking lot two wheels were off the pavement. "It's been a slow day with the weather and all. Not much to do but watch traffic and hope someone's going to pull in. Noticed he was behind you, drove past then came back and parked over there. Must have realized you made a stop before going to the pet store." He forced a laugh. "Didn't want to get dragged into picking out colors."

Tori looked over at the dark vehicle. The windows were heavily tinted and she couldn't tell if the driver was a man or a woman. She leaned forward and tried to see the license number as the SUV suddenly pulled out of its spot, bumped onto the street, and roared away. It turned in the direction they had come, toward Cotton Creek. It was gone before she caught a clear look at the tag.

"Must have pulled in to wait for the rain to stop." Tori's voice was a bit shaky. It was only a slight drizzle when they arrived. "Or make a call from their cell phone." They had shopped for over an hour.

The salesman stepped back. "Thanks for your business. I'll call and make arrangements for delivery when your order comes in," he reminded and hurried back into the store.

"Now for the pet store." Aunt Tilly pulled her sweater tighter and rubbed her arms.

Tori still stared in the direction of the departed SUV. "It's raining," she said needlessly. "And we don't have a dog yet." If Aunt Tilly was going to ignore the drama, so would she.

"There's only one shelf of pet things at the hardware store in Cotton Creek. There's a great big pet store three blocks down. I went there with Mable when she got her cat. You can drop me off at the door and then park close in the handicap spot." She pointed to the tag hanging from the mirror. "We'll just get puppy or small dog stuff." She looked pointedly at her niece. "Not Doberman size. I want one that can fit in my lap or cuddle next to me without pushing me out of the chair. And it'll give that car time to get gone. We can be more alert driving home."

Maybe she wasn't going to ignore the SUV after all. Why would someone be following them? But they still didn't know why someone was breaking into her aunt's house. Should she call Derrick? And say what? A dark SUV may or may not have been tailing them?

They left the pet store with a backseat filled with supplies. Two medium size beds, a dark blue to match the new furniture in the sunroom and a green one to put in Aunt Tilly's bedroom. She had dithered a while, then reluctantly put the deep pink one back. It was okay for a female dog to have a blue bed but if they decided on a male, pink wouldn't do. They didn't know if their new addition would be a male or female. The rest of the backseat was filled with collars—they didn't know what size, but the puppy would grow—a leash, lots of toys, and puppy chow. If they got an older dog, it would have to eat puppy chow for a month. They could return whatever collars they didn't need.

Tori was glad Aunt Tilly was so excited about getting a pet. She hoped her aunt would feel the same way after chewed up shoes and puddles on the floor. But, it would be company after Tori was gone.

The thought had her slumping over the steering wheel. The two attacks had brought her closer to her aunt. And she enjoyed working in the spacious library, if she ever got back to increasing her word count. She glanced in the rearview mirror. Had someone followed them or had they just pulled in to chat on their cell phone?

Tilly also watched in the side mirror and twisted around to check on cars that pulled behind them from side roads.

They made it back to the hotel without incident. Tori pulled in a handicap spot near the front and sat for a moment. She couldn't help looking round the hotel parking lot for a dark SUV.

The rain had stopped, but they decided on a meal at the hotel rather than going to Ed's Eating Place. Tori was ready to try new restaurants, but Ed's was Aunt Tilly's meeting place as well as eating place. A place to run into friends.

Derrick stopped by the hotel and joined them for a cup of coffee as they finished dinner. He returned the keys and let them know the police had released the house. It was no longer a crime scene. He told them he had made an extra set of keys so the surveillance team could get in at night and reminded them not to change the locks. And in case the intruder was watching the house, wait to install a security system.

Tori fingered the keys on the way up to their suite. She had mixed emotions about leaving the safety of the hotel. The 'in case someone was watching' had made her more uneasy. Should she have mentioned the SUV to Derrick? She'd been frightened at the thought someone was following them when the salesperson said the vehicle had followed them into the lot and parked while they were in the store. She clenched her jaw. If someone was following them, they wouldn't have been so obvious. Would they?

Several phone calls later, they had made arrangements to meet Martha, the lady who helped Aunt Tilly with cleaning, and the cleaning service that had been recommended at ten the next morning. They wanted to get there early and walk through the house to check out the damage done by the person who attacked Tori and the additional mess of fingerprint powder created by the police. Aunt Tilly had seen the slashed sofa. What else had been vandalized?

Chapter Eight

Just as Derrick had promised, the crime scene tape was gone. There was no sign of the surveillance team that was supposed to spend the night. The neighborhood seemed so normal. Aunt Tilly headed toward the ramp that led to the back door. Tori lagged behind looking up and down the street. Vera Finley, two houses down, watered the flowers in her front yard. The spray from her hose went wild as she shifted her attention to Tilly and Tori and waved a greeting.

Tori smiled and returned her wave. Her yard certainly didn't need watering after all the rain. Was she keeping surveillance over the neighborhood? Across the street, Missy Vancoff's tabby cat leaped at a butterfly. If only she could remain outside and not face the destruction left by a vindictive intruder. Why hadn't he or she been content to just search?

"You coming?" Tilly called from the back porch. Keys in hand, she waited to unlock the door.

Tori turned around one more time, searching the area. At least the sun was shining. Derrick had said someone might be watching, but she didn't see any strangers lurking. She didn't see anyone except Vera and Vera wasn't a suspect. She gave herself a shake and hurried toward the back door. The window frame for the broken glass was still boarded over. The repair man was coming today to replace it with the tempered glass pane that Aunt Tilly had ordered.

Tori took the key from her aunt's shaking hand and inserted it into the lock. They would both feel safer when the locks were changed, and an alarm system could be installed and motion lights at both front and back doors.

Aunt Tilly turned the dead bolt behind them, "I remember when we never locked our doors."

The women surveyed the kitchen. Black fingerprint dust covered the beige countertop and drawer fronts. One drawer had been left half open. The dust had spilled into the contents. The catchall 'junk' drawer had been emptied on the counter. A small dark stain marred the wooden floor inside the doorway to the hall. Tori reached up and touched the back of her head. The lump was still there but the bandage was gone.

"Glad we've got people coming to help with this mess. I'm not anxious to see what the rest of my house looks like." Aunt Tilly's voice trembled.

Tori nodded. She carefully stepped over the blood stain. "Let's start at the front and work our way back, then I'll check upstairs."

Her Aunt paused and stared at the dark stain. Her mouth clamped in a hard straight line. She clenched her fists and stepped over the spot where Tori was attacked.

In the library, books had been pulled off shelves and tossed on the floor. Tori's computer was askew on the desk. She crossed over and pressed the power button. It sprang to life, requesting a password. Tori gave a sigh of relief, thankful that it hadn't joined the books on the floor. She closed it and joined her aunt in the dining room across the hall.

Drawers has been dumped and chairs knocked over, but except for the broken plate Aunt Tilly was trying to piece together, the china and crystal were safe behind glass doors.

"Was it a special plate?" Tori asked.

"Nothing valuable. Just memories." Tilly carefully put the pieces on the dining table. She turned on her crutches and headed toward her bedroom. Same story. Drawers dumped, mattress pulled off the bed. Lots of black powder.

"How long was I knocked out?" Tori hadn't thought about it before. She'd just assumed that she'd been found right away and hadn't noticed the destruction when she'd arrived home. She'd only walked down the hall to the kitchen doorway.

"More than two and a half hours. We finished early because a couple of the ladies had to get going. I kept trying to call you. Anna offered me a ride which was nice because she lives the opposite way. We got here and your car was in the driveway. You still didn't answer so Anna insisted on helping me in. Thank goodness. I went to pieces seeing you lying on the floor like that. She called 911. They wanted us to wait outside, but no way was I leaving you."

"But what about my 911 call?" Tori questioned. Her memory was cloudy, but she was sure she had made the call.

The front doorbell rang just as someone started knocking at

the back. "Oh. That must be Martha. Her key won't work now that you had the locks changed when you first got here. I'll let her in. You get the front door. Probably the cleaning crew." Tilly pivoted on her crutches and disappeared into the kitchen.

Tori could hear a woman's high-pitched exclamations coming from the kitchen as she pulled the front door open. Two muscled men, obviously related, with crops of dark curly hair and strong jaws stood on the porch. Father and son? Tori would have slammed the door and locked it if the older man hadn't shoved a business card at her proclaiming them to be the cleaning crew. They needed a peep hole. A middle-aged woman stood slightly behind, holding a bucket with cleaning supplies. She was slightly taller than Tori but beside the two men she looked petite. Grey roots in faded brown hair announced it was past time for an appointment at a salon or a do-it-yourself job at home.

Tori stepped back pulling the door open wider and the crew tromped in. A fourth member had been hidden behind the two men. She looked barely out of high school. The girl had the dark curls of the two men but fortunately not their jaw. She wore a scowl that clearly proclaimed she didn't want to be here. She tilted slightly against the weight of her bucket of cleaning supplies which was put down with a thump as she crossed the threshold.

From his position in the hall the older man looked through the doorway of the library and shook his head. "Wow. There are some messed up people to do this stuff." He straightened his shoulders and turned his attention back to Tori. "You have furniture that needs to be hauled off? We'll load that up first." He jerked his thumb toward the still open front door. A heavy-duty truck could be seen backed into the driveway. "If you show us what needs to go we can get it out of the way for cleaning."

"We were just looking through the house, checking out damage." Tori said.

"You can start with the sofa in the sunroom," Tilly announced as she joined them. She tucked a crutch under her arm and gestured down the hall. She followed the men, talking to Tori over her shoulder. "Martha's really upset but she's started in on the kitchen."

The two female members of the crew disappeared into the

library.

Tori and Tilly put away personal items and piled clothes that needed to be washed again while Martha and the crew worked miracles throughout the house. Tilly took advantage of the muscle power and had the men haul away a chair with sagging springs and two lumpy mattresses even though they hadn't been slashed.

Finally, Tori locked the door behind the crew and joined Martha and her aunt . They were in the kitchen already seated at the table, shoulders slumped, with tall glasses of ice tea in front of them. A third glass waited for Tori. She sank into the chair beside her aunt.

They sipped in silence, too tired to talk. Tori had tried to take Aunt Tilly back to the hotel midday when she went to pick up hoagie sandwiches for lunch, but her aunt wasn't going to leave her house with a bunch of strangers, even with Martha there to supervise.

Martha tucked a stray strand of strawberry blonde hair behind her ear and broke the quiet. "Tilly is too stubborn to say she needs help. Next time..." She paused to point her finger at Tori, a serious gleam shone in her brown eyes, "you call me and I'll skedaddle myself right back here."

"Martha, you went to be with your daughter when your grandchild was born. I wasn't going to pull you away from that. Time you took a vacation, too." Tilly's glass clattered as she put it down on the table. The smile she directed at Martha said they were friends, not just employer and employee.

"Not sure how much of a vacation it was helping out with her older children, but it sure was great cuddling that baby every day. Nice having a little girl after three rambunctious boys. But Stella had lots of people in and out. She'd have been fine without me and I could've gone back when the baby's cooing and smiling instead of screaming cause she's hungry or has a poopy diaper."

When Tilly opened her mouth to protest, Martha held up her hand. She turned back to Tori. "You got your orders. Now take Tilly back to the hotel. I'll lock up here."

Tori shook her head and insisted they all leave together. Derrick's statement about someone watching still had her uneasy. She wasn't going to leave Martha alone at the house. She threw in an invitation for Martha to join them for dinner.

Martha followed in her own car, and they enjoyed an early dinner at Ed's Eating Place. It had been almost empty when they settled at a table and ordered the daily special. The evening crowd was starting to arrive as they left.

Tori dropped Aunt Tilly at the front of the hotel and went to park her car. She was on the phone when Tori got up to their room.

"They can still do their surveillance. I'll make your guys a pot of coffee before Tori and I go to bed, but we're moving home tomorrow. Don't know that hanging around all night is going to catch anyone anyway. It was the middle of the day when he broke in and attacked Tori." Tilly stopped arguing and nodded her head to whatever Derrick was saying. "We'll do that." Tilly hung up the phone and added, "and we're getting a dog."

Tori dropped her purse onto a chair and waited for her aunt to enlighten her, but she was off on a tangent about going out to Carl's for a puppy.

"I take it Derrick's not happy about us moving back to your house." She had qualms about it, too.

"He can't expect us to stay forever in this hotel."

"So, are we making coffee for the stakeout team or is he giving up?"

Tilly waved her hand. "He's going to have people driving by. Wants us to go ahead and change the locks and get an alarm installed." She sank down on the edge of the bed and kicked her shoes off. "An alarm! I need an alarm, so I know when someone is breaking into my house," she said disgustedly. "But we're still getting one of Carl's puppies."

Tori's brow wrinkled as she noted the fatigue in her aunt's face and her rounded shoulders. "Why don't you go soak in the tub? Whoops, sorry. That could be hard to do."

"No soaking for me anyway, I'm liable to fall asleep and I'd rather do that in bed." Aunt Tilly pushed herself up, gathered what she needed and shuffled to the bathroom. "I'm going to wrap up this cast and shower off some of this dirt. Be glad when I can get rid of the dang thing."

Tori grabbed her phone as her aunt headed into the bathroom. "I'll leave a message on the locksmith's answering machine," she called after her aunt.

Chapter Nine

The locksmith was waiting when they arrived at the house the next morning.

"Good morning, ladies," he said as he climbed from his truck. "Had a change in schedule so I came early. Hope that's okay."

"More than okay, but you should have let us know. We could have been here sooner. We stopped by the donut shop which made us later." Tori joined him near his truck. She opened the donut box and offered up a variety of tempting pastries.

"Good morning to you, too, Gary." Aunt Tilly swung toward them on her crutches.

Gary's eyes widened at the selection then he chose a cream filled bar with chocolate icing. He spoke around a bite. "My wife talked to Martha. She said you spent the whole day cleaning up the mess that no good felon made. Guess I thought that meant you were back staying in the house."

Tori started toward the back door. "Not until the locks are changed and we have an alarm system. Whoever hit me on the head, stole my key."

Gary licked his fingers then pulled a handkerchief from his pocket and wiped them. He reached back in his truck and grabbed his toolbox and a cardboard box filled with locks and lights. "Well," he said as he followed Tori and Tilly to the back door, "I'll change the locks and put on additional deadbolts and I'll install motion lights wherever you say, but you'll have to wait on the alarm system. I special ordered it but it will take two more days to get here. Not much need for alarms in Cotton Creek so I don't stock them. That way I can get the newest of whatever there is."

Tori dropped the key she had been trying to insert into the keyhole. She turned to her aunt standing behind her. "I guess that means two more days at the hotel."

"It means we'll pack up our things at the hotel and go get our dog."

When Tori bent over to pick up her dropped key, she noticed her aunt clutching the green dog bed in her right hand as she gripped a crutch. She reached out and gently pulled the dog bed from Aunt Tilly's firm hold. "I'll put this in your room."

Martha arrived as Tori finished unlocking the door and they all trooped into the kitchen. Tori stood in the middle of the room and turned around. Her shoulders dropped in relief. Her attacker hadn't returned and the surveillance team left no trace that they had been there. She placed the donut box in the middle of the table and headed into her aunt's bedroom to deposit the dog bed. Tori looked at Aunt Tilly's mattress that still needed sheets and blankets. Would the dog actually use the bed they bought or would it wind up snuggled with her aunt? She smiled and returned to the kitchen. She'd get the rest of the dog things that were still in her car later.

Aunt Tilly was starting the coffee pot and Martha was loading the washer. Gary had put two sets of locks on the counter and was digging in his box. He nodded at Tori as she entered.

"I'm replacing the locks and adding a deadbolt to both front and back doors. Was goin' to put one that needed a key on the kitchen door but Tilly says she had the pane replaced with tempered glass. The guy won't be breaking that to get in."

"Can you put a peep hole in the front door, too?"

Gary pulled another small size box out and waved it. "Got it right here. Gonna put it for Tilly's height. You'll have to stoop a little."

Tilly piped up, "I'll stand on my tiptoes to measure so you won't have to bend over so much."

Tori laughed. "You just stand comfortable. It's not going to hurt me to lean down and look through a peep hole to see who's here." She grabbed some sheets and a blanket that had been washed the day before and headed back to her aunt's room to make up her bed. Tori's bed would be next if they were going to be checking out of the hotel.

She'd rather be sleeping downstairs closer to Aunt Tilly in case someone did try to break in again, but the slashed sofa had been hauled away. Even the recliner her aunt had fallen asleep in her first day home from rehab had been slashed and had gone with the sofa on the cleanup crew's truck.

Tori came down the stairs after straightening her room and putting away clothes that Martha had washed and found Gary staring at the door to the sunroom. "Is something wrong, Gary?"

"I'm thinking, even though I put up motion lights on the back corners of the house, with all those windows, wouldn't hurt to put a deadbolt on this door until I get the alarm installed. You'd be more secure locking it at night and when you go someplace. Sleep better, too."

Tori nodded in agreement. "I hadn't thought of that but it's a good idea. I've been worried about sleeping upstairs with Aunt Tilly down here."

"Course with that super dog she keeps talking about, you probably don't need anything I've done so far." He laughed at his own joke as he headed to his box of supplies in the kitchen.

Before Gary left, he also put a camera aimed at the back door. It was broken and didn't work but if their intruder came back, hopefully, he wouldn't realize that fact.

They ordered pizza for lunch and Aunt Tilly started talking about checking out of the hotel and driving out to Carl's farm to pick out a dog. Martha insisted there was still a lot of work and she would be fine working with all the doors locked, but there was no way they were going to leave her alone.

Mid-afternoon Tori called a halt and convinced both ladies it was time to quit. Well, Martha, at least. Aunt Tilly had been ready to quit and go to Carl's to see the puppies. Tori went through the house checking locks on windows and doors. As they exited the back door and Tori turned the key, she shivered and looked pointedly at the non-functioning camera in case someone was watching. She wasn't looking forward to coming back and spending the night, but she didn't have much hope of changing her aunt's mind.

Driving back to the hotel, Tori kept glancing at her aunt. Tired was written all over her face. Tori should have insisted they quit washing and folding clothes sooner. At the hotel, she pulled into a handicap spot near the front door and hung the handicap tag from her rearview mirror. She took a deep breath and climbed from her car. Retrieving the crutches from the backseat, she helped Aunt Tilly from the car.

Once in their suite, she settled Aunt Tilly in a chair, turned on the television, and handed the remote to her aunt. She pulled the suitcases from the closet and began slowly packing, keeping an eye on her fatigued relative. When Aunt Tilly's chin dropped to her chest and the remote fell to the floor, she pulled her phone out. She called Detective Stone and let him know they wouldn't be staying in the house until the next day and called Carl to say they would be out the next morning to see the puppies. Martha wasn't supposed to show up at Aunt Tilly's the next day but just in case, Tori called and left a message that they would be spending one more night at the hotel and be going to Carl Wilson's farm in the morning. Then after packing everything except what they would need tonight and clothes for tomorrow, she dialed Ed's Place and put in a to-go order.

She put on a lightweight jacket and was debating whether to wake her aunt and let her know she was going to get their food or slip out and hope she slept until she got back when her phone chimed its ring. It was Mae, Ed's wife. In her cheerful voice, she said one of their college workers was leaving early because he had a big exam the next day. They couldn't deliver to the hotel, but if Tori wanted to walk outside and down a block, he'd drop off her order on his way home.

"That would be great," Tori accepted as Aunt Tilly stirred and blinked her eyes.

She sat up straighter and looked out the window at the darkness. "You didn't wake me."

Tori sat in the chair next to her aunt. "No. I didn't. You and Martha over did it today and both needed to recoup. I called Carl and told him we'd be there tomorrow morning to see the puppies. I didn't want the puppy to be in a strange place for the night and it will have the whole day tomorrow to get to know you and get used to your house."

She glanced at her watch. "I have to go. Mae is having our dinner delivered but I have to walk down the block because they can't deliver it at the hotel." She shrugged. "Hotel policy, I guess. I'll be right back and we can talk while we're eating."

Even with her own fatigue, the cool evening air was refreshing and reviving. Halfway down the block, a car flashed its light's. Tori stopped and fear gripped her. Was it her delivery? She should have asked Mae what kind of car the college student had. The interior light came on as the driver's door opened and she recognized George, the young man who bused tables.

She heaved a sigh of relief and hurried forward. George walked around the car and pulled two bags from the passenger seat. "What did Mae send? The whole menu?" Tori sniffed the delicious aroma as she took the bags.

"Nah, just enough that you're going to have to roll yourselves into bed." George laughed.

"We'll never eat all this. Why don't you keep some of it for your own dinner?" Tori peeked into one of the bags.

"Thanks, but she loaded me down, too." George pointed to another bag on the floor. He waved her offer of a tip away and headed back to the driver's side. "Go on. I'll watch 'til you get back to the hotel." He waited before getting into his car.

"Thanks. Good luck with your test tomorrow." She turned and hurried back to the hotel.

***

It would be a nice drive into the country if Tori had gotten her own directions to Carl's farm. But go a mile past the dairy, which was now void of cows and had a for sale sign nailed to the gate, then turn right at the forked tree, which due to lightning had lost half its fork, was a bit frustrating. They were now driving down a gravel road looking for a tilted mailbox.

"Stop! You just drove right past Carl's driveway."

Tori shifted in to reverse and backed up to the perfectly straight mailbox. Evidently, Carl had gotten diligent enough to repair it, probably because the post office refused to deliver to a mailbox that was halfway to the ground.

She pulled into the rutted driveway and hoped her car would still have a bottom by the time they made the return trip. In the near distance, she could see a house and barn, both in need of paint. As they got near the house, a bedlam of dogs and geese greeted them. If the puppy Aunt Tilly chose was one of the barkers, there would be plenty of warning if the criminal attempted to break in again.

Tori pulled to a stop and turned off her motor. She sat staring at the chaos. Even her aunt was hesitating with her hand on the door handle. Carl stepped from the barn and gave a loud whistle. The geese moved to a spot near a wood pile and the dogs quieted. The pups moved to sit near a white dog, obviously their mother. Three large dogs, two tan and one almost black, stood facing the car as if on guard, but tails were wagging.

Carl, clad in denim overalls and heavy boots, clomped across the yard. "Glad you ladies made it." A tattered brown ballcap shaded his eyes. "You gonna be so happy to take one of my little pups home." He walked around to the passenger side and opened the door for Tilly and helped her with her crutches.

Tori eyed the dogs. Not as happy as you are to get rid of one she thought and cautiously pulled the handle to open the door. The dogs remained where they were as it swung open. Tori squared her shoulders and climbed out. Carl and Aunt Tilly were already standing near the white dog. Puppies were tumbling around their feet. Tori skirted around the larger dogs and hurried over to them. Her aunt's face reflected delight as she clung to a crutch and bent over, petting one pup and then another. She arrived in time to hear Carl say, "course if you take two, they'd be company for each other."

"Thank you, Carl, but one is going to be a companion for Aunt Tilly." Tori shot him a warning glare. Carl cast a glance at her aunt and opened his mouth. "One," Tori repeated. When her aunt straightened and looked from her to Carl, she quickly added, "will fit in Aunt Tilly's lap."

Tori looked at the puppies rolling and nipping at each other. She had to smile at their antics. How were they going to be able to choose? One puppy stood off to the side. She looked like a badly pieced quilt. The white, gray and tan of her wiggling body was dotted with black spots. Her head was cocked and she seemed to be studying the humans with her light blue eyes. As if she made up her mind, the puppy trotted over to them. She planted her four feet and barked at the dog Aunt Tilly was petting. Then she stood on her hind legs and waved her front paws as if saying 'pick me up.'

Carl laughed, scooped the puppy up, and held it out toward them. "Looks like you've been chosen, Tilly." The clincher was when the puppy gave two little barks as if she agreed and licked Aunt Tilly's hand as Tilly reached to take the squirming animal from Carl.

Tori reached over and stroked the white stripe that ran from the top of the puppy's head to her nose. "What do you think, Aunt Tilly?"

Her aunt hugged the puppy close to her chest and beamed. "Oh, yes. This is the one."

Carl scratched his head. "She's a good choice. Smartest one of the whole bunch."

There was no way she would be able to pry the dog from her aunt but with a backward glance at the three larger dogs, she had to ask, "Uh, how big is she going to be?"

"No bigger than Daisy, her ma." He pointed to the white dog who sat amidst the pups. Her feet are small and she's startin' out smaller than her brothers and sisters. See that black pup. Look how big his feet are. Gonna be big like those three." He pointed to the three who had stood guard and were now inching closer for some of the attention. "But he'll stop any burglar in his tracks." He glanced hopefully at Tilly.

"Thanks, Carl. I guess we'd better go and let you get back to your chores. Anything we need to know about taking care of Aunt Tilly's dog?"

"Well, feeding twice a day and she's housebroke so if she goes and sits by the door, you need to let her out." He shrugged. "You have any questions, just give me or the wife a call. Sorry I ain't askin' you in for coffee but my wife went into town for groceries and my coffee's enough to make the cows stop giving milk."

"That's alright. We need to get home and get Aunt Tilly's pup settled and we have things we need to get done, too." She smiled but Carl had bent to give the black pup a pat on his head. "Here, Aunt Tilly. Let me carry her to the car. You've got those crutches." Tori started her aunt toward the car before Carl could start pitching again for them to take two dogs.

Tori settled the puppy in the towel padded cardboard box on the backseat floor. She gave her a few pats and backed away.

"I'll sit back here with her in case she starts missing the other pups," Aunt Tilly announced and maneuvered herself in. "Maybe she'd be happier in my lap."

"She'll be safer in her box, especially with us bouncing out of Carl's driveway." Tori put the car in reverse and backed around, crossed her fingers and aimed for the main road, well, the gravel road that led to the main road. When Tori stopped at the stop sign before turning onto the paved road that would lead back to Cotton Creek, she glanced back at her aunt. The puppy was cuddled in her arms. She smiled and shook her head.

"What do you think of the name Sassy?" Aunt Tilly asked as she eased the puppy down into her lap. She sure was sassy with that other pup."

"It's cute but you don't want her to live up to that name," Tori answered. "I had a friend who had a cat named Rascal. She swore her next pet was going to be named Goody Goody."

"Well, she has four white feet but I'm not going to name her Boots or Socks."

"When we get home, we can make a list and see which one she answers to. Did Carl say he was calling her anything?"

"No. He said he's leaving names up to whoever takes the pups."

They picked up burgers on the way home. The leftovers from Ed's that Tori had stuffed into the mini fridge at the hotel would be dinner tonight. Grocery shopping was a must tomorrow.

Tori pulled into the driveway and looked around. Things seemed so normal. When Aunt Tilly opened the rear door, Tori warned, "Hang onto the pup. I'll get her." She grabbed her purse and hurried to help her aunt. Cradling the puppy in one arm, she steadied Aunt Tilly until she had her balance and then led the way to the fenced back yard. When the gate was closed behind them, she set the little dog down. "Okay, this is home now."

The pup wandered and sniffed. When she took care of potty needs, there was lots of pats and praise.

Tori headed to the back door. She paused and studied the lock. Was she going to do this every time they came home? She jumped when something brushed her leg. When she looked down and saw the puppy, she felt foolish. She reached down and gave it a scratch behind one of her tan ears. "Ready to see the inside part of your new home?" Tori opened the door and the pup trotted in ahead of them. Placing the burgers on the counter, she located the water bowl they had bought and filled it.

Aunt Tilly dug around in a drawer and pulled out paper and pencils. When Tori joined her at the table and distributed the food, she was already scribbling names. An extra pad and paper were on Tori's side of the table. Evidently, Tori was expected to help name the new addition to the household.

Aunt Tilly would write a name, take a bite of her burger and look down at the puppy sitting hopefully near her chair. Tori looked over at her aunt's list. It was longer than her own meager one, but there were a lot of names with lines drawn through them that had already been rejected.

Burgers and fries eaten, Tori gathered up paper wrappings and tossed them into the trash. Coming back to the table she asked, "How are we going to do this?"

Aunt Tilly scooted her chair away from the table and managed to turn it sideways. "Pull out that chair." She nodded toward the chair beside her. "And put the pup over there and tell her to stay." She pointed to a spot about six feet in front of her.

"You think she'll listen?" Tori asked as she followed her aunt's instructions and then sat in the chair beside her. "Now what?"

"We'll go through our lists. I'll say a name and then you repeat it. When she responds, we'll put a check mark." They started down Aunt Tilly's list. The pup sat with tilted head as if wondering at the craziness of humans. Halfway through, the pup lay down, nose between her paws.

"Well, that didn't work," Tori said as they finished both lists with no response from the dog.

"She just didn't like our choices," Aunt Tilly smoothed her list. "She has a mind of her own."

Tori scribbled on her list. "Mind. If we add a y, we get Mindy. She pronounced the name with the short sound of the 'i' as in minute. Maybe..."

As she spoke, the dog sat up and gave a little bark.

"Mindy," Aunt Tilly called. The pup scurried over and with tail wagging, put her paw's on Aunt Tilly's knees. Her aunt scooped the pup up into her lap. Half talking to the dog, "Told you she has a mind of her own."

"That's done." Tori crumpled her list and pushed her chair back under the table. "But I wonder if maybe we should have followed my friend's advice and named her Goody Goody.

Chapter Ten

Tori settled Aunt Tilly in an Adirondack chair in the back yard with a glass of lemonade and the puppy to keep her company. She put her aunt's cell phone on the flat arm of the chair. "I'm going in to edit pages. Call if you need anything." Tori hesitated. Her aunt would be too stubborn to ask.

"Go on. Get your work done. The purpose of that rehab place was to make me independent. You can hand me that ball before you go though. Mindy is learning to bring it back to me.

Tori retrieved the ball and went inside. She grabbed herself a glass of lemonade as she went through the kitchen. She had worked through several chapters when the persistent barking of the puppy pulled her out of her concentration. She pushed her chair back and hurried to check out what was happening.

She stepped out onto the back porch. A stranger was opening the gate to the backyard. His thinning blond hair was slicked back and his rumpled jacket hung open. Tori looked around for a weapon. She pulled the screen door open again, ready to duck back into the kitchen and grab a knife, when her aunt spoke.

"Best hold your ground, Talbert. This puppy isn't trained yet and she's just as likely to bite as lick your hand. As if to emphasize her words, Mindy's barks changed to a low growl.

Talbert backed out the gate and pushed it shut. "Didn't see you sitting there. I tried the front door, rang the bell and knocked, but no one answered. I was coming around to knock on the back. I know I'm late coming by to express my concerns after your accident, but things have been hectic at work. It's good to see you up and about."

"Well since I haven't seen you since Mary's funeral, I didn't expect your concern."

Talbert shuffled his feet and rested his hands on the top of the gate. "Uh, uh."

The sound of the screen door slamming shut momentarily shifted his attention from Tilly. "This must be the granddaughter that came to look after you." His forced smile looked more like a grimace on his thin face.

Tori crossed the short distance to stand by her aunt.

"This is my niece. Tori this is my friend Mary's husband. Haven't seen him in nearly a year but he dropped by to share his concern about my fall. Mindy is not feeling friendly toward him so he won't be staying."

"Tilly, I don't blame you for being upset with me, but you and Mary were such good friends it's hard to see you and not think about how much I miss Mary."

Her aunt narrowed her eyes. His voice sounded so convincing. Too bad he couldn't look her in the eye when he said it. Aunt Tilly's raised chin and tilted head said she still wouldn't have believed him. She kept one hand on Mindy's collar and reached up to cover Tori's hand that rested on her shoulder.

"I miss her, too, Talbert. Still don't understand what made her take her car out that night. She didn't drive after dark and certainly not in the storm we had." She made her statement sound like a question.

Talbert rubbed the back of his neck. "I don't either. I would have stopped her if I had been home."

Tilly remembered his excuse of working late and coming home to an empty house only to have police knocking on his door before he could even start calling to find out where his wife might be.

Tilly uncurled her fingers from Mindy's collar. The puppy ran barking toward Talbert.

Tilly winced as the pup lunged at the gate and bounced off. Her hand flew up to hide her smile as Talbert stumbled back.

"Oh. She jerked out of my hand. Mindy, come here." Tilly stood and grabbed her crutch, holding it more as a club than for support. "As I said she's not trained yet. Thank you for coming by."

He glanced at the house. Their protector made another lunge at the gate and Talbert stepped back farther. "I'm glad to see you doing well and your grand... uh niece is here to help you." Throwing a look in Tori's direction, he turned and strode away.

Mindy gave a couple of barks at the retreating figure and came back to sit at Tilly's feet.

"What was that about?" Tori had never known her aunt to be so inhospitable.

Tilly dropped back into her chair. "That was my friend Mary's husband." She almost spat out the word husband. "He never came over with her to visit. She's been dead nearly a year and he comes over now?" She leaned forward and patted Mindy on the head. "You were a good girl." She grinned at Tori. "I told you she would be a good guard dog."

"Her barking is what made me come out to see what was going on."

"She may be smaller than a Doberman but she had Talbert backing up." Tilly reached into her pocket and pulled out a dog treat. "You deserve this, but you need to sit to get it." The pup immediately plopped on her hind quarters.

"Good girl." Tori leaned over and scratched behind her ears. "If the crisis is over, I'll get back to work. That deadline on my other book is still looming." She stopped and turned back to face her aunt. "Why did he head back here instead of ringing the front doorbell?"

Tilly raised a brow. "Talbert said no one answered. He was heading to knock on the back door."

"He said he rang? I know I zone out when I'm writing, but I would have heard someone at the door. Eventually, anyway."

As Tori settled in the chair at her desk, she wondered if the fact that she had parked her car in the garage had anything to do with his trying to go to the back door. She would have heard the doorbell. Had she been too engrossed in her story to hear him try a key in the front? Thank goodness they had gotten the locks changed. She'd give Gary a call and see if there was any news about the alarm system before getting back to her story.

Light in the room was starting to fade when the doorbell chimed. She definitely heard it. With a sigh, she hit save and went to answer it. Looking through the peep hole Gary had installed, she raised a brow and opened the door. "Detective Stone?" With his tan slacks and rolled up sleeves of his white shirt, he looked more casual than the suit he wore when he interviewed her and Aunt Tilly.

He waved one of the bags he held to stop her questions. "Off duty. And it's Derrick." He grinned. "I brought food. Didn't know if you had settled in enough to cook."

Tori stepped back and almost stumbled over Mindy who had appeared at her feet. "You're supposed to bark. There's a stranger coming into our house," she addressed the dog as she waved the detective in. Mindy just wagged her tail faster. Tori shrugged. "I guess she knows anyone saving my aunt from my cooking is welcome."

When they entered the kitchen, Aunt Tilly had the fridge open and was studying its contents. She pulled out one of Ed's to-go boxes and turned to put it on the counter.

"You can put that back, Aunt Tilly. Derrick has arrived with food."

"I thought I heard the doorbell, but Mindy didn't bark."

Derrick put the bags of food on the table and bent to give the puppy sniffing at him a couple of pats on the head. "She knows not to bark at a police officer. Don't you girl?" He straightened. "But I hope she'll become a barker whenever anyone comes to the door."

"She put on a real good show this afternoon when Mary's no-good husband stopped by. Wouldn't even let him in the back yard where I was sitting."

"She even roused me from my work with her barking." Tori laughed as she put silverware and glasses of tea on the table. "So what did you bring us?"

Derrick had begun unloading the food. "I don't know. As soon as I told Mae I was picking up something for you and Tilly, she said Ed would fix something special and disappeared into the kitchen. When she returned, she had these bags."

They settled around the table and began opening containers. Ed's something special was beef stroganoff with noodles, green beans, and yeast rolls. Filling his plate with a second helping, Derrick resumed the conversation. "What did Mary's husband want?"

"Haven't seen him since Mary's death, and now he's all concerned about me and my fall. Not enough to come see me five weeks ago in the hospital, mind you. Or even send a card."

"Sorry about your friend. Was she sick?"

Pain flashed across Aunt Tilly's face before she answered, her voice accusing. "She died in a supposed accident."

Derrick paused with his fork halfway to his mouth and gave Tilly a questioning look.

Tilly continued, "Mary didn't drive at night. No matter how much she might want to go somewhere. If one of her friends didn't give her a ride, she'd miss it. There was a big storm, wind and heavy rain. Mary was supposed to be driving in it and ran off the road."

"Maybe it was an emergency. Some people..."

Aunt Tilly shook her head. "Mary would've called me or one of her other friends or run through the rain to a neighbor's."

"If it'll ease your mind, I'll pull up the report and see what the investigating officers said."

"Unless they say she wasn't driving, they're wrong." Aunt Tilly was adamant.

"It's possible she asked someone to drive her somewhere in her car and when they had a wreck, the driver panicked and ran away. Especially if they thought she was dead."

Aunt Tilly considered his words then asked, "Would they have gotten fingerprints?"

"Probably not if they thought it was an accident."

"But she wouldn't have been wedged behind the wheel if someone else was driving." Her shoulders sagged. "Guess it wouldn't hurt to have a fresh pair of eyes looking at what they said happened."

Derrick's smile barely turned up the corners of his mouth. "If it was a year ago, don't expect much. I can try talking to the investigating officers, but they may not remember much."

Tilly nodded.

Mindy interrupted the conversation with a bark as she stood by the door. As her aunt reached for her crutches, Tori pushed her chair back. "I'll take her out." She flicked on the outside light and opened the door. Mindy scooted out. "Carl was right about her being housebroken." She smiled and followed the puppy.

When Tori and pup returned, Derrick had gathered up the empty bags and used napkins and was throwing them in the trash. "Tilly assured me it was Ed's too large portions and not his choice of food that had you leaving many leftovers."

"That and Aunt Tilly won't have to eat soup and sandwiches tomorrow." Tori laughed. "Before you go, what did you find out about my 911 call?"

Derrick settled back at the table. "Evidently, she hadn't answered yet when you gave your address. When she did pick up, all she heard was a high-pitched voice fussing at kids for playing with the phone. The person apologized for the kids making the call and promised they would be grounded." Derrick shrugged. "The operator said she wondered about the voice sounding strange but figured it was because the person was angry."

Chapter Eleven

Tori came downstairs to the tantalizing smell of coffee and clatter of cutlery and dishes. She hadn't expected to get much sleep until the alarm was installed, but Derrick had checked all the windows and doors before he left and she had fallen asleep almost before she'd pulled up the covers.

"Good morning," her aunt greeted as Tori entered the kitchen. Aunt Tilly was puttering around the stove and Martha was setting the table. Their watchdog was licking her bowl clean. "Get yourself a cup of coffee. Breakfast is just about ready. Martha stopped at the grocery store on her way over and picked up a few necessities."

"Thank you, Martha. That was very thoughtful of you." Tori poured her coffee then asked, "What happened to all the barking Carl promised?"

"She did give a little yelp first thing this morning and went to the back door to let me know she needed to go out. How about buttering the toast that just popped up and put a couple more pieces of bread in?"

"No barks for Derrick and no barks for Martha," commented Tori as she watched Mindy settle on the rug by the back door.

Aunt Tilly finished scraping the scrambled eggs into a bowl and carried it over to the table, hobbling with one crutch. "Mindy's discriminating. She knows good people. Remember how she wouldn't let Talbert even open the gate to the backyard. Besides, Martha's scent is all over this house."

Martha smiled as she placed the platter of bacon beside the eggs and slid into a chair. "I guess that's a compliment."

"Mmm. This smells a lot better than the hotel breakfasts," Tori said as she set the plate of toast and her coffee on the table. Martha and her aunt were already dishing up eggs and bacon. "Maybe you two can accept the challenge and teach me how to cook."

"You stick around long enough and we might be able to do that."

"I'm here until you're back on both feet."

"Humph. That might be long enough to teach you how to open

a box of crackers to go with your can of soup."

Tori caught Martha trying to hide her smile behind her cup of coffee. She didn't try to hide her own grin when she replied, "I warned you that you might prefer my mud pies to my cooking."

Martha choked on the swallow she had taken and grabbed her napkin to keep from spewing coffee across the table.

Aunt Tilly looked from Martha to Tori. Her face was expressionless, but her eyes twinkled. "We bother to teach you, your mother going to let you cook when you move in with her?"

"That'll just be temporary. With a few more books and a part-time job, I'll get my own apartment."

"Why don't you be temporary here?"

"I…well…I…"

"I won't be dragging you off to a bunch of society stuff, so you'll have more time to write and draw your fairies."

Tori's smile stretched across her face. "I'd like to be temporary here."

"Then I don't think we'll be wasting our time teaching this girl to cook, Martha. Might even save my stomach."

"Can't even start unless we send her out to the store with that list we made."

"We knew you'd balk at leaving us alone but we're going to lock the doors when you go. If someone comes, we'll use the peep hole Gary put in and if we don't know the person, we won't open the door. We'll have our cell phones handy and if they try any shenanigans to get in, we'll tap 911.

As if they had planned a demonstration, Mindy ran barking toward the front door just as the doorbell rang. Aunt Tilly stood up and Martha pulled her phone from her pocket.

Tori held up her hand. "I'll see who it is." As she headed toward Mindy's barks, she felt in her pocket for her own phone. "Good girl." She bent and patted the dog then looked through the peephole, thankful that Gary had installed it. All she saw was a teenage face behind a bouquet of flowers. "Quiet." Tori commanded the dog, surprised when Mindy obeyed. Cautiously she opened the door as the dog maintained a charge stance. Maybe she was going to be the great guard dog Carl promised.

"Flowers for Ms. Matilda Statton," the teenager announced as he eyed the dog through the screen door.

"Thank you. Why don't you set the vase down on the porch and I'll get them. The dog is still being trained and she's a bit unpredictable," Tori said, imitating her aunt's warning to Talbert when he tried to enter the gate the previous day. She waited until the delivery van pulled away from the curb before she retrieved the flowers and carried them into the kitchen.

"Flowers for you, Aunt Tilly. Do you have an admirer?"

"Not likely." Her aunt snorted.

Tori pulled the card from the arrangement and handed it to her. "A little late if it's condolences for your broken leg and too early for your birthday."

Aunt Tilly looked at the card and threw it on the table. "What's Talbert up to?" Her eyes narrowed. "Never came around when Mary was alive. I've seen him around town this past year without so much as a nod or hello. Don't know why he showed up yesterday. Sure wasn't to express concern like he claimed." She waved her hand toward the bouquet of yellow and white carnations. "Flowers and an apology? Bunch of malarkey. Toss them in the trash, Tori."

"I. Uh. They're really pretty. Maybe Martha would like to take them home."

"No thanks. I feel the same way about that...person...as Tilly."

"I'll take them to the hospital or rehab."

"Martha nodded. "Then we won't have to look at them every time we throw something away."

"Sit down and eat before your eggs get cold." Aunt Tilly pointed her fork at Tori's plate. "You can drop them off on your way to the grocery store."

Tori frowned and looked from Martha to her aunt. With a sigh of resignation she said, "At least Mindy barked this time. Promise you'll keep the doors locked. We should do that anyway until we find out what's going on."

"I'll only open the backdoor to let Mindy out and Martha will stand guard." She waved her hand toward a corner of the kitchen.

Tori's eyes widened as she spied a shotgun leaning against the wall partially hidden by the refrigerator. The vintage wallpaper with pots, tea kettles and rolling pins helped to further disguise it. "Aunt Tilly! No! Martha can stand in the doorway armed with her cell phone. Where did you get that shotgun?"

"It was your grandpa's. Your dad used it too when he and Hank went hunting," she said, as if that would make the weapon more acceptable. "It's not loaded, but a barrel pointing at someone is going to make them stop."

"Unless he pulls out his own loaded gun. We need to be cautious and keep the doors locked while we may be in some other part of the house, but I think it's safe to let Mindy out while I'm gone." She studied the gun her father had used. "I thought it was Uncle Hank's gun you mentioned to Derrick?"

Tilly waved her hand in dismissal of Tori's words. "Couldn't find bullets for his. Besides, I promised Derrick I'd leave Your Uncle Hank's gun in the closet."

Tori choked on the bite of eggs she had just taken. When she stopped coughing, she managed to croak out, "You said that the shotgun isn't loaded."

"It's not, but we need to be prepared in case..." Her Aunt shrugged.

***

Tori pushed the overloaded cart out to her car. She had added a few extra things that weren't on the list. Well, maybe more than a few. She had suggested picking up lunch but Aunt Tilly had reminded her of all the leftovers from Ed's Eating Place in the fridge. She unloaded everything into her trunk and pushed the empty cart to the cart corral. As she turned back toward her car she nearly bumped into someone. A slight chill rippled down her back when she looked up and saw Talbert Hatchett standing in front of her.

"Oh, I'm sorry," Tori said as she sidestepped to go around him.

"Entirely my fault," he said as he shifted his weight to block her departure. "I was looking at my phone and not paying attention. Tilly's niece. Right?"

Tori took a step back and forced an answering smile. She watched as he slipped a hand into his front pocket. Had she seen a phone?

"How is Tilly? I feel bad about not checking on her sooner. Did she get the flowers I sent?"

Tori felt her face warm. Her voice was stilted as she answered, "They arrived just before I left the house."

"Hey, my shopping can wait." He waved his hand toward the store entrance. "How about grabbing a cup of coffee and you can tell me what she needs. She and my wife were good friends. I know Mary would be doing things for Tilly if she were still alive. Maybe I can fill in for her." Talbert's smile didn't reach his brown eyes.

"I… uh..." She stiffened. "Thanks, but I have frozen food and I need to get home before it thaws." Her eyes narrowed as she added, "Aunt Tilly's fine. She doesn't need anything. I'm there and Martha's there and Police Detective Derrick Stone has been stopping by." Aunt Tilly didn't trust Talbert. Mentioning Derrick might make him back off.

"I really need to get going." She nodded and pushed past him, cringing as her shoulder brushed his arm. She hurried to her car. She slid in behind the wheel and locked the door before starting the motor. As she pulled out of her parking spot, she glanced in her rearview mirror. He was still standing there, staring in her direction. She had to wait for traffic to clear before she could exit the parking lot. She looked over her shoulder to see if Talbert was still watching her, but he was turning away. He pulled his phone from his back pocket as he walked over two aisles to a late model yellow sports car.

She hadn't realized how tense she was from her encounter with Talbert until she pulled into Aunt Tilly's driveway and her shoulders relaxed. Something was odd about their meeting. It almost seemed planned. She grabbed two bags from her trunk, choosing ones she knew held ice cream and frozen food, and headed toward the backdoor.

She looked through the large pane in the door and saw her aunt and Martha puttering around the kitchen. The table was set and Martha was putting ice cubes into glasses. Rather than try to insert her key, she kicked the door a couple of times. Both women turned with startled expressions and Tori immediately regretted her action until Martha beamed a smile and hurried to let her in. "Sorry about that. I didn't mean to alarm you."

Martha ran her damp hands down her denim capris and took a bag from Tori. "No worry." She patted Tori's arm with her free hand.

"Good thing you know that gun is unloaded. I was about to grab it and point it in your direction." Aunt Tilly shook her crutch at Tori. A twinkle in her in blue eyes and a chuckle belied her words.

Tori put her bag on the counter and headed back out the door. "I've got a couple more loads."

"I'll come help." Martha started to follow.

"Thanks. I can get them, but those things need to go in the freezer. If you can do that?"

Tori carried in the last load and locked the door.

"Looks like our list multiplied in the store," Aunt Tilly said, looking at the grocery bags on the counter and floor.

"Just a few extra things," Tori laughed. "You forgot a few essentials like ice cream."

"Well, let's eat lunch before we have to warm things up again. The rest can be put away later."

Martha finished pouring glasses of tea. Tori grabbed two and carried them to the table.

Her aunt and Martha carried on a conversation about friends and events planned. Tori only half listened.

A thought hit her. She put her fork down on the edge of her plate. The encounter in the parking lot with Talbert had felt odd. He had said he was looking at his phone. He had put his hand in his front pocket when she moved to avoid a collision, but he pulled the phone from his back pocket as he walked away.

"Something wrong with your food?"

Aunt Tilly's question jerked her attention back to the leftover fried chicken in front of her and her companions.

"I was thinking about my grocery shopping. When I was returning the cart, I bumped into Talbert Hatchett, literally."

"If you put that cart out of whack when you ran into him, I won't complain so much when I get a wobbly one. I'll grin and think maybe it's the one you whacked Talbert with," chuckled Martha.

"Unfortunately, I'd just shoved my cart into the corral. When I turned around, there he was." Tori frowned at the memory. She picked up her fork and scooped up a bite of green beans.

"And?"

Tori shrugged. "He asked if you'd gotten the flowers and if you needed anything. I told him Martha and I were handling everything."

"Darn tootin'," exclaimed Martha.

Her aunt raised a brow as if she knew there was more. She glanced toward Martha and changed the subject. "Eat up so you can get to your writing. Martha and I have our chores planned for this afternoon. She's leaving early to take her neighbor to a doctor's appointment. I 'spect I can find something in those bags to cook for dinner, but we still have leftovers from what Derrick brought over last night, too."

Tori tilted her head and looked at her aunt. "Since you made the list, I'm sure you will. I'll help put the groceries away and I want to call Gary about the alarm he ordered then I'll get busy writing."

"Never mind the groceries. Martha and I will take care of them. I need to see what all you did buy."

When they finished eating, Tori stood and started stacking empty plates.

"Leave those and skedaddle." Her aunt made shooing motions toward the doorway.

"Aunt Tilly, I came to take care of you, not have you take care of me."

"You came to get me out of that jail house they call rehab. I've got a leg and two good crutches to stand on. Go finish that book so I can wave it around to my friends."

Chapter Twelve

"Tori looked up as her aunt thumped into the room. Doggie nails tapped on the wooden floor behind her. Aunt Tilly looked serious and determined. Tori clicked on save. Her imagination was taking a vacation anyway.

"Martha's gone. Time to tell whatever you left out earlier about your run in with Talbert. You want to talk here or join me for tea and chocolate chip cookies in the kitchen?"

Tori pushed her chair back. "Tea and cookies sound good."

When Tori entered the kitchen, the smell of something good cooking rivaled the fragrance of fresh baked cookies. A pot simmered on the stove. She sat and picked up a still warm treat.

Mindy for once had abandoned her aunt. She sat by Tori with begging blue eyes. "No chocolate for you, little lady." Mindy gave a hopeful bark in answer, but when Tori shook her head and repeated no, she moved to lay down at Aunt Tilly's feet.

Her aunt waited until Tori swallowed her bite of cookie. "You can think about what you are going to say while you chew that next bite, but I want to know what happened."

"I didn't want to talk about this in front of Martha. I don't know how much she knows about your business." Tori put the cookie on her plate and clasped her hands together. "I don't think the meeting with Talbert today was accidental. I don't know if he followed me there, which is a scary thought, or if he was really buying groceries and saw me. In which case, he could have hailed me and waved. I turned around and he was there. I told you he asked about the flowers, but he also asked me to have coffee with him to talk about what you needed. Said, since Mary wasn't there to do for you, he would fill in for her.

"At lunch the idea hit me. You said Mary was the one with all the money. If he's spent all he inherited..." She shrugged. "Maybe he has a gambling problem or something. Anyway, could he be trying to court you for your money?"

Her aunt stared at her, shock raising her brows nearly to her gray hairline. "Good thing I hadn't taken a sip of my tea, I would have spewed it across the table. The man's no-good to the core. Mary had filed for divorce. She died before it was final so he's claiming everything. I know she wasn't careless enough to have not changed her will. She said she did when she arrived here after she had filed for divorce, but the only one found left it all to Talbert."

Tori was unwilling to let her suspicions go. "Maybe Mary wasn't as rich as everyone thought, or it doesn't matter because he's greedy and wants more."

"Mary kept her purse strings tight when it came to Talbert. She wasn't an attractive woman and she had a sharp tongue, but her heart was pure gold. She wasn't popular with the guys growing up. Made her susceptible to Talbert's charms. Didn't take her long to realize he had married her for her money. I think she was too embarrassed to admit she'd been bamboozled and divorce him then.

"And I don't think he's benefitted much since her death. She made her lawyer, Hayden Whitmore, executor, and he's claiming Mary had a new will. Hayden is taking his time settling her estate with the old will Talbert came up with."

"So, now he's after you."

"I don't have a big house like Mary. Don't drive a fancy car. So what's to make him think I'm worth pursuing?" Her aunt gave a slight shake of her head and clenched her fist. "But I agree. He's after something."

"You and what little money you may have?"

"I don't know where he would have gotten a whiff of what I have or don't have."

"If he rings our doorbell like he said he did before, do we let him in?"

Aunt Tilly looked at her niece like she'd aged and gotten dementia. "We've got that peep hole. We don't answer the door."

Tori savored another chocolate chip bite before asking. "What if he circles around to the backdoor and sees you or Martha in the Kitchen?"

Her aunt tapped her fingers on the table. The straight line of her lips curved up into a smile. "I'm going to put a bucket in the middle of the kitchen and stick a mop in it. If he catches us unawares, I'll point to the bucket and then point to the floor. I'm going to lean that shotgun against the wall opposite the door so he can see it, too.

"And if he corners us on neutral territory like the grocery store or a restaurant, we'll let him babble and try to figure out what he wants." She laughed. "Maybe stick him with the check. I'm going to paint a sign that says 'Beware Biting Dog' for the gate."

***

The next day, in spite of having a pantry full of groceries, Aunt Tilly declared they needed to go out for lunch. It wasn't a day that Martha worked and Mindy wasn't happy at being left alone, but she dutifully sat at her aunt's command though she might have been baffled at the command 'guard.'

Using the handicap tag, Tori took advantage of the space right in front of Ed's. She hopped out and started around to the passenger side to help her aunt. She spotted Talbert across the street talking to a man. Aunt Tilly's network must be working and she decided to put their plan into action. Tori had hoped he would drop his overtures toward her aunt and there would be no action. She stopped and stared when she recognized the man he was talking to. Their locksmith who hadn't answered or returned her three calls.

"Well, I'm glad you're finally letting me do for myself." Her aunt's words pulled her attention away from the two men across the street.

"I'm sorry. It's a matter of courtesy, Aunt Tilly. When I get older you can open the door for me." Tori laughed.

"Yeah, my ghost just might come back and do that."

"Did you see who's across the street?" Tori lowered her voice and leaned toward her aunt.

"Of course, why do you think we are here?"

Before they could enter the restaurant, Gary crossed the road calling, "Ms. Tilly. Tori."

"Oops. Wrong one," her aunt said.

Gary stepped up onto the curb and focused on Tori. "I owe you an apology. I lost my phone. Left it at a client's house. Never done that before. It must have dropped out of my pocket. Her four-year old son found it and it took her a while to get my home number to let me know. Sorry. There was a mix-up in the order for your security system but I've replaced the order and put a rush on it. They're going to give you a discount, too, since the mess up was on their end."

"When do you think you'll get it? I know you put up that camera and we have the dog, but we'll sleep easier with the alarm."

"Problem, ladies?" Talbert asked, coming up behind Gary.

Tori caught the satisfied glance her aunt sent her and quickly answered. "No problem. Gary was just discussing the work he has done for us." Tori turned back to Gary. "Thank you for getting back to me."

Gary raised an eyebrow and touched his cap as he stepped back. "I'm late for a job. I'll be in touch as soon as that order comes in." He wheeled around and headed for his truck.

Tori shook her head. "He did some work for us and he was checking to see if we need anything else."

"You ladies are obviously going in to eat. Do you mind if I join you? It's hard to dine alone." The sadness in his tone didn't quite reach his eyes. He ran his hand over his scalp, flattening the slicked-back style even more.

"I think Mae can find us a table for three." Her aunt's smile didn't reflect in her shrewd eyes either.

Mae waved to them as they entered. As soon as she finished helping the customer at the counter, she joined them. "I guess it's great to be back home and I hear you have protection now." Before her aunt could say anything, Mae added, "I heard Carl finally got rid of one of his puppies."

"Yes, we got the best of the bunch. She's turned out to be a great watchdog." Not wanting to hurt Carl's chances of finding homes for the rest, she added a little loudly, "He's still got some great ones to choose from though if anyone's looking for a pet or protection."

"You advertising for Carl?" Mae grinned. "That table over there is finishing up. We'll clear it as soon as they gather up their stuff."

"Talbert is joining us today," her aunt informed.

"One way of getting out of waiting for a table, Talbert." Mae's voice was sarcastic as she looked at their companion.

"Now, Mae. Tilly was Mary's best friend. The least I can do is treat her to a meal now and then."

At least they weren't boxed into a booth with him, Tori thought as they settled at the cleared table. She smiled. And Mae had conned him into treating. The waitress came with menus, water and utensils wrapped in napkins then hurried over to another table where a customer was signaling impatiently.

Talbert picked up the menu but didn't look at it. "So, how are you managing, Tilly?"

"Super dooper, Talbert. Rehab made me independent. I have to shoo Martha and Tori away to let me do things. How are you managing alone in that big house?"

"It's lonesome but I'm getting by." The woe-be-gone look was back.

Tori noticed several ladies around the dining room looking their way. Talbert's act must work with other women. There were several envious looks in their direction.

"But what can I do for you? I've been very neglectful of you. I'd like to make that up."

"Now, Talbert. Just because Mary and I were best of friends doesn't mean you should feel guilty unless you had something to do with her accident."

Tori stifled a gasp behind a fake cough when her aunt, under the guise of a sincere concern, threw out her dart. Talbert flinched. His ashen face matched the white knuckles that gripped the table.

Aunt Tilly continued in a consoling tone. "Like you had an argument and she jumped in her car and left. But you weren't even home."

Tori saw Talbert's hands tremble as he slipped them under the table and into his lap.

"No, I wasn't. But if I had been home and we argued, I would have taken her keys away and not let her go out into that storm. Surely people don't think that I... That I... I can't even say it."

Aunt Tilly reached over and patted his upper arm. "Oh, I'm so sorry. I didn't mean to imply..." She shook her head. "I was trying to say that you don't need to feel obligated on Mary's behalf. I have Martha and Tori and Detective Stone has been stopping by. Now let's change the subject before I put my foot in my mouth again."

She leaned back in her chair and picked up her menu. "This is nice having lunch with you."

At her aunt's raised eyebrow, Tori picked up the conversation. "Do you eat here often, Mr. Hatchett? I'm afraid we've become addicted. Especially since I'm such a terrible cook. But Aunt Tilly and Martha have promised to teach me." She babbled on. "Of course, for Aunt Tilly, teaching me is a matter of self-preservation."

"Please, Tori. It's Talbert. I thought we were past formalities." He relaxed a little and opened his menu. "I don't believe the waitress told us what the specials are."

Tori almost laughed. She and Aunt Tilly rarely even got a menu. It was usually 'Ed will fix you something.' And it looked like the same was happening today. She looked over Talbert's shoulder to see Mae bearing down on them with a tray. She placed a plate down in front of Tilly, another in front of Tori, and slapped a third in front of Talbert.

"Hey. I haven't even ordered yet."

"Since when have you ordered anything except the meatloaf when it was on special?"

Talbert sputtered a little before saying, "I guess this will do."

"Do?" Mae reached over and picked up his plate. "Let me know when you are ready to order." She started back toward the kitchen.

"Mae, the meatloaf is fine. Thank you."

Mae set the plate back in front of Talbert and put her hands on her ample hips. "You sure? Cause we aren't going to comp you this meal."

He picked up his fork and cut into the tender meat. "You are right. This is what I would have ordered if the waitress had told us what the specials are."

Mae winked in Tori's direction and headed back to the kitchen, stopping to chat at a table with three women along the way.

"A bit presumptuous, but I do order the meatloaf special frequently," he huffed out. "She didn't give you a chance to choose either. Is that what you usually get?" He looked at Tilly's plate as if he was trying to figure out what she was eating.

"Ed usually –"

"Yes. It's really very good." Aunt Tilly interrupted Tori and took a bite of her chicken.

Tori raised an eyebrow and stared at her aunt. Aunt Tilly raised an answering eyebrow and shrugged as she buttered her roll. Tori smiled and focused on her own meal. Talbert wasn't going to be able to comp their meals either. "Mmm. Delicious." She added for effect.

"Even if you and Martha can teach me to cook, I don't think we'll be able to give up eating here."

Talbert swallowed the bite he'd been chewing. "You'll have to invite me to taste-test your cooking."

Aunt Tilly suddenly choked and grabbed her glass of tea. When Talbert started to rise, she shook her head and waved him back down. She took another sip of tea and patted her mouth with her napkin. "I shouldn't have laughed at your offer. Actually, she's quite good at heating canned soup and making meat and bread sandwiches."

"Aunt Tilly says the mud pies I made as a child would taste better than my cooking. Thank you for your offer but I'll limit my tasters to Aunt Tilly and Martha." She saw her aunt sit back and relax. Did she think Tori'd accept his offer? "They won't be polite and try to eat it if it's not good. They'll pick up their plates and scrape them into the garbage."

"I'm willing to take a chance. I can scrape my plate with the best of them."

"No. I'd be too embarrassed." She changed the subject to divert him. "I don't believe Aunt Tilly mentioned what kind of work you do."

"I'm a financial consultant. If you need help with what you earn from your books. I'll be glad to advise you."

Tori laughed. "I'm not making enough to even think about investments." Funny, she thought. He didn't even know I was Aunt Tilly's niece, but he knows I write books. Is he looking into what obstacles he has to remove in order to get to her aunt's money? Is a niece less threatening than a granddaughter?

"What about you, Tilly? Talbert dismissed Tori and turned his attention to greener fields. "Are you ready to switch to an investor who can make you lots of money?"

"No. My husband, Hank, was satisfied with Foster's company.

I'll stick with them."

"But—"

"No more business talk. Do you still play golf every weekend?"

Talbert frowned. "That lawyer Mary appointed as her executor canceled her membership. Claims it's his job to preserve her assets."

"Oh, but surely you know enough people for them to invite you as their guest."

He shook his head. "They seem to remember that she filed for divorce, not that we reconciled and were working out our problems."

Tilly ignored his reconciliation statement and pointed out, "There is our public course. I understand it's well maintained."

"It's not the same taking a client there and then discussing business after you've let him win."

"I'm sure the lawyer is just making sure Mary's wishes are followed."

"Her wishes were stated quite clearly in the will I found in her desk. Anger contorted his face. "That lawyer is on a power trip." He relaxed the grip he had on his fork and put it on the edge of his plate. Talbert took a swallow of his tea. When he put his glass down the anger disappeared as if it had never been there.

"Actually, Tilly, I've been meaning to ask you about the papers Mary left at your house when she was staying with you."

Tilly stared at Talbert several moments before she answered. "Mary only stayed with me a few days after she filed for divorce. She went home to make sure you left with only what belonged to you. She didn't say anything about leaving something with me." She took her napkin from her lap and laid it beside her plate.

Talbert opened his mouth but before he could say a word, Mae appeared at their table. "You folks want dessert or are you ready for the bill?"

Talbert pushed back his chair. "I need to get back to the office. You ladies indulge. Mae, put their dessert on my tab."

"I think we're ready to go, too. If we could have a couple of boxes?" She smiled at Mae.

"Here you are Talbert." Mae slapped the bill down on the table. "Cash or credit card. Wanda will take care of you at the register." She picked up Tori and Tilly's plates. "I'll box these up for you in the kitchen."

"Thank you for lunch." Tori couldn't force herself to say it was enjoyable.

"Still willing to be a taster of your mudpies." He nodded stiffly in Tori's direction before switching his attention. "Tilly," he managed a smile, "have a nice day." He snatched the bill from the table and stormed toward the register.

"Wow. Was he trying to leave us with the tab?"

"More likely Ed's Eating Place."

By the time Mae returned with bags suspiciously holding more than their uneaten lunches, Talbert had paid and pushed his way out the door. "How'd you two get tangled up with Talbert?"

"I think he's got his radar out for Aunt Tilly. He was across the street when we parked in front of the restaurant. He practically ran over to tell her hello."

"He wanted to join us and I thought maybe we could find out what he's up to," Tilly replied in lowered voice.

Mae raised an eyebrow.

"Except for her funeral, I haven't seen him since before Mary died. All of a sudden he's showing up at my house, sending flowers." She laughed. "And joining us for lunch."

"You find out anything?" When Tilly shook her head, Mae continued, "You be careful. Right after Mary died in that accident lots of the widow ladies were coming on to him but they dropped him real quick. Or he dropped them when he found out they had no money."

"Don't worry. I'm no fool and I don't believe for a minute he and Mary were reconciling. Let us know if you hear anything." She pointed to the bags Mae was holding. "That looks like you added the refrigerator."

Mae laughed as she handed the bags to Tori. She waved to a customer trying to get her attention. "Back to work."

Chapter Thirteen

Tori pulled into the driveway and scanned the area around the house before turning off the motor. "Why don't you wait here while I check out things?"

"We going to pussyfoot around every time we come home?" Tori's aunt opened the car door and reached for her crutches. "If we see broken glass or forced doors, we'll jump back in the car and dial 911. Otherwise, if anyone's in my house, I'm going to poke them with one crutch and whop them with the other."

Tori choked back a laugh. "And if they have a gun?"

"They better get me with the first bullet."

She shook her head and followed her aunt up the ramp to the back door. "Mindy's not barking. That's a good sign." She could hear Mindy's nails dancing on the floor as she turned the key and pushed the door open. The pup bounced out, gave a one-bark greeting, and dashed into the yard to do her business.

"You wait til Mindy's done her stuff. We'll go in together. You might need me and my crutches."

"If I need your crutches, you lean against the wall and hand them to me. I'll do the poking and whopping."

"You're not taking my fun away from me."

Joking relieved the tension of coming home to an empty house, but it didn't stop Tori from taking a quick tour through it even if Mindy hadn't been barking.

"Looks like Mae topped off our lunch with more food and included dessert," Tori announced as she emptied cartons from the bags. "You want pie now or save it for later?"

"I'll make coffee and we can have pie now. After putting up with Talbert for an hour, I need something to sweeten my day."

"I thought you planned running into him."

Aunt Tilly huffed out a breath. "It was a bad idea. I thought we could maybe get a hint about whatever he's up to. Or a clue that he had something to do with Mary's accident."

Tori paused getting forks from the drawer. "We found out he's a cheapskate and probably broke since the lawyer is delaying about settling things in his favor."

"He never did have much of a work ethic. I think Mary

subsidized his investment business to keep him busy and out of the house. Someone else handled her accounts and investments. I heard Talbert complain about that more than once."

Tori carried the two mugs of coffee her aunt had poured to the table. Aunt Tilly dished up the apple pie while Tori got sugar and cream. Mindy had watched food being put on the table hopefully, but when they sat down, she lay beside her aunt, nose resting on her paws.

"You didn't let me in on your plans."

When her aunt tilted her head and raised an eyebrow, Tori continued, "You seemed pretty sure we would run into Talbert at Ed's."

"You had a run in with him at the grocery store, I didn't think you could act surprised to see him again."

"That wasn't surprise before. That was startled. You think he's stalking us."

"He knows I eat a lot at Ed's. I think he staked himself out across the street, talking to whoever came by as a cover. We'll have to bring up the subject when Gary comes to install our security system."

"You're going to quiz Gary about his conversation with Talbert?"

Aunt Tilly scraped up the last bite of her pie. "If our pizza arrives as he's finishing up the installation of our security system, it would be rude not to invite him to join us."

"Our pizza?" Tori glanced over at the bags from Ed's.

"Course, after eating such a big lunch, it's a good thing our alarm won't get here for a few days. But I've been having a hankering for pizza and Gary can help us eat it so we don't over indulge."

"Do you trust Gary? He's changing locks. He could have a key to nearly everyone's house in Cotton Creek and a few businesses."

"I don't trust anyone right now except you, me, Martha and maybe Derrick."

As she finished that statement, the doorbell rang, startling both women and sending Mindy barking to the door. But when Tori followed, she found the pup wagging her tail.

"Well discriminating watchdog, I hope that's a friend out

there." She looked through the peephole and smiled down at the dog. "I'm glad Aunt Tilly included him on her trusted list, even if it was only a maybe."

She turned the deadbolt and opened the door. "Come in detective." She eyed the white box he carried. "We're in the kitchen having coffee and apple pie." She gestured down the hall.

As they entered the kitchen, Derrick chuckled. "I came bearing dessert, but I see I'm too late."

"Tori, pour the detective some coffee and get him a plate." Aunt Tilly eyed the box he set on the table. "Talbert joined us for lunch at Ed's Eating Place and we needed something to put a good taste in our mouths. A slice of apple pie doesn't mean we've succeeded." She smiled. "What are you offering?"

Derrick laughed and flipped it open.

"Ooh...pecan tarts. I think Tori and I can manage to share one."

Tori put the coffee and a plate and fork down in front of Derrick. "Would you like a slice of pie to go with your tart?" she asked as she reached for the knife.

"One of Mae's?" he pursed his lips speculatively.

She grinned as she slid a piece onto his plate. "Good guess."

Derrick smiled his thanks as he picked up his coffee and took a swallow. "Talbert? Mary's husband, right? How'd you get stuck with him?"

Tilly deftly divided one of the tarts and slid half onto Tori's plate and half onto her own. "He was across the street and joined us before we even got into the restaurant. But we took the opportunity to see if we could figure out what he's up to with all his attention. After Mindy chased him out of the backyard, he cornered Tori in the grocery store parking lot."

Derrick put his fork down. His expression was serious as he turned to her. "Tell me about that."

Tori repeated the tale of her encounter with Talbert ending with, "He had no groceries when he bumped into me and he didn't go into the store afterwards."

Derrick refocused on Tilly. "You think Talbert is the one that broke into your house?"

"I would if I could think of a reason why." She wiped her lips with a paper napkin.

Tori frowned, wrinkles furrowing her forehead. "Did Mary maybe forget something here when she visited? Like a purse or a coat with something in the pocket?"

Aunt Tilly shook her head. "I would have returned something like that. She did come to stay a couple of days after she filed for divorce and told him to pack up and get out. Then she started thinking maybe she'd better supervise his packing so it didn't include the family silver."

Tori grabbed the coffee pot and refilled everyone's mug. "What about the garage sale? Did you buy something he wants back?"

"He'd just have to ask. No. All I bought was a pink sweater that Mary wore all the time. I couldn't stand the possibility of seeing someone else wearing it. And that teapot over there in plain sight." She pointed to the counter near the stove. "Mary always made tea in it when I visited."

"If you think he's stalking you, I'll pull him in and give him a warning." Derrick's phone buzzed. He pulled it out and pressed his lips together as he read the message. "I've got to go. Thanks for the coffee, pie and company." He looked at Tori. "Come lock the door behind me."

He turned when he got to the door and gripped Tori's upper arms. "Make sure Martha is here if you have to go out and be careful when you do." His hold softened almost to a caress. "I'll have the officers doing the drive-by be on the lookout for his vehicle." He stepped back and opened the door. "Lock it," he said pulling it shut.

She didn't hear his departing footsteps until the lock clicked as she turned it.

Tori returned to the kitchen to find her aunt standing by the counter staring at Mary's teapot.

"You know. This is worth a lot more money than what I paid for it."

***

"Good morning, Aunt Tilly." Tori had been lured downstairs with the smell of brewing coffee and frying bacon. The tantalizing smells made it hard to sleep late. When she entered the kitchen, her aunt, looking cheerful in a pink plaid dress, was scraping scrambled eggs into a bowl. Mindy was lying on the rug they'd put by the door to protect the floor from excited paws when they came home.

"Carry these eggs to the table then grab yourself some coffee. Breakfast is ready."

"You must've gotten up early to get this all done. I've seen you slowed down because you have to make two or three trips managing things with those crutches."

"You'd be an early riser, too, if you weren't up so late."

"I know, but sometimes that's when the words start flowing. I hope I'm not waking you when I go up the stairs. I know which steps creak and I try to avoid them."

"Not a problem." Her aunt gave a half smile. "I guess since that first break-in, I wake up at the slightest little noise. Mindy may lift her head but if she doesn't bark, I go right back to sleep." Tilly broke the piece of bacon she carried and dropped the pieces into Mindy's bowl. "There aren't many words in your fairy picture books. What's all the writing you're doing?"

"You've seen my books?"

"Of course I have. Read every one of them. They have a special shelf in the library. Surprised you haven't noticed them." Aunt Tilly hung the flowered dish cloth she'd been using on the rack beside the sink and hobbled to the table on one crutch. The other was lying on the floor by the stove.

"Whoever broke in must not have tossed them to the floor. Those are the ones I noticed." Tori put the bowl of eggs on the table and filled a mug with the fresh brewed coffee. "I'm trying to write a book for middle schoolers. It's a chapter book with a lot more pages." She settled at the table and dished up eggs and bacon. After savoring a few bites, she looked at her aunt. "I still feel bad snoozing away while you're working away doing for me as well as yourself. I did come to help."

"You did help. You got me out of that rehab place. A person can heal faster in their own home. And I'm getting exercise doing useful stuff. They had people climbing up and down fake steps that didn't go anywhere."

"Those fake steps were getting people ready to climb the real thing, like the ones you have to your front porch." Tori laughed.

The phone rang and Tori jumped up to answer it. She looked at the ID. “It says ‘Mary.’ Must be Talbert using her phone.” She found herself whispering even though there was no way for him to hear.

“Let it ring. I guess I’ll have to listen to his voice mail later. Unless it accidently gets deleted. Get the coffee pot while you’re up, would you?”

When Tori sat down after topping off Aunt Tilly’s mug, her aunt gave a dramatic sigh. “I guess I need to dust that answering machine. I’m still clumsy with these crutches.” She looked pointedly at the one abandoned on the floor. “That deleting might just happen.”

“I’ll dust. That way you can blame it on me.”

“Why do I need to blame it on you?”

Tori grinned. “I’ve got a hunch where Talbert is concerned a lot of things are going to happen that you’ll be taking the blame for.”

Mindy jumped up and gave a happy yap as she scrambled to the back door. Her tail wagged her whole back end. A minute later, Martha’s face looked through the large glass pane. Tori was already on her way to unlock the door to let her in.

Martha bustled in. “Good morning.” She bent down and gave Mindy a few pats. “How’s my favorite dog?”

“We still have eggs and bacon. Would you like some breakfast?” Tilly greeted.

“Been a little while since I ate, but I’m good. I’ll have some of that coffee I smell though.” She stowed her purse and the sweater she had worn for the early morning chill in the laundry room. She picked up the crutch and leaned it against the counter then poured herself a mug.

When they finished eating, Tori let the two women chat while she cleared the table and put plates and bowl into the dishwasher. Mindy gulped the tablespoon of eggs she put in her dish. Tori smiled at their chatter. Someone who didn’t know the two ladies might call Martha the cleaning lady but even though she helped Aunt Tilly by cleaning, she was more of a friend and companion. Tori filled her mug with coffee and announced she was heading to her computer.

An hour later the whir of the vacuum cleaner pulled her out of her story. She picked up her cup and took a sip, grimacing at the cold brew. Martha wouldn't be coming in to clean the library while she sat at the desk but the hall and the dining room across from the library weren't off limits and the noise carried. She stood and stretched. Might as well trade the cold coffee for a glass of ice tea.

Martha moved into Aunt Tilly's room as Tori walked down the hall to the kitchen. She had just finished putting the pitcher back into the fridge when the doorbell rang. Mindy ran barking to the front door. When Tori got there, she had stopped barking and stood growling.

Heart racing, she picked up Mindy and looked through the peephole. Talbert stood there impatiently pressing the doorbell again. She gave a sigh of relief as he turned and went down the steps.

But as she headed back to the kitchen to retrieve her tea, she glanced through the dining room doorway and out the window. Talbert was heading to the back. She hurried to her aunt's room still holding Mindy. Both women turned as she rushed into the room. She shook her head when Martha started to turn off the vacuum. "Talbert." She whispered as a banging started at the backdoor.

"I'm getting my shotgun and see if buckshot will go through tempered glass."

"Aunt Tilly," Tori said grabbing her arm. "You said it wasn't loaded!" Mindy escaped from her grip and ran barking to the back door.

"It wasn't then. What good's a gun if you don't put a shell in it?"

"I'm calling Derrick. Let's let him take care of Talbert." She held onto her aunt until she shook her head in agreement.

Derrick answered on the second ring. "Tori, something wrong?"

Tori quickly explained how they ignored Talbert's ringing of the doorbell and how he was now pounding on the backdoor.

"Hold on." The line went quiet.

She shifted her weight from one foot to the other as she waited for him to come back. Should she have confronted Talbert and not involved the police? She'd never shot a gun but she could have pointed it toward the door with its big glass window, except now the gun had a shell in it.

Derrick came back on the line. "There is a cruiser four blocks from your house. The officers will investigate. Where are you?"

"In Aunt Tilly's room. Out of sight. We wanted him to think we were gone or couldn't hear over Martha's vacuuming. But his banging is awfully loud and Mindy is barking up a storm."

"Good dog. You ladies continue to stay out of sight until the officers have removed him from the premises. You did right to call instead of confronting him. His actions sound a little aggressive for a friendly visit. Certainly more than what is called for."

When Mindy's bark changed to a final yap, Tori rushed down the hall to the kitchen doorway, Aunt Tilly and Martha on her heels. She started to peek round the door frame and stopped. Stepping back, she motioned Martha forward. "You look in case he's still where he can see in." Tori winked. "You were vacuuming and couldn't hear the ruckus."

Martha stuck her head around the door frame. "Oh my! Tilly, come see this."

All three women stepped into the kitchen and looked out the window. Talbert was being led through the gate, hands cuffed behind his back.

"Better'n my shotgun." Aunt Tilly and Martha grinned at each other.

Tori frowned. "But why did they arrest him rather than just send him on his way?"

An hour and a half later, Tori had taken away the celebratory bottle of wine, made sandwiches for everyone, and insured they ate them. Aunt Tilly and Martha sat in the kitchen sipping on coffee. The vacuum cleaner still stood in the middle of her aunt's bedroom.

Tori sat in the library, fingering her mouse and staring at the computer screen. Her shoulders heaved as she sighed. Everything she had typed in since Talbert had rung the front doorbell had disappeared with a few taps of the delete key. She jumped when the doorbell rang again and her heart beat double-time but Mindy rushed toward the door with a yap and stood expectantly, tail wagging.

Tori headed toward the entrance. No sign of Martha and her aunt. She hoped they hadn't pulled out the wine to finish it off. One peek and she quickly flung open the door. "Derrick what are you doing here?"

His expression was serious as he entered. He bent to give Mindy a pet and a treat before answering. "Came to check on all of you and give you a report."

Aunt Tilly was making a fresh pot of coffee and Martha was piling chocolate chip cookies on a plate when Tori and Derrick entered the kitchen. They must have heard him arrive.

"Come in and have a seat. This will be ready in a few minutes." Aunt Tilly beamed a smile at Derrick and grabbed extra mugs from the cabinet. Martha set the plate of cookies on the table and emptied the cold coffee from their mugs into the sink. When mugs were filled and delivered to the table, everyone sat and stared at Derrick.

Tori was ready to snatch the cookie plate out of his reach as he picked up another one without saying anything.

"Well, is that creep sitting in your jail?" Aunt Tilly finally asked.

Derrick shook his head no and smiles faded from the elder ladies' faces.

"But your officers hauled him out of here in handcuffs." She pounded on the table.

Derrick held up his hand. "Mr. Hatchett had picked up a large rock and was about to hit it against the glass window in the door. The officers thought he was attempting to break in."

"Which he was," interrupted Aunt Tilly.

"I questioned him for almost an hour and he wouldn't budge from his argument that he was concerned something had happened to the occupants of the house. You weren't answering the door, but cars were there. There was a buzzing noise coming from inside. The dog was barking frantically. The District Attorney wouldn't have pursued any charges and if he had, a judge probably would have only given him community service." Derrick gave a slight smile. "Would you have wanted to inflict his 'helping' on anyone?"

Aunt Tilly looked down, her finger drawing circles around a small scratch on the wooden table top.

"I pointed out to him that a friend could have picked you up. The noise could have been the washer, dryer or vacuum cleaner running. And dogs bark whenever anyone comes to the door. I suggested he call before he visited and warned him to leave if no one answered the front door."

"That's not doing much," Martha grumbled.

"No, but he has waved a red flag and I'll be keeping an eye on him." Derrick reached for another cookie. "Is there anything to make you think it might have been him that broke into your house either of the two times?"

"He never came round when Mary was alive, and I haven't seen him since her funeral." Aunt Tilly rubbed her forehead. "Now he's showing up here and waylaying us when we go out."

"I believe he's after money he thinks Aunt Tilly has since the lawyer is holding up settling Mary's will." Tori reached over and gripped her aunt's hand. "But he did ask if Mary had left anything here when she stayed with Aunt Tilly after she filed for divorce."

"I don't believe there was any reconciliation like Talbert claims. Mary was finally getting rid of that cheating leech." Tilly gave a negative shake of her head. "But why would he push me down the stairs or hit Tori on the head?"

Derrick took out a notebook and pen and started jotting down what they had mentioned. "Did he say what she might have left here?"

"He asked about papers but..." Tilly frowned and shook her head again. "Mary came with a small suitcase and a few changes of clothes. She took that with her when she left."

"Any idea what papers he might be looking for?"

Tori broke the silence that reigned. "He gave the lawyer a will that named him beneficiary. What if he didn't find her new will where she cut him off with nothing? He would need to find the new one and destroy it."

Derrick tapped his pen on the notebook. "Why doesn't the lawyer have a copy of the new will with her signature?"

Tilly wrapped her hands around her cup as she looked at Derrick. "I went to see Heyden when I heard Talbert was claiming to be Mary's beneficiary and selling her things, but he wouldn't say anything. Said even though Mary was dead, it was a matter of client confidentiality." She took a deep breath and continued. "But it was like I'd stirred a can of worms. He kind of rushed me out of his office. But that could have been because his secretary had left him to go take care of her sick mother and he was handling the whole office."

Mindy interrupted by standing on her hind legs and putting her front paws on Aunt Tilly's thigh as if to comfort her. Aunt Tilly smiled down at the colorful dog and stroked her head. "Don't think that secretary ever came back. Just as well, she was one of those women that fawned over Talbert after Mary died. And there were rumors of her and Talbert being seen together while Mary was still alive. Seems like that would be a conflict of interest."

"What's Heyden's last name?" Derrick asked, pen poised over his notes that were dotted with cookie crumbs.

"Heyden Whitmore. His office is across the street and up a half block from Flo's Flower Shop."

Derrick jotted the name down and brushed the crumbs off his notebook onto his napkin. He tucked the notebook and his pen back inside his jacket, stood and grabbed a couple of cookies. "Let me know if you think of anything else or if Talbert bothers you again." He held up his hand with the cookies. "These are really good." He eyed the plate like he wanted to pick it up and take it with him but turned and headed toward the front door instead.

Tori followed to lock up.

Derrick paused with his hand on the knob and twisted around. "Is your alarm system installed yet?"

"I need to call Gary again and I'm wondering if we should get someone else to change locks and install the alarm. He was talking to Talbert outside the restaurant the day Talbert joined us for lunch. There's a camera over the back door and Talbert didn't hesitate to try to break in as if he knew it wasn't working. No one is supposed to know except Aunt Tilly, Martha and me." She shrugged. "And now you."

"Talk to Gary. Talbert Hatchett can spin a convincing yarn about being concerned and wanting to make sure you're safe. Remind Gary it's your security and only you and Tilly should know what you have. Emphasize telling no one and mention

Hatchett's name. That probably should include the police." When Tori raised an eyebrow and opened her mouth, he added, "I notice Talbert's friendly with a few of the officers." With that warning, Derrick pulled the door shut behind him.

Tori turned the deadbolt, pulled out her phone and punched in Gary's number as she walked down the hall toward the kitchen. When it went to voice mail, she left a message.

Chapter Fourteen

Tori put the breakfast dishes in the dishwasher and poured herself another cup of coffee. She watched her aunt and Mindy out the window over the sink as she sipped the strong brew. Aunt Tilly was throwing the ball for Mindy to retrieve. The puppy had quickly learned to drop the ball in her aunt's lap. The two had really bonded and Mindy was almost like a therapy dog for her aunt.

Her phone rang and she walked back over to the table where she had left it. Gary's name popped up and she quickly answered. He had finally gotten the security system. He had a quick job to do and then would be over. Probably an hour, hour and a half tops. The tenseness in her shoulders eased a little.

Tori went outside to let her aunt know and remind her to order the pizza then retreated to the library.

She sat at the desk in front of her computer not even trying to write. She turned her head to look out the window as she fingered her mouse. Sun glistened off the green leaves of the maple tree in the front yard. At least it was nice day for Gary to be installing cameras and security lights. She checked the time at the bottom of her computer screen. It had only been an hour since he called.

Ten minutes later she heard Mindy give her warning barks. By the time she walked into the kitchen, her aunt and Mindy were there watching Gary. He had unloaded the boxes he carried in onto the table and was ready to head back out for a second armful.

"Good morning, Tori." He touched the brim of his Jaguar's cap. "Got a few extras here. Let me get the rest of the stuff from my truck and we can talk about whether you might want them."

Tori held the screen door open as Gary came back with a second load and dropped it beside the other boxes.

"How about a cup of coffee before you get started?"

"Thanks, Tilly. That sounds great. It's been a while since breakfast.

"Well in that case," she said as she handed him a mug of coffee, "you'll have to stop when the pizza gets here and have lunch with us. Told them to deliver it about noon."

His eyes brightened but he answered, "I don't want to be a bother."

"No bother," Tori chimed in. "You might even be able to save me and Aunt Tilly from eating leftovers again. Now, tell us what you have besides wiring the doors and windows and putting cameras by the front and back doors." She sat at the table and nodded toward the boxes.

"The company was real apologetic 'cause I let them know you'd been broken into twice already. They gave me forty percent discount on what I'd ordered and a twenty-five percent on anything I added to the order. They kinda pushed some wide-angle cameras and an upgraded computer system for managing the cameras. Took advantage of that discount and ordered a dozen wide-angles. Only got a couple of the computer programs though."

He pulled a camera from a box. "I'm gonna suggest a wide-angle for your front and back doors. We didn't talk about cameras for the back of your house but I'm thinking with all those windows in your room back there, might be a good idea to put one on each back corner of the house or a wide-angle on the garage and on the corner of the house away from the garage. A couple of motion lights back there, too. And a motion light on the garage would go on, lighting the area, if you come home after dark. A bit of overkill but you've both been hurt. I'll let you think about the extra cameras and lights while I start wiring the windows and doors."

"We don't need to think about it." Aunt Tilly and Tori shared a look and both nodded in agreement. "Do the overkill. We've been turning that deadbolt you put on the door to the sunroom at night and we'll keep on doing that. But I'll rest easier knowing we have security set up back there, too. I'd like to catch whoever's been breaking into my house if he comes back."

Gary grinned, grabbed a box and headed to the front rooms.

By the time Tori gathered up mugs and stuck them in the dishwasher, her aunt had disappeared also. She could hear the muted sound of the television coming from the sunroom. No sense in trying to write. Gary would be moving from room to room. She rubbed her forehead. She could join Aunt Tilly in front of the TV while her aunt shouted out answers or encouragement to the contestants for the game shows or listen to the names she called the cheating boyfriend if she was watching a soap.

She walked over to the open door and breathed in the fresh air. Red and pink geraniums bloomed near the oak tree in the backyard. The door was usually closed and locked but with Gary in and out it felt safe to leave it open. A beautiful day and not just for Gary when he started installing cameras and lights.

Tori whirled around and hurried to the library. She grabbed her sketch pad and pencils and a small camera from the corner of the desk. The screen door clicked softly behind her as she went outside and headed toward the oak tree in the back yard and the Adirondack chair she had pulled into its shade when her aunt was still in rehab, when Tori was unaware of what had happened to put her there. She placed the pad and pouch of pencils in the chair and looked around for inspiration. She liked to take pictures to capture colors and shadows for when she was perfecting the illustrations for publication, but she drew looking at the real scene. She'd add her fairy characters later, too. She settled in the chair and her pencil started capturing the colorful blossoms of Aunt Tilly's garden. The rose buds had opened into a profusion of color and Shasta Daisies waved nearby.

She flipped a page to start a new picture and realized Aunt Tilly was calling from the back porch. The pizza had arrived. Feeling a bit embarrassed that she'd lost track of time, she quickly gathered everything and headed in.

When Tori entered the house, the smell of pizza wafted a greeting rivaling the aroma of brewing coffee. Three medium size pizza boxes sat open on the table, a veggie with pepperoni added to half, a pepperoni with black olives and mushrooms and a meat-lover's special which Gary was eyeing. She hoped he was really hungry, but they'd probably be eating leftover pizza for dinner. Three glasses of tea were on the table. A pie was cooling on the stove top. Aunt Tilly must have made dessert to go with coffee. She put her art supplies on the counter and washed her hands at the kitchen sink. She didn't realize how hungry she was until she slid into her chair and her stomach rumbled.

After a couple pieces of pizza, Aunt Tilly started her

inquisition. "Mmm. This is good pizza. We've been eating a lot at Ed's Eating Place. The food there can't be beat, but this is a nice change. Didn't I see you talking to Talbert Hatchett the other day?"

Gary paused as he was about to pick up another slice and grabbed his glass of tea instead.

"Is he planning to update the security at his house? I know Mary had set up a good one. She had lots of valuable things."

Gary wiped his mouth with a napkin and shook his head. "No. He was concerned about your safety. Talbert said since you and his wife had been such good friends, he felt like he needed to look after you." Gary's cheeks reddened and he looked down at his plate before he lifted his head and looked Aunt Tilly in the eyes. "He sounded so concerned. Afraid I said a bit more'n I should've about the delay. Even mentioned the camera not working." His shoulder rose in a big sigh and wrinkles creased his forehead. "Sorry. I should've just said I was taking care of everything."

Aunt Tilly smiled and reached over to pat his arm. "Talbert has a smooth tongue and he's a good actor. If his consulting business fails, he should head to Hollywood. But Talbert has no say so about what I do or don't do and I'm not about to ask his advice. You're the expert. The next time he approaches you just tell him I'm safe." She chuckled. "No need to tell him the cameras are working now." She nodded toward Gary's plate. "And don't let this conversation spoil your appetite. We're counting on you finishing that pizza and I've got a pie over there just waiting to be cut."

"Thank you, Tilly. I've never blabbed before and I won't ever again."

"I know you won't. How are your children?" She changed the subject. "I hear the college scouts are coming to your son's games. Think he'll get a baseball scholarship?"

"We're hoping so. His grades are real good, too." Gary was more than happy to talk about the achievements of his kids. His shoulders gradually relaxed. After coffee and two pieces of chocolate pie piled high with whipped cream, he headed back to work.

Midafternoon he announced he was finished and showed

them how everything worked, including the computer program that would let them see what was going on with each camera and how to retrieve what was already recorded. Then he had them set the code they would need to activate and deactivate the alarm and advised them not to share it. He stuck a magnet with the phone number of the security company on the fridge in the event they accidently set the alarm off. But to call him if they had any problems or questions.

"Wow, that information was intense!" Tori shook her head when he was gone, along with the rest of the meat-lovers pizza, half the pepperoni, and the last of the chocolate pie. "I guess the main thing we have to be able to do is set the alarm and turn it off."

"As many times as he had us both do that, I think I can do it in my sleep which is what I might be doing if Mindy has to go out real early in the morning. Wrapping that pie for Gary got my mouth to wanting some. You want a piece?"

"I thought you gave Gary the last of the pie."

"Of that pie yes. She opened the fridge and pointed to a second pie. "Grab that and I'll cut us each a piece while you get plates."

Tori grinned and set the pie on the counter. "In that case yes, but no coffee. Now that we finally have the alarm, I plan on getting a good night's sleep. I don't want anything that might keep me awake."

Tori savored her first bite. As she scooped a second one, the doorbell rang, Mindy gave one bark and raced to the front door. "At least we know it's a friendly person. No barking marathon." She glanced toward the pie tin. "And it's not Gary forgetting something. He'd be drooling at the backdoor and I'd feel guilty not offering him more pie." She followed in Mindy's direction.

Tori bent slightly and looked through the peephole. She unlocked the door to let Derrick in. He stepped across the threshold and Mindy danced around his feet, tail wagging wildly until he gave her a few pats. "Aunt Tilly's in the kitchen." Tori waved her hand in that direction.

Aunt Tilly was cutting a third piece of pie as they entered. She waved her knife toward a chair. "Have a seat. We don't have any fresh coffee but there's still some in the pot we can heat up."

Derrick took the large piece of pie from her and carried it to the table. "Heated up will be fine. Better than what's available at the station. I didn't mean to intrude, but this looks and smells great."

Tori poured coffee into a mug and stuck it in the microwave. She grabbed an extra fork while the brew heated.

"Thanks," he said as she set them down by his plate. He took several bites then licked his lips. "The patrolling officers have reported Gary Thomas's truck was here most of the day. Hope that means he's got the alarm system up and running. I noticed the camera at the front door."

"Yes. We'll finally be able to sleep tonight. That's why we aren't drinking coffee." Tori smiled. She took a sip from her glass of ice water as she watched Derrick lift his cup to his lips.

He nodded. "Good idea. Now that it's installed, we'll be cutting back on the patrols so continue to keep your doors locked and the alarm on."

"We haven't had a chance to talk about it yet. We'll turn it on at night, of course, but I was thinking that during the day we would set it if one or both of us is gone." When Derrick frowned, she added, "Mindy will be going in and out all day."

"Gary said not to the share the code with anyone, but I think we need to tell Martha." Aunt Tilly pushed her empty plate away.

"Wait a few weeks before telling her."

"I trust Martha completely. She's like family." Aunt Tilly's tone was argumentative.

"I believe she's trustworthy, too, but explain to her the police have asked that you not tell anyone the alarm code, and when you can tell her she will probably be the only one. Give her the phone number of the company and tell her to call them if she accidently sets off the alarm."

"Gary left the number on the fridge." Tori pointed to the magnet.

"I'm going to give Martha a new key just as soon as Tori can get more made." She turned to Tori. "Which will be tomorrow."

Derrick nodded in agreement. "But I think Martha should keep it separate from her other keys." He glanced at Tori. "Get her a key ring she can find easily in the bottom of her purse."

Aunt Tilly had to smile at that. "Have you seen that thing she calls a purse. She even stuffs an extra pair of shoes in there at times."

"The intruder may have had a key the first time someone broke into your house. Unfortunately, the scene wasn't investigated so we're guessing. You had the locks changed and then changed a second time when he," Derrick lifted one shoulder, "or she broke the glass and came in the back door. They are either looking for something specific because they left your valuables untouched, or they have a vendetta against you."

When Tilly opened her mouth to say something, Derrick held up his hand. "They trashed your house, not just tossing things around but slashing your furniture. Looking for something or angry because they couldn't find it. Both times they could have hidden until they had a chance to get away undetected, but you were attacked and then Tori."

He picked up his cup then put it down without drinking. "We don't want either of you attacked again or Martha to be next."

"But she could still be attacked for what someone thinks she knows or to get her key." Tori pressed her lips together and stared at Derrick, waiting for him to contradict her argument.

"When is the next time Martha will be here?"

Tilly answered, "Tomorrow morning, but we're friends so with all the trouble going on she might just drop in anytime."

"I'll try to get over sometime tomorrow and set up a plan with the three of you. We don't know who's behind all this or what they want so right now our objective is to keep you safe." He stood. "I've got to get back to the station. I'll see you tomorrow and thanks for the pie. If Tori takes off, I'll adopt you as my aunt."

"You catch whoever's doing this and I'll adopt you." Tilly managed a weak smile.

Derrick patted the back of Tilly's hand lying on the table. "We'll catch him. Try to rest easy now that you're both tucked inside a secure home." He nodded to Tori. "Walk me to the door?"

She tucked a wayward curl behind her ear as she rose. "Thank you, Derrick. Knowing you're around and popping in at random times is comforting to Aunt Tilly. I can see it in her face."

"What about you, Tori?" He stopped at the front door. "I hope you feel more at ease, too." He looked down at her with a raised brow.

She chuckled a little. "We both feel more secure."

"See you tomorrow, then." A smile split his handsome features and he exited the house, whistling a nameless tune all the way to his police issued SUV parked at the curb.

Tori swung the door shut. She did feel safe with him dropping in at odd times.

Chapter Fifteen

"After all these years they don't trust me. If I accidently set off that highfalutin alarm, I have to sit there and wait for the police to come roaring up. Going to cost them money with a bunch of false alarms but Tilly doesn't care."

"Perfect." Derrick laughed.

When Tori and Aunt Tilly started clapping, Mindy jumped up and gave several sharp barks.

Martha stood in the middle of the kitchen, hands on her hips and a scowl on her face.

"Won't even give me a key much less the code so I can get in and clean." She was on a roll—acting roll that is.

"Oh, Martha, next time the town's Little Theater puts on a play, you are going to have to try out for a part," Tilly enthused laughingly.

Martha gave a mock bow and sat down at the table with a grin.

"That was great, Martha." Derrick returned her grin. "Now ladies, let's decide where she's going to give her speech so the right ears hear it and pass it along. Martha, you can grumble a little to people but only give that speech once."

"You can give it to us." Everyone looked at Tori.

"I just did."

"No, we can take you to lunch at Ed's. Not today. I have to get extra keys made and I better go to Forest Hills so no one sees me doing that and questions why if we're not giving anyone else a key."

"But tomorrow, we'll go to Ed's and when we're almost through eating, you can stand up, give your speech, and then storm out of the restaurant. Aunt Tilly can come after you. You'll have to walk slow once you're outside or stop like you're wiping tears from your eyes. Act like you're talking. I'll get to-go boxes, pay the bill and join you." Tori leaned back, happy with her scenario.

Derrick grinned as he shook his head. "Not going to work. First, you two won't be able to keep a straight face. And second, someone might think Tilly's out there promising to give Martha the code."

"And I'm not the crying type." Martha huffed. "Nope. What we need for an audience is a bunch of big gossipers. That's exactly who is in my quilting group and we are meeting Thursday night. I'll go in and sit real quiet, like I'm a little dejected, maybe hurt. I'll wait until someone asks if something's wrong and then I'll give my little speech. But" she pointed to Tilly and then Tori, "be prepared for people to come up and tell you off for treating me so bad after helping you for so long and there's some that will stop talking to you."

"If it keeps you safe, that's okay. We'll deal with it." Tilly rubbed her arm and looked across the table at her niece.

Tori nodded. "That's what this whole charade is about."

For someone who didn't cry, Martha was blinking fast at the extra moisture in her eyes. She gave them both a wobbly smile.

Derrick gave the group a satisfied look. "I think you ladies have come up with a good plan. As far as my fellow officers are concerned, this meeting was to convince all of you the importance of not talking about security measures." He shrugged. "Which in a way I guess it was. Tori, why don't you call Gary to have extra keys made. I'm sure he's having keys made all the time and Martha, if anyone approaches you about what's set up, I need you to let me know. Actually, that goes for all of you." He stuck his notebook and pen in one of the leg pockets of his black tactical pants, stood and re-tucked the black t-shirt into the police utility belt around his waist. A gun and several tool pockets along with his badge hung from the sturdy nylon band.

"It's not that I don't trust Gary but I'd like to cut out the middle man and get the keys myself." Tori said as she rose from her seat.

"Tilly," Derrick paused before heading for the front door. "I'm going to talk to Gary."

Tilly shook her head. "He already feels bad enough that he

said something to Talbert. I don't think he's going to say anything again."

"You can call him and give him a heads up, but I want to make sure that if someone does try to get information from him that I'm the one he reports it to. I'm not saying that we have bad cops, but you tend to trust your friends and as I said before Talbert is friendly with several officers and he's a smooth talker."

He turned toward Martha. "After you get your key, it'd be a good idea to knock when you come for a week or two. We'll see how your performance goes but it'll probably be safe enough for you to know the security code." His gaze swept the three women. "Just don't talk about it even among yourselves." With a nod toward the two elder ladies, he stepped aside for Tori to lead the way.

"It looks like you're dressed for some sort of combat."

"Backup for a meth lab raid."

"Please be safe out there." She gave his forearm a squeeze. She hadn't thought before how his job would put him in danger.

"Will do, Tori." He gazed down at her with a warm smile. "You be safe, too." He stepped through the open front door.

She shut it behind him and locked it. A feeling of comfort permeated her being.

When she returned to the kitchen Tilly was saying, "No, I don't think you should practice. You don't want your speech coming out sounding like you rehearsed it. And it's okay if you stumble over a few words. After all, you're supposed to be upset."

"I agree with that." Tori smiled at Martha. "I'm going to get my purse and head to Forest Hills." Tori gathered the mugs from the table and placed them in the sink. "Aunt Tilly, if you let Mindy out for a little while, I can set the alarm before I go."

"You go on. Martha can stand on the porch while I'm out and I know how to set the alarm. While you're there go by the bakery and get us some raspberry tarts."

"Blueberry for me," Martha piped up.

"Get a mixed dozen. The peach ones are good, too. There's a new shop in the same block. I hear their roast beef sandwiches are really good."

***

Forest Hills was a forty-minute drive through the countryside with half grown crops and the occasional open pasture with black and white cows grazing while their calves frolicked close by. Tori slowed to watch their antics. She laughed when a lone goat joined their game. That was when she noticed the dark SUV that had been trailing at her sedate pace also slowed. A shiver trickled down her back as she bit her lip. Was she paranoid to think someone was following her?

She sped up. So did the dark vehicle but not enough to pass her. She wanted to press on the gas and get to civilization but managed to continue at the speed she had been driving. Tori gave a sigh of relief at she passed the 'Welcome to Forest Hills' sign and slowed with the reduced speed limit and increased traffic. She saw the hardware store with two open parking spaces in front but drove past and parked near the bakery.

The trailing SUV continued down the street. She watched until traffic blocked her view. She gave a nervous laugh. So much for her paranoia. She climbed out of her car and went into Betsy's Bakery. She inhaled deeply of delicious aromas and looked at the glass cases filled with pies, cakes, cookies and numerous pastries. Good thing she had been told what to get or she would have had a hard time deciding. As the lady in front of her paid and took her box of donuts, Tori spied the tarts and her mouth watered even more.

The middle-aged lady behind the counter wore a too big white apron. Sprigs of dark hair escaped from her white cap. She chuckled and asked, "First time in the shop?"

Tori laughed, too. "How can you tell?"

"Your eyes have that Christmas morning look."

Tori swiveled her gaze along the case of goodies. "I have a specific order from my aunt for a dozen tarts, mixed flavors, or I would still be trying to decide when it's time for you to close."

"I'm Betsy and this is my shop. Those words make it worth getting up at four to bake."

"Today we have apple, raspberry, peach, and blueberry."

I'll take three of each," Tori said, glad her choice was easy. "I hope some of them make it home. Better make that four of each."

"Hold on," Betsy said. After putting the tarts in a box, she plucked up a blueberry fritter and dropped it into a small brown bag. She handed the bag and a couple of napkins to Tori. "Lagniappe for a first-time customer. Put those in the back seat," she pointed to the box, "and keep this one up front with you."

Tori went out the door smiling. She followed instructions and put the box on the back seat. As she shut the door, she swallowed hard. A dark SUV was parked down the street in one of the spots that had been vacant in front of the hardware store. From this distance, she couldn't tell if anyone was in the vehicle. Still gripping the door handle, she looked around. The sandwich shop was near the bakery, two shops down but she had planned to get the sandwiches just before she headed back. Which might be sooner than she thought. The hardware store might be another trip.

Across the street a small boutique had a sale sign in the display window. She dashed over and hurried inside, nearly barreling into the gangly teenager standing near the door. "Oh, I'm sorry," she said.

"Larry, if you're going to lounge around at least don't block my customers from coming in."

"Sorry, Ms. Claire. If you could hurry Sue Ann up, I'll be happy to get out of here. She's done tried on a half dozen dresses already."

"And I got a half dozen more to try on before I decide." A young female voice shouted out from behind a curtain.

Tori had been looking out the window to see if the SUV would leave. She turned and studied the teenager. Why not? "Excuse me. I wonder if you could do me a favor if you're just waiting for, uh, Sue Ann."

The teen continued to slouch against the wall but turned his face toward Tori.

"I was supposed to get something at the hardware store when I saw the sale sign here. I'd like to shop a little but," she glanced at her watch, "could you get some keys made for me at the hardware store?" She pulled a twenty-dollar bill from her wallet.

"I need three keys. You can keep the change."

The teen grinned and held out his hand. "Sure, I can do that." With key and money in his fist, he started to push on the door.

Tori grabbed his arm to stop him. "Do you think you could go out the back door? And come back that way?"

Larry looked at the twenty-dollar bill and pivoted toward the back of the shop. "Ms. Claire, I'm going to prop the back door open with a rock. I'll be right back."

"Don't you go smoking behind my shop," she admonished, but Larry was gone.

Tori breathed a deep sigh. But now she had to buy something. She spotted a blue sweater the shade of Aunt Tilly's eyes. She pulled it out to check the size. The sweater had an intricate design knitted into the yoke.

She jumped a little when Ms. Claire's voice sounded over her shoulder. "That's handknitted. A real bargain. Marked down forty percent off."

She was following Ms. Claire to the cash register when she saw a large red handbag on display at the end of an aisle. When she stopped to look, Ms. Claire was at her elbow. "It's got lots of handy pockets inside. I can give you a bargain on that, too."

When she named a price, Tori pictured Martha carrying it. It was still expensive but... "Tell you what, I'll take an extra ten percent off."

In spite of Martha understanding, she was hurt not to be trusted. Tori nodded and Ms. Claire grabbed the purse from its hook. Tori paused again at a display of key rings near the register. There was one attached to a small flashlight and a dangling whistle.

"That's a popular choice with women." Ms. Claire commented as Tori placed it on the counter beside the sweater and purse.

Tori was paying when Larry strolled from the back.

"You take that rock out from my door?"

"Yes, ma'am. Sue Ann pick out a dress yet?"

"You be quiet or I'm telling Mama. It's got to be the right one." The voice came from behind the curtain again.

Ms. Claire handed Tori the bag containing her purchases with a thank you. She sighed with a roll of her eyes and headed toward the curtain. Evidently Larry wasn't the only one exasperated with Sue Ann.

Larry slipped a small envelope and the receipt into Tori's hand. If they don't work, he'll make 'em again for you," he said in a low voice and sauntered to his spot by the door.

"Thanks, I appreciate it," Tori whispered as she passed him.

"I appreciate the change." He grinned and patted his pants pocket.

Turning her head in both directions to check the almost non-existent traffic before crossing, she glanced toward the hardware store. The dark SUV was still there. As she put her purchase in the back seat beside the tarts, Tori tried to convince herself it was just someone shopping in Forest Hills. Maybe even someone from Cotton Creek.

As with the bakery, everything smelled so tempting at the sandwich shop she bought extra sandwiches. If they tasted as good as they smelled, someone might want more than one. When she came out of the shop, the SUV was gone. Relieved that she had worried over nothing, she headed home.

Her relief was short lived. She saw the SUV at the gas station at the edge of Forest Hills. And a mile out of town, the dark vehicle was behind her again. She dug in her pocket for her phone. One hand on the steering wheel, she managed to press the contact for Derrick with her other hand. "Please answer."

"Tori?"

"I think someone's following me."

"Where are you?"

"A mile, no maybe two miles outside of Forest Hills heading back to Cotton Creek."

She heard a muffled curse word then Derrick said, "Stay on the phone. I'll see if the police in Forest Hills will send someone out."

After a short time that seemed like forever, Derrick came back on the line. "Forest Hills is sending a patrol car."

"I guess I'd better slow down then. I don't want a ticket."

Derrick stifled a laugh. "Yeah, but if the car following you closes the gap, speed up unless you hear the siren or see the lights of the patrol car. They will probably want you to pull over and answer questions. We're sending an unmarked vehicle. It will pass you, make a u-turn and follow you back to Cotton Creek. Okay, it's a tan Ford sedan. We'll let the Forest Hills police know they are law enforcement."

"I see flashing lights coming behind me. The SUV is coming faster." Her voice had a panicked edge as she kept an eye on her rearview mirror.

"Stay in the middle of your lane and grip the wheel tight in case he sideswipes you."

The dark vehicle swerved toward her as it roared past but didn't make contact. Tori tried to see what the driver looked like but when he swerved, she gripped tighter and focused on the road. Mud was smeared on the license plate. Whoever had been stalking her sped away and disappeared over a rise in the country road.

The patrol car stayed behind her. The siren was off, but the red lights on top of the cruiser blinked. "Derrick, I'm pulling over like you said. I-I'll talk to you when I get to Cotton Creek."

"Good. You're safe now." His deep voice was a shade gruffer than normal. "I'll see you shortly."

She steered over to the side of the road and the cruiser pulled behind her. An officer climbed out and approached her car. He rapped on the window. She forced her white knuckles to relax so she could let go of the wheel and push the button to lower the window.

"You alright, Miss?" His brow was furrowed. Dark brown eyes quickly scanned the inside of the car.

"Yes. No. T-thank you for coming. You didn't go after him."

"Your safety first. You Victoria Statton?"

She looked at the officer with surprise. Of course, he would know her name. Derrick gave it to him.

The second officer had walked up and stood beside the first. "The famous author and illustrator?"

"I'm not famous," Tori gave a weak laugh, surprised this cop in the middle of nowhere was familiar with her work. "But I do write children's stories and I illustrate them."

"My kid, Anna, loves your stories. Wait'll she hears I met you."

The first officer cleared his throat and looked at the man beside him.

The second officer grinned and introduced himself. "I'm

Officer Kenley and he's Officer Pierce. He nodded toward the taller, dark-haired man who had first approached her car.

She smiled weakly at Officer Kenley. With his red hair, freckles and boyish grin, he didn't look like a policeman until the tan sedan that passed them made a u-turn and pulled up behind them. His features transformed to all business as he ordered her to get down and stay in the car.

"But..."

"Down."

Tori obeyed. From her uncomfortable position sprawled across the gear shift, she shouted, "They're Cotton Creek police." Lifting her head a little, she peeked over the back of her seat.

The officers separated and approached the other vehicle with their weapons drawn. A feminine hand stretched out the window holding a badge still attached to a lanyard. She stepped out of the car wearing clothing similar to S.W.A.T., but without the bulletproof vest. Her long blonde hair was pulled up in a ponytail. A man, almost identically dressed, stepped out of the passenger side dangling a badge out to his side. They must've been on the same drug raid as Derrick that morning.

The Forest Hills officers holstered their weapons and the four officers spoke for several minutes. The male officer got into the driver's seat of the Ford as the other three came toward Tori.

She straightened up and had her hand on the door handle when Officer Pierce barked, "Ms. Statton, when an officer tells you to get down, you get down and you stay down until he tells you otherwise." Color flushed her cheeks as Tori ducked her head. "These officers are Cotton Creek law enforcement, but they could have been cohorts of your stalker. The communication that they would be coming in an unmarked car failed to reach Officer Kenley and myself." He nodded toward the female officer beside him. "Officer Enslow will drive your car. We will follow through our jurisdiction. Officer Morrow will follow us at a distance. When we turn back, he will move up."

Tori started to protest until she remembered the larger vehicle swerving toward her. The Forest Hills officers shook hands with Enslow and moved back to their vehicle as Tori got out and walked around to the passenger side.

The trip back to Cotton Creek was tense. Tori kept a watchful eye, but there was no reappearance of the dark SUV.

Chapter Sixteen

When they reached Cotton Creek, Officer Enslow drove to the police station. As she pulled into the parking lot, she announced, "Detective Stone is waiting in his office for you."

She wanted to go home, but the officer kept her keys. Officer Morrow parked in the slot beside them and they escorted her inside. At the door to an office, Morrow nodded goodbye and headed down the hall. Tori called a thank you after him and turned to the female officer beside her. "Thank you, too." Enslow nodded her acceptance and rapped on the door frame. She stepped back to let Tori precede her.

Derrick stood as they entered and swept his worried gaze over Tori. He took a step to move around the desk but stopped when Officer Enslow cleared her throat.

"Only trouble we had was no one informed the Forest Hills officers that Cotton Creek police would be arriving in an unmarked car," Officer Enslow informed before Derrick could ask. "A bit dicey for a few minutes but after they checked our IDs, they were cooperative. They had a different viewpoint on what was happening though. Seemed to think the guy trailing her might've been trying to kidnap her because Miss Statton is a famous author and artist."

Tori blushed at her words and shook her head in denial.

Derrick raised a brow. "That's an angle we wouldn't have thought about, considering everything else that has happed. Unless we have two perps with different motives, she would have been taken when she was knocked out." Derrick sat back down behind the desk. "But it's good to have an outsider's input. Be sure you include that in your report. Thanks. I appreciate you and Morrow taking on the assignment." He dismissed the officer.

Officer Enslow handed Tori her keys and left, heading down the hall in the same direction Officer Morrow had gone.

"You have an office now?"

Derrick gave Tori his lopsided grin and shook his head. "Would be nice, but this is Sam's office. He had some family matters he had to go take care of. The chief handed me most of his cases and said since the files are in here, I should work here."

He settled back. "I talked to Sam before he left and he said it was fine so long as I didn't organize things. Said he knows where everything is." Derrick pointed to the piles of papers and files lined against the wall.

Tori leaned over. Each pile had a note on top. "Back right corner." She read aloud. She straightened and looked at Derrick with a raised eyebrow.

"So I know where to put them back." His expression turned serious. He rummaged through the top drawer of Sam's desk and finally pulled out a recorder. "Probably would have been faster to go get the one from my desk."

Tori tilted her head. "Derrick, I really need to get home. I have Martha's and Aunt Tilly's lunch in my car. Can we do this later?"

Derrick nodded. "I can come by later this afternoon."

Tori sank into the chair in front of his desk. "No, I don't want them to know about it."

"Tori, they have to be told. They have to be aware when they are out, especially Martha. She's more likely to be alone." He untangled the microphone cord and checked to see if the batteries worked. "You want to go ahead with your statement now?"

Tori held up a finger. "One minute." She pulled out her phone and texted her aunt, 'Been delayed a little. Be home soon with sandwiches and tarts.' She slipped her phone back in her pocket. "Okay, let's get this over with."

Derrick recorded the preliminary information of people present, time and date. "Miss Statton, tell the events of your trip from Cotton Creek to Forest Hills, what you did in Forest Hills and your return trip."

Tori heaved a sigh and spoke quickly. "I left Aunt Tilly's shortly after you did. A great day for a drive in the country. There was a dark car way behind me but not much other traffic. There was a goat in a field trying to get some calves to play with him. I slowed way down to watch them, maybe even stopped. I checked my rearview mirror before I started up again. I thought the car behind me would have caught up but it was still a distance back."

Tori continued with her account of the trip. When she recounted the SUV swerving toward her as it passed, Derrick clenched his fists but said nothing until she told of Enslow's insistence she come in and give her report to Detective Stone.

"When he swerved, did you get a glimpse of the driver?"

Tori shook her head. "Like I told the Forest Hills officers, I was concentrating on holding onto the steering wheel and staying in the middle of my lane. I did try to see the license plate, but it was too dirty to read." Tori stood. "Can I go now? Aunt Tilly is going to be worried in spite of my text."

Derrick reached over and turned off the recorder. "Okay." He came around from behind the desk. "We'll need to go over this again. I still have questions. And the report from the Forest Hills police will probably raise more questions, too."

Tori ran here hand through her hair. "What on earth could an old lady have that anyone would risk murdering for? She's certainly not rich."

"I don't know, Tori, but we'll catch the perpetrator."

She turned at the door to look back at Derrick, hesitated then issued an invitation. "I bought an extra sandwich if you want to join us, but you can't say anything to Aunt Tilly or Martha about this."

Derrick shook his head regretfully. "I'd like to come but I can't promise not to say anything. Martha particularly needs to be warned and one of Tilly's friends may offer to pick her up for bridge or whatever."

She bit her lip and looked down as she fingered the keys in her hand. "Okay, so come."

"I'll be five minutes behind you." Derrick smiled.

Tori parked her car in Aunt Tilly's drive and pulled her keys from the ignition. The smell of roast beef and sweet pastries had stirred hunger pangs as she drove home from the police station. She retrieved lunch from the back seat and hoped Derrick stuck to his five-minute promise. She slipped her fingers through the handle of the boutique bag and added the brown bagged lagniappe to her load. Even if she had remembered her treat, her stomach had churned too much to eat it on the return trip to Cotton Creek.

Martha opened the door as Tori climbed the porch steps. "Bout time. We were wondering if you'd pulled to the side of the road and were eating all the goodies yourself."

"I was tempted." Tori managed a laugh. She placed the bag of sandwiches and box of tarts on the table. The box was immediately opened and both ladies *aahed* over the pastries.

"What's in the little bag?" Martha pointed to Tori's special treat.

"Betsy, that's the owner and baker, called it lagniappe. Something extra since I was a first-time customer."

"Lagniappe. If those tarts taste as good as they look and smell, I'm ready to head over to Forest Hills and get me something extra."

Tori winced. Derrick was right. Martha was joking, but she and Aunt Tilly needed to be told about someone trailing her. "I saw Derrick when I got back into town and invited him for lunch. I got extra sandwiches," she said as she dropped the bag with the sweater and purse on a chair."

Aunt Tilly stopped puttering with napkins and silverware and raised a brow. "Something you not telling us?"

"Yes. I'm hungry. Hope he gets here in a hurry." Saved by the bell, Tori thought, as the doorbell rang. She rushed to answer it, Millie running at her heels.

They entered the kitchen as Martha was putting glasses of tea around and Aunt Tilly placed a wrapped sandwich on each plate.

"Good thing you got here. Don't know if we would've waited for you." Aunt Tilly grinned as she motioned for him to sit. She put the two extra sandwiches in the middle of the table next to a bowl of chips and the tarts and passed around packets of extra sauce. The smell of brewing coffee over on the counter couldn't compete with roast beef and sweet tarts. She sank down into her chair. "After my doctor's appointment tomorrow, I hope to trade these crutches in for a cane."

Tori looked at her aunt. "You didn't tell me you had an appointment."

"Haven't had a chance to tell you. His office called while you were gone. They moved my appointment up."

Conversation lagged as four hungry people dug into the food. Aunt Tilly kept glancing at Tori and Derrick but she held her tongue. Derrick finished his sandwich and eyed the two sitting next to the tarts. Tilly reached over, picked one up and put it on his plate. "I imagine you need that to chase down crooks," she said.

He grinned a thank you and unwrapped it.

Aunt Tilly managed to make it halfway through her tart. She put her fork down with a clink and said, "Out with it. I know something happened. What?"

Derrick finished chewing his bite of tart. He looked at Tori, but she pressed her lips together. He put his fork down. "Tori was followed to Forest Hills today. She thought it was just someone going in her direction When the same vehicle started following on her way back, she called me. I called the Forest Hills police and asked them to check it out. Whoever was following her took off when they showed up. They escorted her through their jurisdiction and then our officers took over. We don't know who or why someone followed her."

Aunt Tilly's face paled as Derrick talked. She sat for a minute then turned toward Tori. Her voice tearful, she said, "I want you to stay here with me, but you have to go home. I can't let you get hurt."

Tori gasped, "No." She looked at Derrick. His expression said he had the same answer as Tori. "That's what today was all about." She got up and hugged her aunt. "That's what he wants, Aunt Tilly. We're putting up obstacles so they don't have access to you or your house and they're giving me all the credit. He wants me out of the way. A key gave him access to your house until I came and had the locks changed. He doesn't know you're the one that ordered it done. And now we have a dog and an alarm and the police are patrolling."

She sat down again and cast a weak smile in her aunt's direction. "Nope. I'm not going anywhere."

"That's a logical explanation." Derrick clasped his hands together on the table and leaned forward. "The Forest Hills officers had another theory. That whoever followed her wanted to kidnap Tori because she's a celebrity, a famous author and artist. Tori says she's not famous and most authors don't make that much money. Regardless, she's safer here, protected by the security you've set up. And, Tilly, you're safer with Tori here."

Tori appreciated his support. Just for that, he could have the last sandwich and an extra tart. She felt like giving him a hug, too. She laughed to herself. How would he respond to that?

Aunt Tilly still looked doubtful. "You tell him about someone following us down to Henderson when we went furniture shopping at Riley's?"

Derrick's head jerked toward Tori. "You've been followed before and you didn't report it?"

"I... We weren't sure that someone was following us. The salesman commented that he thought the driver of the car was with us because he pulled into the parking lot shortly after us. He thought maybe it was a husband or boyfriend who didn't like to shop and was waiting for us. But he parked far away and stayed in his car. When the salesman made his comments, we all looked that way. The vehicle suddenly squealed out of the lot and headed in the direction of Cotton Creek. It was raining. He could've pulled over to make a phone call." She shrugged. "We went on to the pet store."

"A phone call that lasted the same amount of time it took you to buy a sofa and whatever?" Derrick waved his hand in frustration. "What did this car look like?"

Tori's voice stuck in her throat as she remembered the vehicle. Aunt Tilly answered for her. "A black SUV. At least, it looked black with the rain."

Derrick rubbed his temples then focused on Tori.

"We watched for it on the way home," Tori croaked, "But we didn't see any sign of it."

"Anything out of the ordinary, anything suspicious you report it to me. Anything. And you do it when it's happening, not when you get home and certainly not a week later. Riley's in Henderson, right? You have the salesman's name?"

"Paul was the one that came forward to help us in the store. The other salespeople stayed near the register talking. I doubt if they paid attention to anything outside." Tori supplied the information.

He jotted in his notebook and slammed it shut. "Everyone is safer if Tori stays right here."

"He's right, Tilly." Martha added her support. "We'll all three be looking after each other and have 911 on speed dial."

Derrick took a deep breath and asked, "Martha, Tilly never

said, do you live alone?"

"Yes, I do. I've got me a little apartment over the bookstore"

Derrick frowned. "Most of those apartments over the downtown businesses have the entrance in the back."

Martha nodded. "There's a light back there and several parking spots."

"If for some reason you get home after dark and that light is out, you keep on driving back around to the front and call me. I'll come or send someone to make sure you get in safely."

"What's the police chief saying about all our extra protection?" Martha tilted her head.

"So far, nothing. His officers messed up investigating Tilly's first break-in. Two women have been attacked. If we get a crime spree, we'll have to pull some of the officers off to work other areas but right now all he's ranting about is why haven't we found this guy."

Tori took a sip of coffee and twiddled her fork. "Maybe..." She raised a brow and looked at her aunt.

"Maybe you can come stay here until this is all over." Her aunt continued for her.

"Thanks, Tilly, but I got other jobs I'm coming and going to. And a cat that sits by my door waiting when it's time for me to be home. Besides, after I give my little speech to the quilting group and those ladies start gossiping, no one's going to believe we're friends anymore."

Derrick pushed his chair back. "Thanks for the lunch, ladies. Martha, keep an eye watching behind you. Anything suspicious, call the police or drive to the station."

"I'll be home by dark unless Mrs. Willowby is entertaining. Then she usually finds something extra for me to do when it's time for me to leave."

He frowned. "Make an excuse and tell her you have an appointment or need to pick someone up."

Martha shook her head. "She pays well when she keeps me overtime and I don't want her finding someone else to help."

Derrick looked at Tori and nodded toward the door. "Come lock up." He paused with the door half open and grabbed her hand. "Don't leave the house without telling me, even if you think a short run to the store or post office is safe. Whoever the culprit is, he's desperate and he isn't hesitating to attack you or Tilly."

She nodded and bit her lip. "I agree, but I won't be a prisoner in this house."

Derrick stared at her for a moment. "I'm not saying don't go out. Just let me know and stay where there are people." He waited for Tori's agreement.

She nodded and he gave her hand a gentle squeeze then turned away. Tori locked the door behind him and watched through the window as he climbed in his police issued SUV and pulled away.

Chapter Seventeen

Three days had passed without incident. The only excitement was when Riley's finally delivered their new furniture. Last night she was able to sleep without nightmares of being forced off the road by a dark monster wearing a mask. Tori rubbed her temples. The dream hadn't invaded her sleep. She wasn't going to let it ruin her day. She sat in front of her computer reading the last paragraph written.

A friend had picked up her aunt for a bridge luncheon and she had gone off happily leaning on a cane, leaving her crutches behind. Aunt Tilly had texted that they had arrived safely.

The house was quiet. The alarm was set and Mindy lay at her feet. All she needed was for her brain to get creative. The last two days she had sat outside and drawn illustrations for her next fairy story while her aunt trained Mindy and taught her tricks, but it was her middle school adventure tale that she wanted to finish. It had become a challenge.

Slowly, words came as she typed and a scene developed in her mind. Her characters began to think and act and talk. She was roused out of her concentration when Mindy stood on all fours, ruff on her neck raised and a low growl in her throat. Tori's fingers tightened on the front edge of the desk and she looked toward the door then over her shoulder.

She moved to the window and cautiously looked out. No one was out walking their dog or working in their flower beds. No strangers. Not out front anyway. Mindy remained by the desk, alert and growling. She picked up her phone that lay beside the computer and punched in Derrick's number. The phone rang several times. She was about to hang up and dial 911 when he answered.

"Derrick," she whispered and immediately felt foolish. She was locked inside with the alarms set.

"Tori?"

"Sorry. The alarm hasn't gone off, but Mindy is growling and I don't think it's at a mouse. She hasn't left me or started barking. I didn't see anything or anyone out the front window. I haven't looked out any others."

"Hold on. I'll see if anyone is close by and can respond." He left the line open and she could hear him consulting with someone. When he came back on he sounded exasperated. "It'll be fifteen maybe twenty minutes before someone is there. Where are you? Where's Tilly?"

"I'm in the library. Aunt Tilly's gone to her bridge group."

"Can you lock the library doors?"

She looked up at the double doors that opened into the hall. "I'll see." She walked over to close them. There was no lock but she could close the doors and wedge chairs under the knobs. She pulled a nearby chair to the door she had closed and wedged the back under the knob. She looked around and grabbed the chair that sat in front of the desk and carried it over. Before she could close the other door. Mindy dashed through it. She could hear Derrick's voice getting frantic as he called her name when she retrieved her phone and ran after the dog. "I'm here. There aren't any locks so I was trying to put chairs under the knobs. I needed two hands."

Relief filled his voice when she answered. "Good thinking. Next time let me know you are putting the phone down. Move so someone looking in the window won't see you. I'm on my way."

"I'm not in the library now. Mindy ran out and she's barking."

"Go in your aunt's bedroom and lock the door."

"This is an old house. The only door that locks is the one to the sunroom. Gary put a dead bolt on that one because of all the windows." She tiptoed down the hall trying to keep the old oak floor planks from squeaking. "Derrick, it may not be anything but a strange sound only Mindy can hear." She had just wanted to have an officer walk around the house if the patrol was near. She picked up Mindy and commanded, "Quiet," in a stern whisper. The animal obeyed but remained stiff in her arms, ears perked up and nose lifted. Tori took the opportunity to peek out windows in her aunt's room and the kitchen and dining room, quieting Mindy when she added a growl to her bark as she continued down the hall. She gently pushed the door to the sunroom shut and turned the dead bolt.

It seemed forever before she heard Derrick's voice. "Tori, I'm here. I'm going to hang up. The officers are already walking the grounds."

"Is that who you were barking at?" Tori asked the dog. As she stared out the large window in the kitchen door, she began to feel foolish. She couldn't call the police every time Mindy barked. Except, she hadn't been barking, she'd been growling. Coffee. Maybe fresh brewed coffee would pacify them for a wasted trip. She put Mindy down and started a pot. Were there any cookies left? She lifted the lid of the cookie jar and smiled. It was almost full.

Mugs were ready by the pot and cookies on the table but they hadn't rapped on the door to let her know it was a false alarm. She looked out again. They were all gathered by the back gate that led to the neighbor living behind them. Another officer joined them as she watched. She turned off the alarm and went out leaving an unhappy Mindy in the kitchen. Cautiously, she went down the steps and started across the yard. An officer saw her and said something to Derrick.

Derrick looked over at Tori and held up his hand in a stop motion. He said something to the officer kneeling on the ground and walked toward her, studying the ground as he stepped. "Are you alright?" he asked as he neared her.

She nodded. "I am now. Sorry I panicked." She looked over at the men near the gate. "Did you find something?"

"Better to call if you think something's wrong."

"I don't want to be like the boy who cried wolf." She tried again. "What are they doing?"

Derrick hesitated. "There's a footprint. One of Tilly's sprinklers left a muddy spot inside the gate." He shrugged. "It could be nothing. Someone taking a shortcut through your yard or someone who knows Tilly is gone. Whichever, we want to check for more footprints so you need to stay in the house or at least on the porch."

A friendly bark sounded from the kitchen screen door. I'm going to have to take her out. If you want to check near the porch, I can take her there or out front."

"Actually, I'd like to borrow her."

When Tori raised a brow, he explained, "She's not trained to track but she's a smart dog and she seems to alert you and Tilly when anyone comes on the premises. I'd like to see what she does when we set her down near the footprint."

"Okay, but she may just follow you around." Tori laughed. "Is that going to make you look guilty?" She turned and headed back into the house. Mindy danced around and stood on her hind legs to greet them.

"Hey, girl." Derrick bent and gave the expected behind the ear scratches. "Want to try a little police work?" He stood and noticed the mugs set out by the coffee pot and cookies on the table, now covered by wrap. "Having party?"

Tori shrugged. "Thought after a quick walk around the yard, I'd offer the officers some coffee and cookies, but they're taking so long the coffee will probably be like what you get at the station."

"I doubt that, but they'll appreciate the thought and the cookies."

He snitched one from under the wrap. "Do you have a leash for her?" He nodded toward Mindy. "And you'd better put that away." He pointed toward the shotgun leaning against the wall.

Tori grabbed the gun.

"Hold on a minute." He took the gun from Tori and clicked it open. His mouth pressed into a straight line as he emptied the shells into his hand then gave it back to Tori. She stuck it in the laundry room as she got the leash from its hook just inside the door.

"I'll let her run free in your yard, but I may take her through your neighbor's backyard. Officer Enslow knocked on their door. No one answered and from the looks of the tall grass, they haven't been home for a week or more."

"Aunt Tilly said they always visit their son and his family for a couple of weeks this time of year. A neighborhood boy is supposed to be cutting the grass, but he seems to be a little lax in the backyard."

Derrick picked up Mindy and took the leash from Tori. "Stay on the back porch if you come out to watch."

She rubbed her arms as she watched from the top step. It was a little chilly, but she wasn't going to miss anything by going in for a jacket.

He headed across the yard toward the officers. They had

finished whatever they were doing with the footprint and were gathering up their equipment. Derrick said something to them and put Mindy down.

Mindy sniffed. Nose to the ground, she walked to the gate. After a minute smelling the gate and scratching it with a paw, she turned around and sniffed where Derrick had put her down. She then ran behind a bush. After a few seconds, she dashed out and headed to the back corner of the house. She barked at an upended tub and ran around to the other side of the house. Derrick and a female officer followed. With her blond ponytail, she looked like the officer who had driven her back from Forest Hills.

Frustrated that she could no longer see Mindy, Tori wanted to jump off the porch and run after them. Instead, she did her own dashing through the house and watched out Aunt Tilly's bedroom window.

Mindy had both front paws up on the fence, jumping and barking as if to say 'lift me over.' Derrick and the officer had put on gloves. Derrick picked something off the fence and dropped it into the evidence bag the other officer held. He then hooked the leash on Mindy's collar and whistled for her to follow. All three disappeared behind the house and Tori ran back to the porch.

"You have some treats for a smart dog?" Derrick asked when she popped out the door.

Tori hurried back in and returned with a half-filled bag.

"We're going to see if she can pick up the trail from the other side of the fence. Who lives next door?"

"Bill and June Wells but they both work."

"We'll knock before we go in their backyard. Just in case. Don't let these guys eat all the cookies. He nodded at the rest of the investigating team. When you've finished feeding them, they'll canvas the neighborhood to ask if anyone saw anything."

"Hey, you got a head start. We saw you wiping crumbs off your face." One of the officers grinned as they tromped up the steps and into the kitchen.

***

Two officers were still munching cookies when Tori heard the quick tapping of her aunt's cane marching up the ramp to the porch. "Tori...Tori," she called in a breathless, panicked voice.

Tori pushed the screen door open, still holding the coffee pot. "I'm here. I'm alright." She gave her aunt a one-armed hug.

"There're police cars out front. And Derrick's car."

"Everything's okay." She stepped back from her aunt and saw the friend who had given her a ride at the bottom of the ramp. "Hi, Mrs. Thornton. You want to come in for coffee and cookies?"

Isabelle Thornton looked at her watch and answered with a disappointed expression. "I'd like to, but I have to pick up my grandchildren from school and take them to their piano lessons. "If everything's alright, I'll be going. Tilly, call me later."

Inside, the officers had put their mugs in the sink and picked up their hats. "Thanks for the refreshments. We'd better start canvassing the neighborhood before Detective Stone gets back." The younger one put his hand on his stomach. The cookies were really good, Ms. Statton. Tori said you made them." He waved and followed his partner. They took the steps two at a time and hurried to start following Derrick's orders.

"Tori, what's going on?" She stopped and looked around. Her voice rose in a panic again. "And where's Mindy?"

"Mindy's fine. She's with Derrick." Tori breathed in relief as she heard happy barks and toenails scrambling up the steps. Derrick and Officer Enslow were coming through the back gate. "I'm going to make a fresh pot of coffee." She busied herself as the two entered behind Mindy who was soon ensconced in Aunt Tilly's lap on the cushioned window seat.

"Good to see you home, Tilly." Derrick glanced at the table. "Looks like they left us a few cookies. They ate all the chocolate chip ones though."

Tori set the cookie jar on the table and replenished the plate. "Not all of them." She wiped her hands on a dishtowel and tossed it on the counter. "Fresh coffee in a few minutes. Did you find anything?"

"Stop. Tell me what happened from the beginning." Aunt Tilly demanded.

Tori poured up two mugs and set them down in front of Derrick and Officer Enslow. "Would you like some coffee?" she asked her aunt.

"I want to know what happened."

Tori sighed and poured two more. She put one down in front of her aunt and sat at the table. "I was at my computer in the library. Mindy jumped up and started growling. It was different from anything she'd done before. I called Derrick. I thought maybe if a patrol car was in the area, they could check it out."

"What did you see on the cameras?"

Tori put her hand to her mouth and stared at Aunt Tilly. She hadn't even thought to check. Hadn't thought about the cameras until her aunt asked.

"Are the cameras on and working?" Derrick asked.

"Tori nodded. "I'm sorry. I didn't even think. Maybe I wouldn't have had to call."

"We got a couple of things we didn't have before. I'd like to see what's recorded, but first, I'll have some of Tilly's cookies." He grinned and reached for the plate. "My mouth's been watering ever since I had that sample."

"It's on my computer. I'll get it." She went to the library, saved and closed the story she was working on. She wanted to stop and look at what the cameras recorded but the cookies wouldn't last long and they would be invading her space if they came into the library. She carried her computer and mouse into the kitchen and opened the program that showed what the cameras had caught and recorded.

The split screen showed what was currently visible in the range of all cameras. She paused to think. What had Gary told her about reviewing what had been recorded? She may have to call him.

"Problem?" Derrick's voice coming from behind startled her and she jumped. He put his hand on her shoulder. "Sorry."

"I—I'm just trying to remember how Gary said to do this."

"Let Enslow take over. She's a whiz at analyzing surveillance tapes."

Tori reluctantly switched chairs so Office Enslow could sit in front of the computer. A few key taps and a bit of reversing and they were watching the back gate open. A figure slipped in wearing a baseball cap with the bill pulled down and moved behind the bush Mindy had sniffed. After several minutes, the person emerged. He or she had traded the cap for a ski mask pulled down to hide his face. Head swiveling, the intruder cautiously approached the house. He crouched for a minute then stood. He grabbed the windowsill and pulled himself up to look in. The intruder must have heard Mindy barking because he suddenly dropped down and flattened his body against the house. The person took two steps toward the gate then turned and ran around the house instead.

They watched it three more times. Derrick pressed his lips together and shook his head. "We need to have our techs enlarge and enhance the-images. Tori, we're going to have to take your computer in so we can use our equipment to enlarge and possibly identify something about you intruder.

Tori looked at him with a horrified expression. "No." she almost screamed. "My story is on there and I have a deadline." She glared at him. Then in a calmer voice, "Besides what the cameras see is being recorded on my computer until I can buy another one. That would be like turning off half our security system.

"The file would be large to email," Officer Enslow said. "Do you have a flash drive? We'll copy the section we need."

Tori nodded. "Yes." She jumped up and ran to the library, yanked open the top desk drawer, grabbed a new, unused one and dashed back to the kitchen.

Enslow took the package from her and opened it. She slipped the external drive into the computer. A few more taps on the computer and several minutes later she had copied the recordings from all cameras. Resetting the program, she said, "It won't hurt to review everything in case the intruder cased the house earlier."

"That's not a comforting thought." Tilly finally put Mindy down on the floor. "And where is my shotgun?"

Officer Enslow jerked her head up and looked at Tilly then turned toward Detective Stone with a questioning expression.

Derrick ignored her reaction and announced they would head back to the station after they checked the windowsill where the perpetrator boosted himself up. He reached down and rubbed Mindy behind her ears. "Smart dog. You did a good job today."

Tori locked the door and reset the alarm. She sat at the table with her aunt. Neither said anything until Tori grumbled, "And I was getting a lot of writing done, too. Maybe I should start writing mysteries."

"No, you're doing fine with those fairies. Mysteries usually have a murder or two. Besides, we have our own mystery. Why is some criminal so persistent in trying to break into my house and who, the devil, is he?" She rapped her knuckles on the table, "or she?" She took a sip from her mug and grimaced at the cold liquid.

Tori got up to get her a fresh cup but her aunt shook her head. "No, I don't really want any coffee. She sat back down and pulled out her phone. "I'm going to call Gary and have him put a padlock on the gate. We don't have to lock it once the neighbors in the back are home." She left a message when his voice mail picked up.

She gathered up the cups and put them in the dishwasher. "I really need to go buy another computer for the security cameras. It will be more convenient to check. We can even leave it running all the time." Tori hesitated. "But I can't leave you here alone."

"Well, let's go." Aunt Tilly looked down and chuckled. "I've still got my jacket on and my purse is right here. I hate to leave Mindy though."

"Super pup will be fine." Tori really didn't want to leave her either after today. "She's so smart, we can probably teach her to shoot that shotgun of yours."

"And where is my gun?"

"In the laundry room. Derrick didn't think it should be in here with all the other officers around. It's still handy, right inside the door with a raincoat hanging over it." She didn't mention the missing shells that Derrick had pocketed after taking them out of her aunt's weapon. "Be right back." She disappeared upstairs to get her purse and jacket.

Her aunt had been patient in the electronics store as Tori and the salesperson compared merits of the different computers and additional software. Clutching her purchases, she pushed through the exit and held the door open with her hip while her aunt hobbled through using her cane. Tori scanned the parking for a big black SUV, hoping not to find it. She was thankful that Aunt Tilly's handicap parking had given them a spot near the entrance.

She put her packages on the backseat and slid behind the wheel. As she buckled up, Aunt Tilly announced, "While you were spending all that money, I called Ed's Place for takeout. Not up to cooking and don't want to sit in the restaurant answering a lot of questions about today." Her mouth twisted in distaste. "Or put up with Talbert if he's lurking around."

"Great planning." Tori drove to Ed's and waited patiently for the couple who stood by their vehicle in front of the restaurant to unlock doors, climb in and finally pull out of the parking space.

"You go in and pick up our dinner. I'll wait here in the car."

Tori shook her head. Her aunt's face showed the fatigue and stress of the day, but Tori was reluctant to leave her alone.

Aunt Tilly pointed to people on the sidewalk, stopping now and then to look at window displays of shops that would soon be closing. "Lock me in. If someone threatens, I'll honk the horn. You grab a knife off someone's plate and come running."

Tori laughed. "I'll grab Ed or a waiter and come running." She returned shortly, loaded with food bags. She put them on the floor in the back and leaned toward her aunt over the seat. "I need to run down to the drugstore. In case I can't hear the horn a half block away, Mae will come running with a waiter and a cast iron skillet. Will you be alright for a few more minutes?"

"I'm fine." She waved Tori away. "Go."

Tori almost ran the distance. When she got back, Mae had come out of the restaurant and was talking to her aunt. She wore her white apron and a cap covered most of her hair but no sign of a skillet. "Thanks, Mae," Tori smiled.

Mae stepped back from the car. "No problem," she said and headed back inside the restaurant.

Tori handed her aunt the bag from the drugstore. "We're going to have to think of something special to do for Mae."

"She dotes on her granddaughter. Give her an autographed copy of one of your books."

"I have a new one coming out next month. I'll get an advanced copy and autograph it. Her granddaughter will have the book before anyone else, but something for Mae, maybe Ed, too. Do they ever take time off from the restaurant?"

"Not very often. Some holidays. But then, they try to make them family days. I'll be thinking. Maybe a spa day for Mae. That's something she'd never do for herself." She picked up the bag and shook it. "What's in here?"

"Pepper spray to carry in our purses. I got one for Martha, too."

Chapter Eighteen

"Finished." She felt like cheering. Yesterday, when she was computer shopping and saw the new technology available, she decided instead of getting the cheapest that would handle the security cameras, she would get a new one for her writing and leave the camera surveillance on the old one. When she powered up the new computer, it was so much easier to move her programs and manuscripts to it. Gary had installed the security program on her laptop. He explained what he did but it had been complicated then and seemed impossible when she thought of doing it herself.

She and Aunt Tilly needed to decide where to set up her old computer, now the security computer. The kitchen would be best if there was somewhere to put it away from the everyday work. Tori wandered into the kitchen carrying the computer and cord. She could hear Martha singing in the. laundry room. She was looking around for a place to put the computer when Martha wandered out carrying a basket of clothes.

"Oh landsakes. You startled me. I thought you were in the library working on your story."

"I was transferring all my work to the new computer. I think the kitchen is a good place to put this one that monitors the cameras."

Aunt Tilly walked into the room. "Finished already?"

"A lot easier to transfer my work than to install the monitoring system. Some of the programs are still on the old computer so it can be used for more than just monitoring. Now that we're all together, we can decide where to put it. I was thinking somewhere in here."

"You need it in there with you where you're working. If you'd been able to see what that... that confounded trespasser was doing, you could have grabbed my shotgun and when he pulled himself up to peek in the window, he would've been looking down double barrels. We'd have some DNA when he peed his pants."

Martha chuckled and put the basket down. "Would have been embarrassing, him hightailing it back to his car with a wet front.

Anyone seeing him would have remembered him for sure."

"If I'm home alone and working, I'll move the computer back into the library." She winked at her aunt and grinned. "And I'll know what to do." She looked over at the gun which was once more leaning against the wall by the hall doorway, probably loaded again, too. Her expression turned serious as she continued, "but, we're in here or passing through more than anywhere else. "We need a spot where it's not in the way of cooking or doing dishes or whatever."

Martha put her hands on her hips and looked around the room. "How about over there on top of the bookcase with all the cookbooks."

Tori looked in the direction of Martha's pointing finger. Perfect, except the top of the case had cookbooks lined up and held in place with an antique iron on one end and a cherry pitter on the other.

Martha marched around the end of the table and over to the object of discussion. She eyed the shelves. "Tilly, you don't use some of these books very often." A diplomatic phrasing of never. "We can move about a foot and a half of them to a shelf in the library. I noticed a few in there already. But you're going to have to say which ones." Martha would've had no trouble choosing books to move but she obviously wasn't going to step in that cowpie.

She walked back over and picked up the laundry basket again. "You can set that computer on the counter over there." She tilted her head. "There's an outlet behind the cookie jar." She paused and her forehead wrinkled in a frown. "We're not the only ones in the kitchen. Most guests wind up in here. Don't reckon it'd be good to have them gossiping about the cameras."

Tori set the computer on the counter and opened it. After a minute, the screen showed five small camera scenes. "If the doorbell rings or someone knocks at the door, you can check to see who it is," she pointed to the screens showing the area in front and near the back door, "then you close the top." She demonstrated. "When the company leaves, you open the laptop again." She lifted the top and after several seconds, views of the outside areas reappeared. "If the screen stays dark, give this little button a tap." She pointed to the power button on the side.

"Now you're getting complicated. Maybe I'll just throw a dishtowel over the thing."

Tori laughed as Martha departed. "Give it a try," she called after her.

Her aunt looked around as if searching for another place. With a shrug and a sigh, she hobbled over and looked at the books. "Might as well get it done."

Tori pulled a chair over for Aunt Tilly to sit on. As her aunt sat down, she pulled a second one over. "Stack the ones you want moved on this chair and I'll move them to the library later."

"Shouldn't have to move my stuff around because of some crook. You need to help that Detective find out who's disrupting our lives and what in the world they're after." It sounded like 'Rehab Tilly' was back until her aunt bobbed her eyebrows up and down several times.

"Shouldn't be a hardship. He's good looking and smart. Bringing us food is nice." She took a couple of books from the top shelf and put them on the chair. "I think he likes you, too."

"Aunt Tilly, don't you start matchmaking. Derrick is more conscientious than that officer who investigated your break-in. And your friend, Captain Sam Lauris, asked him to check into your complaints."

At the reminder, her aunt smiled. "Sam was your dad's friend and teammate. They'd come over after football practice with a couple of other players and empty my cookie jar. That chip in the lid is from them all trying to get their hands in there at the same time. I expect Derrick would do the same if we put the jar on the table instead of a plate of cookies."

She added two more cookbooks to the stack and put out her other hand as it wobbled. "Would you move these books over to the table?"

"Why don't I go ahead and put them in the library?"

"No, I want to give them another look. I might change my mind before I banish them."

Tori moved the books then sat at the table. "Aunt Tilly, if you haven't made anyone angry, have you thought of anything someone might want to steal or something they believe you have?"

Aunt Tilly put the book she was holding back on the shelf and turned to face Tori. "Talbert asked if Mary left anything here, but as I said, she came with a small suitcase and left pulling it behind her. Martha and I both tried to convince her to stay. No one else has asked or hinted about something I might have"

"Could Mary have left something here? Hidden it?"

"What? Her will or divorce papers? The lawyer supposedly has copies of those." Aunt Tilly added another book to the stack and began rearranging the ones on the shelves.

"Did his secretary ever return and say where she filed them?"

"No. I hear Heyden hired Louise Waters so, if she's permanent, I guess Darla's not coming back." Her voice was muffled as she leaned over to shift books on the bottom shelf. She grabbed a book and straightened up. "Heyden may have let her go and is just telling everyone she left to take care of her mother. I understand she and Talbert dated for a while after Mary died. That seems to me like it would be questionable enough." She added the book to her stack.

"Can you fire someone because of who they're dating?"

"Depends on what she might have been sharing." Aunt Tilly put two more books on the pile and looked at Tori. "And I've wondered if she misfiled Mary's will or was she so into Talbert that she would actually destroy it?"

Tori's mouth dropped open. It took a minute before she asked, "Would she do something like that?"

"Darn tootin' if Talbert promised to marry her and they'd share Mary's wealth." She turned back to her task and moved books from the top to lower shelves. "There, that give you enough room for your computer?" She dusted her hands together and stood.

"Definitely." The top was now bare except for the iron and cherry pitter. "You still want to look at these books? Tori picked up one pile hoping it would spur her aunt into saying no.

"Go ahead and move both piles to the library. If I want them, I know where they are."

When Tori returned to the kitchen after her second trip, she unplugged the computer from its spot near the cookie jar and moved it to the cleared place on top of the bookcase. She plugged it in and flipped it open. When it sprang to life, she turned to her aunt. “I guess Mary’s business is Heyden’s problem. Ours is who’s breaking into your house and why.” She sat at the table as her aunt puttered around pulling out a mixing bowl and ingredients for something she was about to make. The canister with sugar and unopened bag of flour were pulled forward signaling it was going to be something good. “What about something Uncle Hank may have had or known and written down?”

“Hank’s been dead for eighteen years. If that was the case, they’d have broken in long ago. Now get yourself up and put on an apron so you don’t muss up your nice clothes.”

“What?”

“You starting the lesson without me, Tilly?” Martha asked, walking into the kitchen. “And why didn’t you have her get everything out?”

“Didn’t want to give her a chance to back out. It’s all ready. All she has to do is measure and mix.”

Tori looked from one woman to the other as it dawned that they expected her to cook whatever they had in mind. She opened her mouth to protest and closed it. It had been her own idea to learn to cook. But that was before when Aunt Tilly was on crutches. Resigned, she stood and took the apron Martha held out to her. “What are we cooking?”

“You are making chocolate chip cookies.” Aunt Tilly grinned.

“No way. Yours are so good. Everyone will be comparing mine to yours.”

“Then you have a challenge. Recipe is in the holder. You read and we’ll interpret.”

Tori walked over to the counter where nuts, bolts and wire were soldered together and painted red to resemble a crawfish. Its claws held a three by five inch card. “You don’t use a recipe.”

“You won’t need to either after you’ve made them a few times. Stop procrastinating and read. Even if you flub, people will eat your crumbs.”

“Unless I burn them to a crisp.” She picked up the card. “One cup butter.” She grabbed the measuring cup her aunt had placed beside the mixer bowl.

“You don’t need to measure the butter.” Martha informed her.

"Each one of those sticks is a half-cup. Take the paper off two and put them in the bowl."

Tori did as Martha directed. "Three fourths cup sugar and..." She looked at the counter. Yes, there was both white sugar and brown. She carefully measured both kinds of sugar and dumped them in the bowl with the butter. She read the next line, scanned the counter and headed to the fridge.

"Where are you going? I put out all the ingredients."

Tori pointed to the card. "Cream. You forgot the cream." As she reached for the fridge handle, she heard a snort. Tori turned around. He aunt had a hand over her mouth hiding a grin. Martha was rolling her eyes. Hands on hips, Tori asked, "What?"

Aunt Tilly waved her back over to the mixer and bowl. "Read the whole sentence."

"Cream butter and sugar together. Add egg." Her expression was baffled as she read the directions again.

Her aunt smiled at Martha. "She's going to be living with me a long time if she's staying until she learns to cook." She turned back to Tori. "Cream is what you do, like stir the soup or beat the egg."

"So?"

"So cream means to mix the butter and sugar together. Move the top of the mixer down so the beaters are down in the bowl. Now turn it on."

"Wait," cried Martha. "Let's do a little preventive instruction." She nudged Tilly over and pointed to different buttons on the mixer. "This controls the speed the beaters turn. You need to start slow so the butter doesn't splatter out over the counter and floor. You can increase the speed after the butter is creamy, uh... smooth, uh... mixed with the sugar." She shook her head and addressed Tilly again. "We should have started with scrambled eggs."

"If she's going to catch Derrick, she needs be able to bake chocolate chip cookies."

"Martha glanced at Tori who was trying to decipher what to do next. "Catch not chase away."

"Hey, I'm not trying to catch Derrick. I just want to help out Aunt Tilly. Any man I marry is going to have to be happy with takeout every night. We can get takeout food or he can take me out."

Sugar and butter creamed with egg and vanilla added, Tori read the next step. She looked back and forth between the recipe card and counter and finally tapped the card. "This says sifted flour." She pointed to the bag on the counter. "That's all-purpose flour. Does it make a difference?"

After explaining the operation of the sifter, getting the flour and baking soda added to the sugar and butter mixture, and stirring the chocolate chips in by hand, Aunt Tilly demonstrated dropping the dough onto the cookie sheet using two spoons.

Tori sniffed as she pulled the first pan from the oven. The kitchen smelled like it did when Aunt Tilly baked but the misshaped and varying sizes of her cookies didn't resemble the same sized rounds her aunt achieved.

Martha looked over Tori's shoulder as she put the pan on the stove top. "The proof is in the eating. Put the next sheet in and when these are cool, we'll give them a taste test. Use the spatula," she pointed to the proper utensil, "and shift the cookies to the plate so you can drop the next batch on this pan."

Chapter Nineteen

She was taking the last batch of cookies out of the oven when the doorbell rang. She glanced toward the monitor and groaned. What was Derrick doing here? There was no place to hide the misshaped cookies. Maybe she could throw a dishtowel over them. She leaned over and took a deep breath. At least they smelled good.

She could hear Mindy's nails tapping down the hall as she raced to the door. At least someone was happy to see him. Well, Tori was glad to see him, too, but she hadn't even been brave enough to taste her cookies, even though Martha had claimed they were good.

"You gonna answer the door?" Martha grinned at Tori.

"No. I'm going to lock myself in the library and pretend to be writing."

"Hey. I ate some of those cookies. They're pretty darn good."

"Cream? Sifted flour?"

"Pfff." Martha waved her hand. "You put me in front of that computer and I'd be the same way. If you told me a week ago to move the mouse, I'd have screamed and jumped on top of the desk."

Tori couldn't help but laugh and with Martha's firm hand in the middle of her back, she couldn't help heading down the hall toward the front door.

Martha had grabbed the duster as they exited the kitchen and planted herself blocking the library doorway in case Tori tried to follow through on her threat. Tori flipped the lock and opened the door.

Derrick stepped in carrying a large manilla envelope. His glance slid between Tori and Martha. "A welcoming committee?"

"I wasn't sure Tori heard the doorbell when it rang a second time. I guess we were both coming to let you in."

Derrick lifted his chin and sniffed. "Mmm. Is Tilly baking cookies?"

Tori answered 'yes' the same time as Martha answered 'no' causing a puzzled expression to flash across Derrick's face.

"Come on to the kitchen. I'll start some fresh coffee to go with those chocolate chip cookies. Martha led the way. She pointed to a chair at the table. "Have a seat. The coffee will take a few minutes unless you'd rather have ice tea."

"Coffee sounds good if it's not too much trouble. I can use the caffeine."

Martha bustled over to the coffee pot as Tilly entered from outside with a bouquet of fresh cut daises in her fist.

Derrick took a detour over to the plate of cookies on the counter near the stove and scooped up a handful. Tori grimaced as he took a bite.

"Tastes as good as they smell and still warm. My timing's great today."

Tori gave a tentative smile that widened as he popped a second one into his mouth.

"Tori, don't just stand there. Put that plate on the table and get down some mugs," Martha directed as she went to the fridge. She grinned as she pulled out the cream and set it and sugar on the table, sending a wink in Tori's direction.

Tilly stuck the stems of the white flowers in a vase and placed it in the center of the table. She dropped into a chair and pointed to the large envelope Derrick still held. "Is that some information as to who is after something in my house?"

"I'm hoping you can tell me." He opened the envelope and pulled out pictures as Tori and Martha placed mugs of coffee in front of Tilly and Derrick and joined them with their own mugs. These are enlarged images of the person who attempted the latest break-in. He or she, but we are pretty sure it's a man, did a good job of concealing his face. However, maybe you can recognize something. A piece of clothing or a gesture." He handed each of the ladies a handful of pictures, took a couple more cookies and settled back in his chair.

Tori took a sip of her coffee and reached for a cookie, finally being brave enough to taste her own baking. She took a small bite as she pulled her pile of pictures closer. Her eyebrows rose in surprise and she grinned.

"Told you." Martha said and rolled her eyes toward Derrick as he licked crumbs from his lips. She took one with more chocolate morsels than the others and ate as she flipped through her stack of images.

When they had all gone through each stack, they passed them back to Derrick except for one that Aunt Tilly had set aside. She picked it up again and studied it. "There's something here, but I can't quite put my finger on it."

Tori got up and looked over her aunt's shoulder. She shrugged. "I haven't been here long enough to recognize gestures or clothing. Martha, come take a look."

Tori stepped aside as Martha took her spot. The two women stared at the picture. After a while, Martha commented, "He's got that cap pulled down to hide his face, but it's too small for him. His ears are sticking out the same as my son's when he put on my grandson's baseball cap."

Derrick got up and moved behind the two women. "So, it's probably someone who's not used to wearing that kind of hat."

"Or he's already got the ski mask that covers his face on the top of his head." Tori was crowding in again. "You can't see any of his hair sticking out." Her comment ruined Martha and Derrick's deductions.

Martha pointed. "One ear is really sticking out. Maybe he tried to tuck them under the hat but one popped out more because they normally stick out from his head."

Tori asked, "Can you magnify that part more and see if any hair is sticking out, too." She picked up the pile of pictures and shuffled through them. "There are no profile pictures. A profile, even with the mask, might show a protruding or receding forehead or chin. The nose hole may give a clue of nose size." As an artist, she used these features to portray different characters even if they were fairies.

"The jacket he's wearing is bulky so it's hard to tell his upper build, but his pants legs are slimmer." She continued. "We should be able to tell his height by measuring where he came to on the window before he started pulling himself up."

Martha stared at her. "Wow. Were you a PI before you became a writer?"

Tori laughed. "No. When I was in college, one my classes required us to volunteer at a library. I was reading a story to a small group. The words described the elf as being a foot tall but the picture showed him mid-thigh next to the human. A little six-year-old pointed to the illustration and said 'that's not a foot.' That little boy made me very aware of relative size when I'm drawing."

"Well, you and that little boy just might help us get a physical description of this guy even if we don't have a face. Tilly, do you have a tape measure. I can get measurements of the window while I'm here."

"Hank's toolbox is out in the garage. He had a nice metal one."

Tori stood. "I'll get it." She walked over to a drawer and rummaged for the keys to the garage.

"A red toolbox. It's on the shelf just inside the door." Aunt Tilly further directed.

"I'll go with you. If you don't mind, I'll measure and you can record for me." Derrick picked up his notebook and followed Tori out.

As Tori stuck the key in the lock, he questioned, "You and Tilly keep everything locked?"

The blinds over the window rattled as she opened the door. "Aunt Tilly didn't want that scalawag deciding whatever he's after might be in the garage and tossing Uncle Hank's tools around or slashing up our car seats, A new car costs more than a new sofa and her car's not worn out like her sofa was." She grinned. "Her words." She flipped on the light and started to reach for the toolbox, but Derrick beat her to it.

He put it on the cabinet under the shelves, next to the door and opened it. The tape measure was tucked into the tray on top. "We'll leave this here so we can put everything back where we found it. He gestured for Tori to lead the way. "Why the blinds?" he asked as they walked to the back of the house.

"Aunt Tilly didn't want them to be able to look in and tell if one of us was gone. She had her handyman replace the glass with tempered glass and reinforce the door, too."

Derrick took out his notebook, flipped it to an empty page, and handed it to Tori with his pen. He turned and extended the tape under the window.

"You mean I get to write in THE notebook?" When he ignored her comment as he jiggled the tape to keep the end on the ground, she asked, "Want me to hold the bottom of the tape. We women are good at multitasking."

"Thanks. That would be helpful."

When they finished measuring to different heights on and around the window, Tori pointed, "Did your officers move that tub. Aunt Tilly had it nearer the back porch to fill with potting soil and flowers. I don't remember him moving anything or climbing up on it but..." She frowned and lifted a shoulder. "Maybe Aunt Tilly moved it when she had Mindy out."

"I'll measure it just in case."

While she returned Uncle Hank's tape measure, Derrick had donned gloves and moved the tub into the garage to protect any fingerprints and to prevent it being used as a boost to seeing in windows. He left the pictures and Martha and her aunt had looked through them again several times, always leaving the one picture Aunt Tilly claimed to remind her of something on top.

***

Tori, Aunt Tilly and Martha sat in the back booth at Ed's Eating Place. They had decided that after a cooking lesson they deserved a night free of more cooking and Martha was happy to join them at the diner. Relaxing with a glass of wine in front of each, they didn't bother to look at the menu. Talbert had suggested they should be upset that Mae was so highhanded deciding what they were going to eat, but so far everything had been delicious and a lot of it with a twist not on the menu.

Aunt Tilly and Martha sat with their backs to the door and Tori crowded against the wall, but purses and jackets were piled on the seat beside her in the event that Talbert spotted them. If a wanted friend showed up, they could be moved.

True to form, Mae bustled out to let them know Ed was fixing something special for them. "I must be getting psychic. Something told me to save this booth and not let the waitresses seat anyone here. Talbert's already poked his nose in earlier, but if you parked out front, he'll be sticking it in again. Don't know what that man's up to unless you won the lottery. Not that you wouldn't be a prize to some man."

Aunt Tilly laughed. "You don't have to sugar coat it, Mae. We all know he married Mary for her money and then spent it on any bimbo that would raise her skirt. But I'm like you, sure would like to know what he's up to." She twisted her mouth into a smile. "And I haven't won the lottery."

Mae waved at a family entering the restaurant. "Back to work." As she turned away, a waitress pushed through the door from the kitchen with a large tray and headed in their direction.

Martha looked at the food piled on her plate. "Oh, my goodness. I shouldn't have eaten all those cookies." She tilted her head toward Tori. "But if I hadn't, I might not have gotten any more the way Derrick was inhaling them."

Tori felt her cheeks warm as Martha accompanied her words with a wink. She ducked her head and picked up her fork.

After several bites, Martha said, "I can certainly see why you eat here so often. Mae's choice is excellent. I see the waitresses taking orders so I guess she doesn't order for everyone."

Tilly swallowed the bite she was chewing. "Sometimes she senses a mood a person may be in and chooses food but I think she uses certain people as guinea pigs for Ed's experiments. I can't complain. We've always been served delicious food. It's like having a personal chef."

Suddenly there was a waitress at their table. She whipped out her pad and held her pencil poised.

"I don't think we need anything." Aunt Tilly looked up at her.

"Shhh. Keep your voice down," she whispered. "You know who just walked in. Angela is making him wait so she can seat him in a booth, hopefully with his back this way. Mae says he's been pestering you." She wiggled her pencil as if writing. "I'm supposed to be blocking his view."

"We appreciate your effort. Tell Angela thanks, too."

"He's a lousy tipper." The waitress lifted her shoulders in a shrug. "I'm Betty, by the way. Haven't worked here long but I like it here and it sure didn't take long to get a handle on Mr. Hatchett's ploys to duck out without tipping." In answer to the man at a table calling 'Miss', she turned and said, "Yes, Sir, I'll be right with you." She glanced toward the front of the restaurant before turning back. "Looks like Mr. Hatchett has decided not to stay." She smiled. "We haven't seen much of him since his cousins came to visit."

"Talbert's cousins? Mary never mentioned his relatives."

Betty shrugged. "They joined him for lunch the other day. Two men all dressed in suits but looking more like linebackers. Must have had bad news. Talbert got real pale. Even left without finishing his food. You ladies enjoy your meal," she said before hurrying away to wait on the man who had been signaling her.

"Well that was interesting." Martha lifted her napkin from her lap and patted her lips. "Personal guard service to run interference along with your personal chef." She leaned back in the booth. "I'm going to take the rest home. I want to save room for a piece of lemon pie if they still have some."

Tori had just scooped up the last bite of her dessert when her phone buzzed. She frowned as she saw Derrick's name pop up on her screen. She quickly swallowed and answered. After a pause she said, "We're at Ed's. Just finished eating. Why? When? No, we'll..." He had hung up after telling her to stay at Ed's. He would call after the police checked out the situation.

"That was Derrick checking where we are. Our house alarm went off. He wants us to stay here until he calls, but I'm going. Aunt Tilly, why don't you go home with Martha. I'll pick you up later."

"No! I'm going with you!"

"Me, too." Martha hopped up before Tilly pushed her off the end of the bench. She waved her hand to get their waitress' attention.

Mae came rushing over. Their waitress hurried behind her with their boxed leftovers.

Tori shoved her credit card at Mae. "I'll be by to sign tomorrow. We have an emergency at home."

Mae pushed the card back. "I'll put it on your tab."

"Thanks, Mae, and add a big tip for Betty and Angela." Tori helped her aunt with her sweater and turned to assist Martha who was already pushing her arms through her jacket sleeves. "I'll get the car and meet you two out front." Tori threw the words over her shoulder as she grabbed the boxes of food and rushed toward the front door, ignoring the fact that the attention of everyone in the diner was focused on them.

When she pulled to the curb, both ladies climbed in the back. As soon as they were buckled up, Tori took off. Her headlights cut through the night. At the stop sign she glanced at them in the rearview mirror. Both women were gripping the door next to them, lips pressed together. "Sorry. I guess it's better that we get there safe than in a hurry." She eased off the gas pedal.

As she tried to turn onto Aunt Tilly's street, a police vehicle, with the red and blue lights swirling in the darkness, was parked blocking the way. Tori rolled down the window as an officer approached. They could hear the alarms faintly in the distance. "Sorry Miss no one allowed..."

"We live here. Those are our alarms that are going off." Tori interrupted.

He peered into the car. "Which one of you is Ms. Statton?"

Tori twisted around and pointed to her aunt in the back. "I'm Victoria Statton, her niece. I live with her." Tori could see her aunt smiling in the dim light at her words.

He nodded in Aunt Tilly's direction. "Just a minute." He turned and walked back to his cruiser. After a few minutes he backed his vehicle so it wasn't blocking the road and waved them through.

Tori drove slowly. As they neared her aunt's house, neighbors crowded the sidewalk. Police vehicles were double parked in front of her aunt's home. She parked in front of Alice Wilson's house next door. "Wait here until I talk to Derrick. No need him yelling at all of us because we didn't stay at the diner, though I think he'll be glad we came so we can turn off the alarm."

She climbed out and ran toward the house. The motion lights Gary had installed lit up the area around the house. She was stopped again as she hurried up the driveway. Frustrated, Tori explained to the officer who she was and asked for Detective Stone. He punched in a number and walked a few feet away. With his back turned, she was tempted to make a dash for the backdoor.

While she fidgeted at the delay, she noticed Bill Wells, the neighbor on the other side of Aunt Tilly, and Charlie Clotsmore, the neighbor who lived behind and who had been on vacation when the last break-in attempt occurred, giving each other a high five. She didn't get a chance to wonder what they were congratulating each other about. The officer moved back to her and pointed. "Detective Stone is over there by the back steps.

The gate to the backyard was propped open. As she passed through it, Derrick scowled and met her halfway. "Should have known you wouldn't stay at the diner."

Tori grinned in return. "Need someone to turn off the alarm?"

"Not until we have secured the house. We need you to let us in. Probably would have broken in the door ourselves if we'd had the code to stop that noise."

"How about, you secure the kitchen and I'll turn off the alarm. Then you can check the rest of the house." She handed him the keys she still held in her hand. "You think someone might really be in there"

"Depends on how stupid he is," Derrick shrugged. "He tried to break into a house that has alarms, or he threw something in the broken window. Will you listen if I tell you to stay here while we check the kitchen?" He sighed. "At least your aunt stayed at Ed's."

Tori shook her head. "Nope. She and Martha are in the car. She'll probably show up as soon as the alarm stops making that racket to see about Mindy." As he climbed the steps to the porch, she called out, "The light switch is on the right just inside the door."

A nod indicated he heard.

Four officers slipped in with guns drawn. After several minutes, one of the men stuck his head out and said something. Derrick turned and waved her forward. Tori hurried up the steps and to the door.

Derrick grabbed her arm before she could enter. "Turn off the alarm, get the dog and come back outside. You can waylay your aunt by the gate."

Tori felt like saluting him. She disengaged the alarm. It was quiet inside but Tori could hear clapping and cheers from the neighbors outside. Panic hit her as she realized Mindy hadn't been barking at the back door and didn't come running when she entered. The barks she heard coming from another room didn't reassure her.

An officer poked his head around the door frame. "Sir, we have a problem. There's a mini-mutt at the end of the hall who thinks she's a Doberman guarding the door there."

Tori smiled in relief and headed through the door to the hall. The officer's arm stopped her. "Sorry, Miss, we haven't been able to clear the area."

Tori dropped to the floor and peered around the officer's knees. "Mindy, come girl."

Mindy broke her guard stance and looked back at Tori. "Good girl. Come on." The dog looked back at the door and growled. "It's okay Mindy. Come here, girl." Mindy took a hesitant step in Tori's direction, then ran to her. Tori scooped her up in her arms and hugged her. "Good girl," Tori repeated.

She grabbed the leash laying on the counter by the back door. "Can you tell me what happened?"

"Someone seems to be determined to break into your house." He shooed her out the door. "We'll talk later."

"Gary put a deadbolt lock on that door that Mindy was guarding because of all the windows in the sunroom. We lock it at night and when we leave." She left Derrick standing in the middle of the kitchen as she carried the pup out.

Aunt Tilly and Martha had somehow gotten past the officer that had stopped her and were waiting by the gate. "How did you get past the officer guarding the driveway?" Tori asked as she handed a wiggling Mindy to her aunt and snapped the leash to her collar.

"That's Harry, Martha's cousin's boy. Used to come over with his mother. When he got tired of climbing in the tree over yonder, he'd come in for lemonade and cookies. Knows us both and wouldn't think of stopping us."

Tori smiled. "Just can't get used to everybody knowing everyone else." She scanned the crowd and noticed the neighbor who lived behind her aunt dodging his way toward them.

He crossed his arms on the top rail of the fence and leaned in. "Hi, Tilly. Glad to see you're okay."

"Charlie, you and Ruth are back. Welcome home, but after this mess you might be ready to leave again."

"Nawh, but I need to apologize for the hole I put in your house."

Tilly put Mindy on the ground and turned back to her neighbor. "Charlie Clotsmore, what are you talking about?"

"We got back about noon. Ruth went grocery shopping and

heard all about the break-ins that've been going on. When your alarms started going off, I grabbed my pa's shotgun. I couldn't get through the back gate so I climbed up on the bench Ruth has in the backyard. Lights were blazing and some feller was knocking the glass out of one of your windows. Looked like he had a brick in his hand. Dang bench was shaky and I missed the leg I was aiming for. Should have aimed for his butt it was bigger." His face reddened. "Pardon me, ladies."

"Thanks for scaring him off anyway and never mind about the hole. A little wood putty and paint will fix that. And now that you're home, we can take the lock off the gate. The crazy criminal was cutting through your yard to get to ours."

Charlie waved to Bill and motioned for him to join them. "Yeah, he got away from my bullet, but he jumped over the fence and ran into Bill's surprise." He laughed. Charlie reached out and pulled Bill into the group when he got close. "Tell them about the surprise the guy got when he leaped over the fence."

Bill puffed out his chest a little. "When the police told me the intruder got away before by jumping over into my backyard, I borrowed my brother's dog. Figured just the size of him would scare anyone away but turns out Dog's a bit aggressive when a stranger invades his territory. I heard a lot of barking and growling and screaming. I rushed outside in time to see someone go over the back fence." He rubbed his neck. "By the time I got there and looked over, he was gone."

Her aunt speared Tori with a look. "Knew we should have gotten one of those big dogs from Carl to keep Mindy company."

Tori shook her head. She wasn't going to drive to Carl's farm for another dog. She'd have to say something to Martha to make sure she wasn't conned into taking her aunt. "With Mindy in our house and Charlie and his pa's gun behind us and Bill and Dog next door. I think we're safe." Her voice raised in question at Dog's name.

"My sister-in-law wouldn't let my brother give him a name because she said they weren't keeping him so he's just Dog."

Charlie's shoulders slumped. "Fraid I don't have Pa's gun anymore. That detective confiscated it. Called it evidence. He straightened and grinned. "But I've got Grandpa's shotgun."

Chapter Twenty

"Maybe we should hang a sign on the door saying Branch Office of Cotton Creek Police." Derrick, Aunt Tilly, and Martha sat at the kitchen table while Tori poured coffee refills. "We can even advertise as 'the branch with good coffee.' Tori slipped into her chair and used her mug to warm her hands.

"The whole town knows we have an alarm installed now. I don't understand how anyone could have expected to get in and have time to search for anything. He'd have fifteen minutes, maybe twenty if he wanted to risk the police seeing him running away." Aunt Tilly's voice reflected the tension in her rounded shoulders. "And he didn't find anything when he pushed me down the stairs or gave Tori a concussion and however many times he must have looked when I was in the hospital."

Derrick put his mug down and looked at Tilly. "He has effectively disabled your alarm. Maybe he's counting on you not being able to get it fixed quickly. I called Gary. He thinks he can rewire so it bypasses the broken window until the glass is replaced. Mr. Wells, the neighbor with the dog, had a piece of plywood in his garage. Hope it was alright that I told him to go ahead and nail it up over the broken window."

Aunt Tilly lifted her chin. "I've got good neighbors. But..." She looked Derrick in the eyes. "You need to give Charlie back his gun."

Martha and Tori nodded in agreement.

"Tilly, he can't go around shooting a gun in the neighborhood. He shot your house."

"Only because that scalawag moved and Charlie missed the leg he was aiming at. And that bullet hole in my house is lot smaller than the hole in my window."

"Charlie missed his leg, but Mr. Wells' dog didn't. The police will be checking with doctors in Cotton Creek and nearby towns to see if anyone was treated for a dog bite." The doorbell rang and Derrick rose to answer it. "That'll be the team that will be posted out front tonight. Come on, Mindy. Let's go make friends."

They heard male voices and heavy footsteps in the hall. Derrick entered with the two officers. Officer Morrow, carrying a wiggling Mindy, had been the other cop with Officer Enslow escorting Tori back from Forest Hills. She smiled a greeting as Derrick introduced them to Martha and Aunt Tilly. "I thought if they came in and made friends with Mindy she might not rouse you when one of them makes a trip around the house to check things and if she did you wouldn't be alarmed."

"We appreciate you keeping us safe tonight. You boys sit and have some coffee. I think there are two more cups left in the pot then we can make a fresh pot and fill a thermos for you."

Thanks ma'am. We'd be glad to empty your pot but no need to go to the trouble making another one." Officer Morrow said as he put Mindy down and gave her a scratch behind one tan ear then rubbed the white stripe down her nose.

Martha stood. "No problem at all. I'll get the coffee. Tori, you see if there are any cookies left in that cookie jar."

Tori set out a plate piled with a mixture of chocolate chip and oatmeal raisin cookies as Martha put a mug in front of each officer and pushed the sugar bowl and cream pitcher closer to them.

"Hey," said Derrick. "Why didn't you bring these out before? Now I have competition eating. them."

Tori grinned. "Hey. You took Charlie's gun away."

"But I'm replacing it with these two." He pointed toward the two officers. His expression turned serious. "Two qualified and experienced guns."

"Charlie's been hunting and shooting his whole life, almost since he was out of diapers." Aunt Tilly continued in her neighbor's defense.

"And his gray hair says it's been a long life."

Officer Denton, who came in with Morrow, raised an eyebrow at Detective Stone's statement but said nothing.

"Is that senior discrimination?" Tori asked.

"Wouldn't dare insinuate that." Derrick back peddled. "Questioning his judgement in firing a weapon in a populated neighborhood. And since he missed his target at thirty..." He shrugged, "...forty yards, his eyesight." He noticed the cookies disappearing and grabbed a handful.

Tori started to mention the shaky bench but decided that would only add to his argument about shooting in a neighborhood. Tomorrow she would go over and help Charlie stabilize the bench. Maybe even move it closer to the fence. They had already taken the lock off the gate between the two homes.

Martha stood. "Tori you get the thermos down and fill it with the coffee. I noticed they both drink it black." She winked at the two officers. "I'll make sandwiches in case they get hungry later on."

"Thank you, ma'am, but that's not necessary," Officer Morrow said halfheartedly.

She waved away his words and turned to Derrick. "I suppose you're going back to the station instead of home. I'll make you one, too." She pulled makings from the cabinet and fridge and said over her shoulder, "Anything y'all don't want on your sandwich give a holler."

Tori watched the officers head down the steps and toward their patrol car. She didn't know what all Martha had put into that bag, but she saw sandwiches, chips and cookies go in. She had included insulated mugs to keep the coffee warm after they poured it up.

Derrick lingered behind. "I thought I was special, but you ladies are hospitable to everyone."

Tori scrunched her nose at him. "Sorry about no cookies. We were so stuffed from our dinner we didn't think about anything to eat. And, well, it was kind of shocking to have someone try to break-in after we finally got the alarm installed." She laid her hand on his forearm. But you *are* special. You're a friend."

Derrick looked at her for a minute then said, "I guess I'll settle with that for now. Don't worry about anything tonight. Those guys are very good at their jobs."

Tori leaned back against the door she had just shut and locked. What did he mean, 'he'd settle for now?' Did he really want more than friendship? She chuckled. Martha would say it was her chocolate chip cookies. She pushed away from the door and headed toward the kitchen. They needed to talk about what they were going to do about the vulnerability of the back windows.

As she entered, she heard her aunt. "I'll sit in there with Hank's shotgun and wait for him to stick his face up before I put bars on my windows."

Tori gathered up the mugs and empty cookie plate and started putting them in the dishwasher. "What about tempered glass in the lower part of the windows or maybe replace the windows with ones that have tempered glass.? It will be expensive but maybe we can get a deal since we've done two doors. And it's time you let me help with cost?"

"What's to stop him from moving up to the front windows?" Aunt Tilly rubbed her temples.

The doorbell rang. "Derrick must have forgotten something," Tori said as she pivoted and headed after Mindy to answer it. The dog gave a few barks accompanied with tail wags.

"Take a look before you open it." Aunt Tilly's words followed her down the hall.

"We've got two armed policemen out front. Wouldn't it be nice if that vandal walked up to the front door while they were here?" Tori yelled back. She peeked and was surprised to see Bill and Charlie. Tori opened the door and beckoned them in. She stuck her head out and waved to the officers before shutting the door.

"Geez!" Bill exclaimed. "Thought we were going to be arrested for visiting our neighbor. They questioned us to the third degree."

"Sorry about that but they're there to protect us and just doing their job." She waved her hand down the hall. "Aunt Tilly and Martha are in the kitchen."

Bill"s face turned pink. "Yeah, I guess I'm overreacting, but seems like I met all the policemen when they visited my backyard and when they tried to get a blood sample from Dog's mouth where he bit that guy who was trying to break into your house."

"My hero neighbors," Aunt Tilly greeted as they entered the kitchen. "Have a seat." She pointed to the chairs vacated by the officers who were now ensconced in their vehicle out front.

"Bill was saying they may have been able to get the intruder's blood sample from Dog's mouth," Tori said as she looked in the cookie jar to see if there was any left to offer Bill and Charlie. She hesitated then emptied it, adding the broken cookies to the unbroken ones on a saucer. When she eyed the fresh pot of coffee brewing, Martha whispered, "This one's decaf."

"Well, Dog wasn't too cooperative, but I think the tech guy managed to not get bitten so if they did get anything, it's going to belong to that perp," Bill rambled.

"What brings you two over?" Martha asked as she put mugs of coffee in front of the two men.

"We're trying to organize a neighborhood watch. That crook seems focused on your house. If you hadn't been here so long, I'd start to think the owner before you buried some gold or something then got Alzheimer's and forgot all about it when his kinfolk hauled him away to a care place. We neighbors have to look out for each other. Even if he doesn't start breaking into other houses, we want to catch him."

Charlie nodded his head in agreement. "And I'm getting a dog, too. That ought to stop anyone from coming into our backyard."

Aunt Tilly smiled. "We got Mindy from Carl Wilson. I'm sure he still has some puppies he wants to give away. And we've always been a nosy neighborhood, we just need to get nosier. Start sitting on our front porches again and talking across the fence instead of watching television."

Everyone was quiet for a few minutes, the men sipping from the mugs Martha had put in front of them.

"If you are going to be talking to neighbors, I think you should ask people a block or two over to watch for parked cars that don't belong, especially dark SUVs. If they can safely get license plate numbers, write them down and give them to the police, Tori said. "Mindy tracked the scent through your backyard, Bill, and over two blocks then lost it. Detective Stone said that's probably where he had parked."

"Another thing, Tilly. If you want, I can take a couple of boards off the fence and Dog can guard both our yards."

"Thank you, Bill. That's thoughtful of you, but then Mindy could get out and I want to keep her close." Hearing her name, Mindy lifted her head. Aunt Tilly reached down and gave her a pat.

Bill nodded and pushed his chair back. "We'll be going. We want to talk to more people before our wives expect us home."

***

Tori couldn't believe it. She was driving out to Carl Wilson's farm. Charlie sat in the backseat and his wife, Ruth, occupied the front passenger seat asking questions about the puppies. Tori had described the ones she remembered, including the larger black puppy Carl had tried to talk her aunt into taking as a companion for Mindy.

She'd offered to drive Ruth and Charlie to the farm because she was hoping Carl would lend, with the emphasis on lend, her one of the large dogs that had them staying in the car until Carl called them off. She had called him earlier to make sure he still had puppies. His voice had perked up when she said she was bringing her neighbors to get one. It had taken a lot of talking to dissuade her aunt from joining them. Needing room for the dog and not leaving Martha alone, especially with the alarm not turned on yet, had been the prime arguments.

Her aunt's disappointed face lingered in her thoughts but there was no way she wanted to give her a chance to decide she needed another dog. Mindy was great as a companion for her aunt and as a watchdog, warning them before the alarm system could be set off. They'd stocked up on extra treats for her.

She turned into the rutted drive leading up to the house. The three older dogs were there before she turned off the motor. Even though she knew they weren't going to attack, she waited for Carl to appear before getting out of the car. Charlie and Ruth took her cue and waited, too, even though Ruth bounced in excitement.

Tori forced herself to approach the three guards. She extended her hand, palm down as Carl had instructed on her last visit, then cautiously gave each a pat on the head. She received a lick from the light brown dog with a bit of white on his nose. Was he Mindy's dad? Tori was proud and relieved she had passed the hurdle of making friends or at least started to make friends with them. "Good boys and, uh, girl," she said and headed in the direction of the puppies Ruth was oohing over.

While Charlie and Ruth were picking up puppies and happily receiving licks, Carl approached Tori. "Thanks for bringing these two. Looks like they'll soon be dog owners. How's Tilly and her pup doing?"

"Great. We named her Mindy. She's smart and turned into a great watchdog."

Carl looked to be in a good mood. Tori was hopeful he would lend her one of his large dogs, though she was starting to wonder if the intruder gave them a treat and a pat would they boost him in the window?

"Carl, how good are those three?" She pointed to the large dogs now lying in the grass beside her car. "As guards? They look fierce but are actually real friendly."

"They remember you. If I hadn't been here, you wouldn't have gotten more'n a step from your car that first time." He grinned. "Makes me feel better when I'm in the back pastures. Not that we have any trouble," he added.

"Well." She dragged the word out. "You know all the trouble we've been having with break-ins and all." When Carl nodded his head, she continued, "Mindy's great in the house, but I was wondering if you would lend us one of your big dogs to guard outside. Not to keep," she quickly added.

He stared at her for a minute, then gave the Clotsmores a quick glance. "You had another break-in." It was a statement not a question.

"He didn't make it into the house." She nodded in Charlie's direction. "Charlie and Ruth live behind us. When he heard our alarm go off, his gun was handy so he took a shot at the culprit."

Carl's brow furrowed and he scratched his head. "Everyone in town knows you have an alarm now. What's this guy's game?"

"Detective Stone thinks he was trying to disable the alarm. With the window broken, we can't turn it on without it blasting out over the neighborhood. But that's getting fixed today."

"Sure you don't want another pup? That black one Tilly took a shine to... Whoops. Looks like it's too late," he said as a grinning Charlie and smiling Ruth walked toward them carrying the black puppy Carl had tried to talk Aunt Tilly into taking to keep Mindy company.

"He going to be a fair size." Carl warned. "But he got a good disposition and he's smart."

"Does he have a name?" Ruth asked, reaching over to rub the

puppy's nose.

"Nope. I leave that to whoever takes the animal. He's had his first shots, so let me get the paper from the vet." He disappeared into the house. His wife, Trudy, came out with him and invited them in for ice tea.

"Thanks, but we've had more trouble and I don't want to leave Aunt Tilly and Martha alone too long. I just came to ask Carl if I could borrow one of the larger dogs to guard the yard. Just for a little while" She didn't want Trudy to think she was getting rid of two dogs.

Trudy answered, "Take Ash. He looks ferocious when he bares his teeth but he's a sweetie."

"I was thinking Dandy would be a good choice." Carl pointed to the brown dog that had given her a lick. He's not a sweetie," he looked at his wife, "but he's not going to bite your hand off if you pet him. Give him a few treats. Have Tilly and Martha do the same so he knows who he's protecting."

"What about this guy that's determined he's going to find something in Aunt Tilly's house?" Tori rubbed her forehead, questioning her own sanity at the plan to take on the care of another dog.

"Him, he'll probably bite. Won't let go once he latches on until you give the command 'release' then tell him 'guard.' Nobody's getting away. Problems. Call me." He chuckled. "Your perp might have teeth in him until I get there. Just don't let Tilly spoil him or you got him for keeps." He gave a chuckle.

They left with Charlie holding the pup and Dandy sprawled on the backseat beside him. Carl had buckled a worn collar around Dandy's neck and handed Tori his food bowl along with a list of commands he responded to that Trudy had jotted down.

Tori paused before pulling out onto the road and scanned the area. Frequent glances in her rearview mirror hadn't shown anyone following. "Have you gotten things that you'll need for your puppy yet?" She glanced at Ruth then looked in the rearview mirror at Charlie.

He answered. "No. Ruth was already to go shopping yesterday, but I wanted to make sure we got a dog before buying stuff."

"Carl gave us both enough food for a couple of days. The

hardware store has some basic supplies." Tori hesitated. The last time she and Aunt Tilly went to Henderson someone had followed them. Charlie and Ruth would be with her this time. She looked in her side and rearview mirrors. He didn't have his gun, but... Her shoulders heaved in a big sigh. "There's a great pet shop in Henderson if you want to make a quick trip."

Ruth beamed and answered for them both. "Oh, that would be great if you have the time. You've already driven us to get our puppy."

"I need to get a leash and a water bowl for Dandy and if I don't get him a bed, Aunt Tilly is going to send me back out after one." She slowed and pulled to the side of the road. "Let me just check and make sure things are okay at home and if Martha can stay longer."

She dug out her phone and tapped the contact for her aunt. After explaining their plans, she had to tell her which dog they had chosen. She laughed when Aunt Tilly asked if they had named him. "Not yet. We'll talk when I get home. Yes. I'll be careful and Charlie's with us."

Shopping was uneventful. The trunk was stuffed. Smaller packages were on the floor near Dandy and at Ruth's feet. Charlie had managed to put a few things back on the shelf. Ruth had pouted but moved on to grab something else.

Tori pulled into her aunt's driveway after depositing the Clotsmores, puppy, and their shopping at the house behind. Charlie promised to come over and unload the large bag of dog food. She hoped the police caught the troublemaker before Dandy finished it. She grabbed the leash and fastened it to the blue collar she had bought. "Come on Dandy. You're going to be our guest for a while. Let's go meet everyone."

She led him around the backyard to show him his territory and let him take care of necessities. She rapped on the door and waited while Aunt Tilly punched in the security code. Evidently Gary already had the alarm working again. Martha opened the door then jumped back at the sight of Dandy, but the big brown dog was wagging his tail. Did he sense a kitchen with friendly people or was it whatever smelled delicious in the pot on the stove?

Aunt Tilly clamped a hand over her open mouth. "Oh my, Tori. If you were going to get another dog, why didn't you get another puppy?"

"This is Dandy, a very temporary dog who will be guarding outside. As soon as he finishes chewing up our intruder, he goes back to Carl's farm," Tori said over the yapping of Mindy who was greeting Dandy or maybe establishing her territory.

Chapter Twenty-One

Tori finally felt relaxed enough to sit in front of her computer and focus on the plot of her story. The glass in the broken window had been replaced and Gary had reset the wiring for the alarm while she was gone yesterday. Dandy and Mindy remembered each other and got along. Dandy seemed content to roam the back yard even though his roaming space was greatly diminished compared to the farm.

Her fingers paused on the keys. She could smell Aunt Tilly replenishing their cookie supply. A terrified shriek from the front of the house had her jumping up from her chair. Sounds of a dog barking joined the shrieks. She hurried to the door. Dandy was in the back. Did Dog get out of her neighbors' backyard?

She flipped the locks and jerked the door open as Mindy joined the barking and tangled in her feet.

Her aunt came from the kitchen and peered over her shoulder. "Just happened to look out the window. Carl's dog cleared the fence pretty as you please."

They both stifled their laughs. Talbert sat on top of his sunflower yellow sports car, legs curled up. Dandy was braced on the hood barking. Mindy bounded against the screen door wanting to join the fray. "No, Mindy. Stay," Tori commanded. She scooped up the pup who thought she was as big as Dandy and handed her to her aunt.

"I'd like to leave him up there for a while, but I guess he needs rescuing." Tori wiped the grin off her face and pushed through the screen door. "Close it so he doesn't see you and beg to come in." She headed down the steps. "Talbert, what in the world is going on?"

"Get this dog away from me! Get him away!" His screams sounded like a bad opera soprano.

"Dandy, come boy." Geez. This may take a phone call to Carl she thought when Dandy sat down on the hood instead of coming to her. She slapped her thigh. "Good boy. Come on." Dandy at least turned his head toward her this time. She tried again. Dandy gave two barks in Talbert's direction, causing him to cringe more, and jumped off the car. "Good dog." She lowered her voice and slipped him one of Mindy's treats that she kept in her pocket.

Dog continued to bark from the neighbor's backyard. Bill's wife came out to her front porch to investigate the commotion. "Everything alright?" June hollered.

Tori smiled and waved in her direction. "Yeah. Dandy hopped the fence to guard the front yard as well as the back."

"D-D-Don't let that other dog get out!" Talbert stuttered with a quick glance behind him. When he started to inch forward, Tori slipped a hand around Dandy's collar. Talbert saw she had control of Dandy and wasted no time scooting to the hood and sliding off the opposite side of the car.

Tori watched as he maneuvered to the driver's door. He seemed to be limping. Had he hurt himself climbing onto his car? She started to ask but he slid into the car and slammed the door. With the windows closed and Dog barking, he wouldn't be able to hear. June came down her steps and joined Tori in time to watch his vehicle squeal away.

"Between your dog and the monster Bill borrowed from his brother. I'm about to relent and let Bill get one. She nodded in the direction Talbert left. "What did he want? He didn't stick around to talk to you or Tilly," she chuckled. "But you don't seem too disappointed." She bent and gave Dandy a few pats. "You are a good boy, sending that leech on his way." She took a step back. "I'd better get back. I've got a cake in the oven, but Dog was putting up such a ruckus, I had to check."

"Thanks for being so alert yourself. And if you decide to get a dog, Carl still has several." Tori called after June's retreating back. She expected some resistance from Dandy but when she tugged on his collar, he trotted obediently beside her to the backyard. The gate was latched so he must have climbed over the four-foot fence, but Aunt Tilly said he jumped.

Her aunt came out the back door as she shut the gate and released Dandy. She put Mindy down and the two dogs ran in circles as if nothing had happened. Mindy's short legs moving three times as fast as Dandy's lazy lope.

"We may have a problem other than Talbert. Dandy proved he is a great watchdog today, but I don't want to take a chance of him jumping the fence and running away. I may have to take him back to the farm."

Aunt Tilly shook her head in disagreement. "If we give him enough treats and feed him something besides that stuff Carl sent, he'll stick around. A smart dog like Dandy knows a good thing."

Tori raised a skeptical brow but smiled. "That may keep him here, but we can't have him greeting anyone that walks up to our front door the way he did Talbert."

"Mindy goes after Talbert the same way but look at her with Derrick and the officers. I don't think she barked more than once or twice when Bill and Charlie came over the other night. She certainly didn't attack them the way she tried to when Talbert was going to come in our backyard, and she barks up a storm if he comes to our door." She laughed. "That's how we know to hide."

Tori's smile disappeared at the reminder. "Derrick said he told Talbert to stay away unless we invited him. He didn't get a chance to say why he was here, but he didn't call first." She shrugged. "Or maybe he did since we don't answer when we know it's him."

She called the dogs and headed toward the porch. Inside, they lifted their noses to the smell of her aunt's baking, sugar, cinnamon, chocolate. Cookies still sat on cooling racks and two baking pans loaded with oatmeal raisin cookies were on top of the stove where her aunt had hurriedly placed them when the commotion started.

"Sorry guys, not for you." She gave each dog an appropriate treat and filled their water bowls. Aunt Tilly poured herself and Tori each a glass of ice tea. "I guess I'd better call Derrick and let him know what happened." Tori set a small plate of cookies on the table and joined her aunt. "He'll hear some version of it soon enough."

Aunt Tilly sat, fingers idly tapping the table, a slight frown marred her forehead.

Tori eyed her worriedly. She finally asked, "You concerned that Talbert might sue over Dandy attacking him?"

"Phff." Her aunt waved her hand and focused on Tori. "He was told by a law officer to stay away. Far as I could tell from the window, Dandy didn't lay a paw or tooth on him. I've seen him more these last couple weeks than I did the whole time Mary was married to him." Aunt Tilly gripped her glass of tea like it was a lifeline. "Never did like him. I tried to tell Mary. All her friends tried to warn her not to fall for his lies, but Mary wasn't a beauty and she wasn't popular in high school. Came home from college to take care of her ailing dad, so she didn't get to meet a nice guy there."

Her voice grew sharp with anger. "Talbert started pouring on the charm as soon as her dad passed away. She was still grieving and didn't stand a chance. That charm isn't going to work on me so if he's after any money he thinks I have, he's wasting his time. Wish he would sue. I'd sue him right back. Get some of Mary's money and donate it to charity the way she intended."

"He did ask you if Mary had left anything here when she stayed with you after she filed for divorce."

"And I told him no."

"Could she have hidden something here and planned to get it later but was killed in that accident before she could?"

Tilly shook her head in denial. "She would have told me."

Not ready to get back to her computer, Tori puttered in the kitchen. She filled the cookie jar and put more in a container while Aunt Tilly baked the last batch. When she ran out of things to do she grabbed her sketch pad and started doodling at the kitchen table, still not ready to retreat to the library.

The front doorbell sent both dogs rushing down the hall. "No barking." Tori laughed. "We know it's not Talbert."

"My bet's on Derrick." Tilly glanced toward the computer on top of the bookcase and smiled. "You get the door. I'll put these cookies on a plate," she said as she slid a spatula under the ones on the pan she had just pulled from the oven.

After a peek, Tori opened the door and let Derrick in. "We said it was only a matter of time before you heard about the trouble with Talbert."

"If he smelled Tilly's cookies, I can't blame him for showing up." He picked up Mindy whose tail was thumping against her back and reached down to scratch Dandy behind his ear. "So this is the ferocious dog Talbert was raving about."

"Talbert came to you?" Tori's voice was incredulous. "I was

going to call you, but he must have driven straight to the police station."

"I intercepted him on his way to make a formal complaint, as he called it."

Aunt Tilly stuck her head into the hall. "You two going to lollygag out there or you coming in here to share what's going on?" She nodded toward the table as they came through the doorway. "You want tea or leftover coffee?" she asked Derrick.

"Coffee sounds good." Derrick headed for the chair nearest the plate of cookies.

Aunt Tilly put the mug of coffee she'd warmed in the microwave in front of Derrick. "Stop eating those cookies long enough to tell us what happened."

Derrick took a swallow of coffee. "I'd just come out of the chief's office. There was a loud ruckus going on in the lobby, yelling and what sounded like pounding on Teresa's desk. I went to see if she needed assistance. Talbert was there. He wanted to file a complaint. Wanted that dog shot. I won't repeat his description of the dog. Officer Morrow was about to cuff him, but I grabbed him by the arm and dragged him back to Sam's office. Told him to sit down and shut up until he could talk without shouting. When I finally got the story out of him, I reminded him that he was in violation of a police order to stay away from the Statton residence. He would need to include that in his report and he would need to go to the ER and obtain a doctor's evaluation of any bites or other injuries he had received. That shut him up and I'd swear he turned a little pale." He picked up another cookie. "I figured I'd better come check out the monstrous dog and get your version of what happened."

Tori grinned. "To bad we didn't get a picture of Talbert on top of his car and Dandy standing guard on the hood. The threat of it going public would be enough to make sure he doesn't sue."

"Picture! Don't know what our camera recorded, but I've got a whole movie!" Aunt Tilly pulled her cell phone from her pocket and handed it to Derrick. She and Tori both leaned over Derrick's shoulder as he punched a few buttons.

Derrick's hand came up to hide his smile, but his shoulders shook as he tried to stifle his laugh. They watched it twice then

Derrick sent the recording to his own phone. "I saw you slip the dog a treat, but I think it calls for another." As he reached into his pocket, Mindy jumped up. She knew what that meant. "Come on, boy. You, too," Derrick said as he gave Mindy a small chewy bone and pulled out a larger one for Dandy. "How did he get the name Dandy? That's kind of misleading."

"According to Carl, the first time he pooped in the house when he was a pup. Trudy put her hands on her hips, looked at the mess and said, 'That's just dandy.' Trudy was quick to add that she also said, "Your pup, you clean it up.' He got housebroken real quick."

"I know two dogs can be a lot of trouble, but I think Dandy's a keeper."

"Except he jumped the fence when Talbert started up the sidewalk. I'm afraid he'll get out and get lost." Tori's brow wrinkled. "I need to talk to Carl."

"We're going to the expense of new windows. Maybe we should put in a higher fence , a six footer like we have across the back and on the sides."

"Might make it harder for your intruder to get in or out of your back yard but I have a feeling it won't stop Dandy."

"With all his complaining, he ever say why he was here?" Aunt Tilly crumbled the cookie in her saucer.

Derrick eyed Tilly's crumbs, pulled the plate of cookies closer to him and took a couple, as if he was afraid she would crumble them all. "He said it was personal."

"Personal? He asked if Mary had left anything here. I don't know what that could be, but I told him no." She glanced over at Mary's teapot that she'd bought when Talbert had his big yard sale. "At one time I would have given him back her teapot if he'd changed his mind. It's Spode and I only paid a dollar and fifty cents for it, but not now." She wiped her fingers on her napkin and pushed the saucer of crumbs away. "A sale is a sale."

Derrick took another cookie and pushed back his chair. His glance landed on Tori's sketch book. He smiled as he slid it toward him. "Is this an illustration by the famous artist?" His expression turned serious as he stared at her drawing. He glanced up at Tori and back at her drawing. "Even if you gave him wings, he wouldn't look like a fairy."

Tori blushed and pulled the sketch away from him. “I was just doodling.” She looked down at what her worried mind had created. A figure crouched behind a bush. Her pencil had shaded where a head should be with no attempt to draw features, but a knife was gripped in the figure’s hand. A policeman stood between the bush and a few lines that looked like she had started to draw a building. Tori ripped the picture out of her sketch book and started to crumple it.

Derrick reached out and took it from her. “I’d like to have it if you’re going to toss it.”

She started to protest but gave a shrug and a nod instead.

Derrick turned to Tilly. “If you decide to meet with Talbert to find out what he wants, make it for lunch at Ed’s and let me know when. Another officer and I will be having lunch at the same time. Don’t try to ignore us. We’ve been here enough you probably know everyone on the force. Wave and say hello or even come over to our table.”

“Do you think he’ll talk in front of me? There’s no way I’m letting him meet with Aunt Tilly alone.”

Chapter Twenty-Two

"Do you think he'll show knowing I'll be here, too?" Tori held the door open for her aunt.

"Oh definitely. I invited him as our guest. He's not going to pass up a free meal. Probably order the most expensive thing on the menu." She waved at Mae across the room. "I alerted Mae we wanted a table right smack in the middle of the room."

"Good afternoon, ladies." Mae winked as she approached them. "Just the two of you today?" She grinned.

"No. We have a guest joining us today."

"Speak of the devil." Her lips barely moved as she murmured the words. She tilted her head toward someone entering behind them. "This way ladies. Be with you in a minute, Talbert."

"I'm joining Tilly today." He stepped closer to follow.

When Mae stopped at the table Tilly had requested, Talbert spoke up. "What about a booth, Mae? Much easier to carry on a conversation."

"Oh, this is fine." Tilly sank into one of the chairs and leaned her cane against the armrest. "I'll be glad when I don't need this thing anymore but I'm glad to be off those crutches."

"This is a nice apology." Talbert said as he sat in a chair close to Tilly.

Tori sat facing him and raised a brow.

"Apology?" quizzed Tilly.

"Well, your dog did attack me." Talbert became indignant.

"My dog was defending my property against someone who had been told to stay away from my house by the police. I've replaced enough windows broken by a crazy intruder. I didn't need you imitating that scum."

Talbert winced at her words. Perspiration dotted his forehead.

The new waitress, Betty, put in a timely appearance with water and menus. "Ed is already fixing you and Tori something delicious, Miz Tilly. You want the special, Mr. Hatchett?"

"No. I believe I'll have the steak, rare, baked potato, fully loaded, and a salad with the house dressing."

The waitress whipped the menus off the table and stepped

back, turning so Talbert couldn't see her face, she mouthed to Tilly 'you must be paying.' She clapped her hand over her mouth as color tinged her cheeks.

Tilly looked at the waitress and smiled. "Thank you, Betty."

She turned to Talbert. "Let's put the dog incident aside and enjoy our meal. Detective Stone said you had something you wanted to discuss with me." She looked across the room and waved. "There he is now. Ed's is a popular place today." Tori smiled and joined her in waving.

Talbert looked over his shoulder and quickly turned back. "You are friends with the police?" His knuckles turned white as he gripped his glass and took a sip.

"It pays to stay friendly with the police as many times as they have answered our 911 calls lately." She picked up her napkin and shook it into her lap. "I feel like we should be on first name basis with Detective Stone as often as he has been by to ask questions about break-ins and attempted break-ins."

Tilly flicked her hand. "But we weren't going to talk about that," she said. She chatted away about the weather and the flowers she was going to plant as soon as she got rid of her cane. Finally taking a breath, she announced, "Here comes our meal. I wonder what delicious lunch Ed has cooked up for us today."

"How can you tolerate the high handedness of them fixing whatever they want instead of letting you order?"

"As I told you last time, it is always delicious and gives us a chance to try something new. We're lucky Ed has chosen us to be his tasters. I'm sure if I really wanted something from the regular menu, they would be happy to accommodate."

Talbert's posture was rigid with disdain, but his nose twitched and he licked his lips as he eyed Tilly's plate.

Tori sniffed appreciatively. "This smells so good, Betty." She picked up her fork and took a bite of stuffed chicken breast with a mushroom sauce as Betty put Talbert's steak in front of him. "Mmm, and tastes as good as it smells. Tell Ed thank you."

Talbert kept glancing toward Tilly as he emptied his plate of all but the potato peel. Tilly sighed as she put her fork down, her plate only half-empty.

Tori soon did the same. "That was so good," she said, "but Ed always gives us so much."

Betty deposited a bill at a table near them and came over. "Boxes to go, ladies?"

"Definitely." Tilly smiled up at their server. "That was delicious but Ed always over estimates our appetites."

"Dessert?" Betty rattled off available choices.

"Just coffee for now. Tori and I will take dessert home, but I think Talbert would like his now." She nodded in his direction.

Betty scribbled down their choices and headed toward the kitchen.

"Now, Talbert, what is it that you came to my home to discuss?"

"Well..." He looked down at the table, hesitating. He lifted his chin and continued. "You remember I asked if Mary left anything at your house when she stayed with you after..."

Betty interrupted when she appeared with three mugs of coffee and a serving of chocolate pie. "Anything else?" She smiled at Tilly.

"Thank you, Betty." Tilly gave a negative shake of her head. "We're good." As Betty left, Tilly raised an eyebrow in Talbert's direction and tilted her head.

He swallowed the bite of pie he had taken and cleared his throat. "I was wondering if you've had time to look around and maybe found something Mary...Mary forgot to pack?"

Tilly straightened her shoulders. "I haven't even looked. Mary is...was pretty organized. I don't believe she would have forgotten anything." She stared into Talbert's eyes until he dropped his gaze. "I do have her pink sweater that I bought at your yard sale and..."

Talbert waved his hand. "No. She was missing some things when she came home. Before I decided to get rid of some of the clutter."

Tilly pressed her lips into a straight line but said nothing.

"I... I didn't mean that the way it sounded." Talbert blustered. "It was a way to share some of her things with her friends."

Tori's mouth dropped open at the blatant lie.

"Would you mind if I came and looked around the room she stayed in?" His voice was tinged with desperation.

"Yes, I would mind. Martha has cleaned that room several times since Mary stayed with me. Dusting and vacuuming. She even had her daughter come and help flip the mattress." Her tone was rigid and angry. "You think I'm either stupid or lying. I do not appreciate either opinion." She picked up her purse and stood. "Finish your pie. We have dogs we need to get home to."

Tori stood to follow her aunt. She refrained from picking up his pie and smashing it in his face. Derrick had stood and was heading toward their table. Tori gave him a slight shake of her head to stop him but turned back to their lunch guest. "Don't bother my aunt anymore. If she has to take out a restraining order, it won't do your reputation or business any good."

"I didn't mean anything by my request. Your aunt took everything the wrong way. She always was a bad influence on my wife."

"Problem here?" Tori felt Derrick's grip on her arm.

"Yes! I accepted an invitation to lunch and Tilly misinterpreted everything I've said and now this..." He pointed a finger at Tori.

"Careful Mr. Hatchett. The ladies evidently have another appointment and are leaving. Why don't you enjoy the rest of your lunch?"

Talbert opened his mouth as if to say something. His focus shifted between Tilly's niece and the detective several times. He turned back to the table and picked up his fork. "So that's how it is." His voice was low, but loud enough to be heard.

"Thank you, Detective Stone. I'm sorry we interrupted your lunch. I think Aunt Tilly and Mr. Hatchett have come to the agreement they will remember and grieve Mary separately."

***

Tori sat curled up in the corner of the new taupe sofa. Her mind wandered from the flickering screen of the television. Soft snores from her aunt told her she was watching the movie alone. They had turned out the lights but from the glow of the television, she could see Mindy at her aunt's feet, looking hopefully at the half-eaten bowl of popcorn tilting in her aunt's lap.

Maybe things were settling down. After lunch yesterday, her aunt had fumed for hours at Talbert's audacity in asking to search her house. Tori shifted her weight to stretch her legs and Dandy rested his chin on her knee. She rubbed behind his ears and stroked down his neck. "I think he finally got the message," she said softly to the dog. "But he never said what he thought Mary left behind. Maybe another copy of her will," she speculated. Dandy whined as she paused in her petting. She started rubbing again. "If there's no new will, he inherits everything and according to Aunt Tilly that's millions."

She picked up the remote and clicked off the television. She leaned her head back against the sofa then straightened. If she relaxed too much she'd doze off with her aunt. "I guess I'd better wake Aunt Tilly and both of us can get a good night's sleep in our beds." She continued her one-sided conversation with Dandy and reached to turn on the lamp.

Dandy tensed. The hair on his neck rose under Tori's hand as he stood. He gave a low growl and ran down the hall to the front door. Mindy barked and jumped up. "Quiet girl." Mindy quieted but her bark woke her aunt.

"What's going on?" Alarm sounded in her aunt's voice.

"I don't know. I'd just turned off the TV and turned on the lamp. I was going to wake you when Dandy heard something. Call 911. I'm going to see if I can see anything."

"Get my shotgun."

"I just going to look out the front window. Call 911," she repeated. Tori could hear her aunt talking as she lifted the edge of the drape. "My, God! He's started a fire! We need the police and fire department," she yelled.

She ran to the door and snatched up Mindy. She quietly turned the deadbolt and opened the door. Pushing the screen door open, she let Dandy out. The motion light went on as Dandy butted his way out and leaped off the porch. She could see him racing after the fire starter as the alarm blared. They disappeared into the darkness.

Dog next door started barking. She could hear him jumping against the fence.

She heard a distant bark, a scream and a yelp before she was pushed out of the way and her aunt stepped out onto the porch, shouldering her shotgun. Tori shifted her hold on Mindy to one arm and grabbed her aunt's sweater. "No, Aunt Tilly. The police are coming. Here. Take Mindy. Get her leash and Dandy's and wait outside. The fire crackled, growing as more of whatever the arsonist had piled up caught fire. I'm going to get the hose."

She lifted the heavy hose from the rack that hung on the side of the house and struggled to drag it toward the front of the house. Her burden was taken from her as Charlie appeared.

"I've got this. Turn on the water. Where's Tilly?" he hollered as he rounded the corner of the house, uncoiling the hose as he ran.

Tori turned on the water and looked around. Her aunt and Mindy were still inside. As she ran up the steps to the porch, she saw Bill dragging a hose from his house toward the blaze. "Aunt Tilly," she called frantically.

The alarm went silent and her aunt hurried toward her still carrying a struggling Mindy. "I had to turn off that infernal noise."

Tori put her arm around her aunt's waist and pulled her out the door and away from the house. The neighbor from across the street had come with a rake and was attempting to pull the burning debris away from the house. Sirens sounded in the distance.

Tori took the leashes dangling from Aunt Tilly's hand and fastened one to Mindy's collar. "I'm going to see if I can find Dandy."

It was Aunt Tilly's turn to grab Tori. "No, you're not. I left my shotgun in the house so Derrick wouldn't have a conniption. What do think he's going to do thinking you ran after that arsonist? Dandy may have him cornered. Then what?"

Tori stared in the direction Dandy had disappeared. "I heard him yelp. What if he's hurt?"

"Then he'll need a big strong policeman to carry him home."

While they had argued, the firemen had arrived and taken charge of putting out the fire. Minutes behind them were two police cars. Derrick's Ford Escape squealed to a stop behind them. He climbed out dressed in jeans and sweatshirt, obviously off duty. He stood for a minute surveying the area and then strode across the yard toward the two women.

"What the hell's going on now?" He glanced at Tilly. "Sorry, Tilly."

"Hell's full of fire so that a good question. I guess, if he can't break in, he's going to burn us down."

"You two okay?" When they both shook their heads, he turned toward the fire which seemed to be out except for smoke and a few flares.

"Hold on, Derrick. Before you go investigating, you need to send someone after Dandy. I've been hanging onto Tori to keep her from taking off after him."

"He's the one that alerted us something was going on. I let him out and he chased after the guy but he'd already started the fire."

"Morrow." Derrick called the nearest officer over. "Seems Dandy went after the arsonist and hasn't come back yet." He turned and asked, "Which way did they go?"

Tori pointed in the direction they had disappeared. "Take Mindy. She'll track Dandy for you." She handed officer Morrow the leash attached to Mindy's collar and the extra leash for Dandy.

"I heard a bark and a scream and a car door slam, but it didn't sound close. Dandy also gave a yelp like that guy had done something to him." She choked out the last words.

"Call for backup if Dandy happens to have that guy cornered," Derrick lowered his voice as he walked away with Officer Morrow and Mindy, but Tori heard him say, "or if he hurt the dog."

She watched as Mindy tugged on her leash pulling the officer in the direction the arsonist had run until the darkness of the neighborhood swallowed him and Dandy. She moved back to stand beside her aunt like two lost figures. Derrick was talking to the fireman who seemed to be in charge. The three neighbors who had rushed to put out the fire stood off to the side talking. Two firemen crawled under the front porch near where the fire had started.

Tori felt her aunt lean against her and slipped her arm around her waist. "I think it's probably safe to go back inside where you can sit down."

"Not until that officer returns with Mindy and Dandy." She trembled against Tori.

"Then let's go sit on the steps." Tori led her aunt toward the house. She settled her aunt on the top step and went into the house. She grabbed the afghan thrown over the arm of the sofa and carried it out and draped it around Aunt Tilly's shoulders. For mid-June, it was still a bit nippy at night.

As she settled beside her aunt, Tori said, "Uh oh. Are you sure you don't want to go inside?" She nodded toward a white van that had just pulled up. "We are finally newsworthy. The media has arrived."

"Surprised they haven't come before. Half dozen police calls for someone determined to break in and steal what?" She shrugged. "I still have my silver service and my jewelry in spite of some deranged person ripping up my old furniture."

"Let's talk to Derrick before making statements to the press. Publicity might make this criminal step things up."

"He tried to burn down my house. How much more stepping up can he do?"

Tori jumped up. "There's Officer Morrow with the dogs." She dashed down the steps and ran toward them.

As she got close, Officer Morrow held up his hand gripping Dandy's leash. "Hold up. Don't touch Dandy." He gave Dandy the command to sit." Dandy obeyed. Then he lay down and whined as he rubbed his face against the grass.

Tori froze. "What wrong?"

Anger blazed in Officer Morrow's eyes. "That no good... He maced Dandy. Here, take Mindy." He thrust the smaller dog into her arms. "I had a hard time keeping her back so she didn't rub against Dandy and get it in her eyes, too."

"What's going on, Morrow?" Derrick had come up behind her as she took Mindy.

"Maced." His voice was terse as he answered and nodded toward Dandy. "I called my vet. I didn't know who you take Dandy to. He'll meet us at his office and wash out Dandy's eyes, bathe him and give him something to ease the pain." After a glance at Derrick, he looked at Tori. "If that's okay with you?"

He reached into his jacket pocket and pulled out a plastic bag containing a large piece of fabric. "Dandy had this in his mouth. Looks like the perp left with a draft cooling his backside. Didn't see anything else with my flashlight and two dogs to handle but I marked the spot so we could look around in the daylight."

Derrick stuck his hand into his pocket where he kept dog treats. He gave Mindy one and carefully placed several in front of Dandy. "Good boy, Dandy. We'll have you feeling better."

"Let me give Mindy to my aunt and get my purse." She turned to Derrick. "Can someone stay with Aunt Tilly until I get back?"

"I'll stay."

"I'll get a blanket for the back seat so he doesn't rub mace on it," she called back as she hurried away. When she came out, Officer Morrow stood beside a patrol car.

"We can take my car." Tori said as she shook the folds from the blanket.

"I can drive a little faster in this." He grinned and opened the rear door.

Chapter Twenty-Three

A pink glow was starting to lighten the sky behind her aunt's house as they pulled into the driveway. A patrol car with two officers was parked in front, but Derrick's vehicle was still there.

Tori waved at them as she led Dandy up the walk toward the porch. She stopped at the bottom of the steps and stared at the darkened patch of grass. Dandy gave a low growl. She reached down and put a hand on his head to quiet him. The edge of the porch was scorched showing how close it had been to have the house on fire.

She felt Morrow's hand on her back as he urged her forward. "Don't dwell on that. Your neighbors controlled the blaze until the firefighters got here. We'll be back in the daylight to investigate. In the meantime, those officers are keeping watch." He nodded toward the cruiser parked at the curb.

The front door jerked open as she tried to insert her key. A rumpled Derrick greeted them. He held up a finger to his lips as he stepped back and motioned them in. "Talked her into going to bed a couple of hours ago." His voice was barely above a whisper. "How's Dandy?" He rubbed the dog's head and neck and laughed quietly when Dandy sniffed the pocket where he kept the dog treats. "Two left and you deserve them," he said as he held his palm out with the goodies.

"Vet said he'd be fine. Thanks again, Ted." They were now on first name basis.

Officer Morrow nodded. "You're welcome, Tori. I'll be off." He turned his head toward Derrick. "See you at the station in a couple of hours."

"Get some rest. Come in late."

"Nah. I want to look over the sight where I found Dandy before joggers contaminate it." He headed down the steps.

"I'm going to head home to get a couple of hours sleep, too. Try to get some sleep yourself. Those guys will be out front until officers come to investigate the site in the daylight."

"Thanks for staying with Aunt Tilly. I don't know how you managed to get her to go to bed, but thanks for that, too."

"She was stubborn, but when I told her you would be needing

her today, she picked up Mindy and went." He gave a tired smile. "Lock the door and turn on the alarm. You'll sleep better with double security." He pulled the door shut behind him.

She locked the door, turned on the alarm and headed for the sunroom. "Come on, Dandy. We'll share the sofa."

Tori woke to the smell of brewing coffee and frying bacon. She groaned as she tried to roll over without falling off the edge of the sofa. Her sleeping companion was gone. Probably licking his chops in the kitchen hoping Aunt Tilly would drop something. She sat up and ran her fingers through her hair trying to smooth the tangles that were a result of tossing and turning before she finally fell asleep.

She stumbled into the kitchen and over to the coffee pot. She poured herself a mug and leaned back against the counter as she took her first sip.

"Morning. You manage to get any rest?" Her aunt greeted.

"Doesn't feel like it but according to that clock, I must have gotten some."

"I can hold up this breakfast if you want to get a quick shower. I took egg sandwiches and coffee out to the officers parked out front all night. They're gone but we have a couple more searching around in our front yard. A fireman, arson specialist he called himself, was here early, too."

Bleary-eyed, Tori caught a glimpse of her reflection of the black microwave door. The blurred image showed her wild curls haloing her head. "Are you saying I look a bit bedraggled?" She hid her grin behind another sip of the dark brew.

Aunt Tilly paused in the transfer of bacon to a paper towel lined plate. "If that fire starter sticks his nose back in our yard, your appearance will help Dandy chase him away," she answered with her own grin.

Tori attempted to smooth her tangled curls again then lifted the front of her shirt and sniffed. "Right. I guess a day and a night in these clothes means I better in case any of the investigators come in to ask questions. She took a couple more swallows and put her mug on the counter. "I'll hurry. Breakfast smells good and Dandy looks like he'll eat it if I take too long."

"After last night, he deserves it."

Tori showered, dressed in a blue t-shirt and jeans and slid her feet into a pair of sandals in record time. She had just slipped her last piece of bacon to the two hopeful dogs at her feet when the doorbell rang. She started to get up but Aunt Tilly waved her to stay and headed down the hall. "You've been up all night. Just sit there. I'll get it."

Derrick and Officer Ted Morrow followed her aunt back into the kitchen.

Ted nodded in Tori's direction then focused on Dandy. "I came to check on our fellow here." He knelt and gave Dandy a few pats. He put his hands on each side of Dandy's face and studied his eyes. "I think you're going to be alright. We'll get that guy and the chief is going to have to hold me back from spraying a little mace in his face." He rubbed Dandy's head and laughed when Mindy stuck her head between them. "You want a little attention too, huh? You did a good job of finding your friend last night." He patted her head and stood.

"You two want some breakfast?" Aunt Tilly asked.

"No, but we'll take some of your coffee," Derrick answered for both of them.

Tori waited until they were settled with their mugs. "Did you find anything in the daylight?"

"Nothing new. The investigator for the fire department is out there now. He's looking at different things. Maybe he'll come up with something." He took a swallow and put his coffee mug down. His shoulders heaved as he took a deep breath then lifted his gaze and focused on Aunt Tilly. "This perpetrator is after something or he's a stalker fixated on you. He has been dangerous from the start, attacking you and then Tori and now he attempted to set your house on fire."

"I thought a stalker followed you around, made phone calls, maybe broke in and stole something personal." A cold chill gripped Tori. "We've been watching but I haven't noticed anyone following us around." She paused. "Well, I haven't noticed a dark SUV. I guess he could have switched vehicles."

"I threw in stalker because someone followed you to Forest Hills and I'm assuming the person in the parking lot in Henderson followed you there, but maybe he thought you had whatever he's after with you."

Ted shifted in his seat and cleared his throat. "Have you had a disagreement with anyone? Even something you think was trivial?"

Aunt Tilly sat for a few minutes. She finally shook her head. "A couple of run-ins with Talbert and the dogs when he tried to come visiting. Mindy wouldn't let him in the back yard and Dandy chased him up onto the top his car." Her grin was contagious as Tori and the officers joined her with chuckles. "The incident at the restaurant was... Well, he's been asking if Mary left anything here. She stayed with me almost a week after she filed for divorce, then she decided she'd better go home and make sure Talbert wasn't packing up the silverware. Those were her words when she told me she was moving back home. Easier to keep him from taking things than to try to get them back," she said. "At the restaurant, he asked if he could come and look around the room Mary stayed in." She took a sip of coffee and put her cup down with a bang. The liquid sloshed out. She stared at the mess then wiped at it with her napkin. "Blew my top at the nerve of him. Told him off."

Derrick and Ted shared a hard-to-read glance.

"My neighbor, Alice, was a bit miffed because I didn't give her a key when Tori had the locks changed. She got over that quick. And she's been gone for the last three weeks. Should be home this weekend." Aunt Tilly shook her head and smiled. "She's going to be mad she missed all the excitement." A sigh escaped as she said, "I wouldn't have minded missing it one bit."

"The next question is, what could he want?" Derrick had pulled out his notebook and was making notes.

Tilly leaned forward. "I haven't said anything to Heyden, Mary's lawyer, and I'm not going to but Talbert was dating his secretary mighty soon after Mary died. And if the gossip is right, before that, too. It makes me wonder if somehow, he sweet talked her into destroying the lawyer's copy of Mary's will. She left town saying she needed to take care of her sick mother and hasn't returned." She leaned back in her chair. "A lawyer doesn't lose important documents. It would be the end of his career and the beginning of a lot of lawsuits."

"Maybe that's it," Tori said. "He hasn't found Mary's copy and he thinks she left it here."

"Like I told Talbert at the restaurant, Martha has dusted and vacuumed that room once or twice a month since Mary stayed. Even had her daughter come in to help flip the mattress. And when you came and dusted for fingerprints, we washed everything in the drawers because whoever pushed me down the stairs had mauled what I had stored there with his grubby hands." Her face flushed as her temper rose. She took a deep breath and picked up her coffee.

"'Can he search my house, indeed? Makes me wonder if he *is* the one breaking into my house."

Derrick and Ted exchanged another look before Derrick asked, "Do you think it could be Talbert breaking in?"

"When he first started coming around, I thought maybe he believed Aunt Tilly had money. Not as much as Mary apparently had but enough to try to get her as a client or get me out of the picture and marry her if Mary's lawyer doesn't turn over her assets to him."

A rap on the glass of the back door had them all turning in that direction. Martha shielded her eyes as she leaned forward and peered in through the windowpane, a concerned look on her face.

Tori hopped up and unlocked the door. Martha breezed in. "Oh, my!" Martha's brown eyebrows nearly reached her hairline. "I really didn't believe it until I drove up and saw the police and that fireman out front and all that black grass." The red purse Tori had bought her when she went to Forest Hills landed on the counter with a soft thud. "I would have been here sooner, but it is my day to help Mrs. Willowby and it seemed, as usual, every time I picked up my purse to leave, she found something else that needed doing for the dinner she's having tonight. That woman sure likes to entertain." Martha finally acknowledged Derrick and Officer Morrow. Her brown eyes shot them a steely glare. "Well, I hope you guys got some clues this time."

"We're working on it, Martha." Derrick gestured to an empty chair. "Maybe you'll have some input."

"There's a wacko running around Cotton Creek getting away with breaking into houses and hurting people and now he's into burning down houses. That's my input!" She dropped into the chair he had designated.

Tori pushed the door shut and relocked it. She poured a mug

of coffee without asking and set it in front of Martha. She moved the cream and sugar closer to her before sitting again.

Martha's smile softened her expression. "Thank you, dear." She turned her attention back to the two men and raised an eyebrow.

"Tilly, tell me about Mary's stay with you. Martha, if there's anything you noticed, I'd like to hear it, too."

"Mary finally had enough of that cheating spendthrift." Tilly leaned back in her chair and crossed her arms. "She showed up here with her suitcase and asked if she could stay a few days. Of course, I said yes. I refrained from bringing out the champagne because she was embarrassed, and her self-confidence was crushed." Aunt Tilly's lips turned down at the corners with remembrance. "She said she'd changed her will and filed for divorce. Mostly, I let her talk, but she didn't do much of that. We watched a lot of television. Well, I watched. Mary sat there with her mind elsewhere. She'd been here almost a week when she came down with her suitcase and said she needed to go home and hurry Talbert's packing and make sure her things weren't going into his boxes."

Martha shook her head. "I tried cooking her favorite foods. She ate enough to be polite but not enough to keep her going for long."

Derrick stared into his almost empty mug for a minute then eyed the coffee pot before asking, "You think she changed her mind about the divorce?"

Tilly and Martha exchanged looks then both shook their heads. "She left here saying it was her house and if he didn't leave, she'd hurry him up by throwing his things out the door. I thought he had already moved out but he said he came home the night of the accident to find her and her car gone. He's been saying they reconciled, but I don't believe it."

"That doesn't matter one bit." Martha announced. "Haven't you heard? Heyden Whitmore had Talbert served with an eviction notice and demanded restitution or whatever they call it for everything he sold. Evidently Mr. Whitmore's secretary, the woman that's taking the place of the one that took off to take care of her sick mother, found Mary's will misfiled. Don't know whether she still temporary or permanent now."

Derrick raised a questioning eyebrow in Ted's direction.

Tori and her aunt stared at Martha, then Tilly broke into a grin. "I thought Talbert had talked Heyden's secretary into destroying it when he was cheating on Mary and dating her. Evidently she had a few scruples or she wised up to the fact that Talbert was big on promises that he never intended to keep."

Derrick's phone rang. Everyone quieted while he answered. He started to rise but dropped back into the chair. "Take him down to the mercantile and buy him a new pair of pants. Tell him he still owes Ms. Stella a week of sidewalk sweeping and send someone to her shop to recover whatever she trimmed off to patch them. Hopefully, she didn't wash them." He listened for a few minutes. "Make sure he understands that he's not under arrest but keep him at the station until I get there. I'll be a little longer here." After another pause, he said, "Yeah, buy him a burger. He was probably digging in that dumpster hoping to find something to eat." He clicked off his phone with a grin.

"Dumpster Pete found a pair of pants in the bin behind Yum Burgers. Like new except for a big hole in the seat. He took them to Stella Bolton's sewing shop and bargained with her to patch them."

"If the arsonist wasn't in them, how is that going to help? Martha crossed her arms across her breast.

"We'll know more about his size. So far with that ski mask and bulky jacket. We're guessing. And we'll be looking for someone not anxious to sit down. He might even be limping. Dandy tore a pretty big piece of cloth from those pants. He probably got some ass…" He cleared his throat. "Excuse me, ladies. Chances are he got some flesh with it."

He pushed his mug aside and pulled his notebook closer. "The lawyer's name is Heyden Whitmore. Do you know his secretary's name?" He looked at Martha. "The one that left. Is she back in town?"

"Darla Simms. I haven't heard if she's back. All the gossip's been about Talbert blowing his cool because he has to move out. He's still claiming he and Mary reconciled and now he's saying she tore up the new will right in front of him."

"Darla Simms?" He tapped his pen as he stared at his notebook. He picked it up and flipped backward through the pages. He stopped turning and read something. "She's his alibi. He claims to have been with her the night of Mary's accident." His words were spoken slowly as if he were piecing them into a puzzle.

"Why did he need an alibi if it was an accident like the police claim?" Tilly frowned.

"Because you and several other of Mary's friends raised such an uproar, the police did a little more investigating. They didn't just close the case."

Aunt Tilly's cheeks flushed and she looked down into her coffee mug. Evidentially that was exactly what she had thought. After a moment, she lifted her chin, looked Derrick in the eye and asked, "Did he explain what he was doing with Darla if he and Mary had reconciled?"

"According to the report, he was letting her know he had reconciled with his wife and wouldn't be seeing her again."

Martha and Aunt Tilly shared another look. "Well, he didn't stop seeing her very long. In fact, it was mighty soon after Mary died. Did they talk to Darla to confirm his claims?"

Derrick shook his head. "She had left town to take care of her sick mother."

"So it's probably another of his tall tales or if I'm going to call it like it is, another lie."

"That hussy," Martha said. "Dating a married man. Wouldn't be surprised if Talbert talked her into getting rid of Mary's will. I think she was hedging her bets by misfiling the will instead of destroying it. She must have gotten suspicious with Mary dying and him wanting the new will to go missing."

"Hold on, Martha. There's no proof Mary's death was anything other than an accident. You don't want to get sued for slander," Ted cautioned, breaking into the conversation.

Martha and Aunt Tilly both glared at the officer. Aunt Tilly cleared her throat and broke the silence. "Mary didn't drive at night. Period. Something about her eyesight. Check with Dr. Marsten, her ophthalmologist. And she did not drive in the rain and rarely rode as a passenger when it was raining. When she was a teenager, her mother was killed in a car accident caused by heavy rain conditions. She was in the back seat and couldn't get out until another motorist saw the vehicle off the road and called for help. She was there for a while with her mother dead in the front seat."

"Okay. You've made your point. We'll talk to Darla Simms and we'll see what Heyden Whitmore can to tell us." Derrick pushed his chair back and Ted followed suit. "I've got a man being held at the station that I need to question. I don't know how much longer the inspector from the fire department will be, but we are through. You can go ahead and call your insurance agent and get started with repairs and cleanup when they're finished.

Chapter Twenty-Four

Tori stood beside her aunt on the front porch and looked down at the large black patch. The rainy week had coaxed green sprigs to dot the evidence of what could have been. The porch and rail had been repaired but the weather had prevented the bare wood from being painted. Dandy wiggled beside her and nudged her hand.

"I know, boy." Tori stroked down his back. "It's been a tough week waiting for something else to happen." She moved to the swing and sat. The edge of it had been scorched but not burned. A little sanding and paint would fix that. Dandy remained by the steps as if on guard.

With a sigh, Aunt Tilly turned and settled in her rocker. She pulled her blue sweater from Forest Hills closed to ward off the chill of the damp day. Mindy followed, secured by her leash. Aunt Tilly bent and scooped the little dog into her lap. "I know, you're insulted because you are on a leash and Dandy is free to roam but you're the home guard and Dandy is the attack force." She rested her head against the tall back of the rocker.

"At least we haven't had to put up with Talbert after that altercation in the restaurant. He must be busy packing, too, with that eviction notice. I hope Heyden has someone supervising that packing. But I am curious as to what he wanted to look for. I assumed it was Mary's will so he could destroy it. But he claimed Mary tore it up in front of him. I'm sure that was another one of his lies. It must have him upset that Darla only misfiled Mary's will." She chuckled. "A blow to his ego, too that he hadn't charmed her into destroying it."

They sat for a few minutes. The silence broken by the chirp of birds nesting in the large maple that would be shading the front yard if the sun were out. "But we haven't seen Derrick either. Ted has called again to see how Dandy was doing after being maced but wouldn't answer my questions about the case." Tori added.

A patrol car approached and slowed as it rolled by the house. The officers returned Aunt Tilly's and Tori's waves. Dandy stood long enough to woof at the vehicle then sat, ears perked and alert. Aunt Tilly smiled at the dog and asked, "You think Carl would let us keep Dandy?"

When Tori had brought Dandy home almost two weeks ago, she had stressed to her aunt that he was a temporary dog. She'd been wondering the same since the arsonist had tried to burn down the house. "I don't know how happy Dandy would be in a fenced back yard. He's had a whole farm to run around," she said.

"We could give him a T-bone steak a couple of times a week."

Tori's responding laugh made her feel better. "That's what we need, a fat watchdog. It would probably limit his jumping over the fence though." Her phone buzzed and she looked at the screen. "I guess we're about to see Derrick. He just texted he's coming over with lunch." She smiled. "Must be missing your cookies."

"I hope he's bringing good news with him."

Tori nodded in agreement. "Someone under arrest would be great."

Mindy jumped off Aunt Tilly's lap and stretched to the end of her leash. Dandy stood with a woof and a tail wag.

Tori looked down the street and saw Derrick's Ford approaching. Could Mindy tell it was Derrick by the sound of his car? And a block away? Better to think that than they had a psychic pup.

As Derrick parked his car and climbed out, Tori gave Dandy the command, "Stay."

He wiggled his body and shifted his weight but remained at the top of the steps.

Derrick retrieved a bag and a flat white box from his back seat and grinned as he walked to the porch. His tiredness showed in his face and the set of his shoulders. "What a greeting. It would be even better if the women were as excited as the dogs."

"Humph. We don't have tails to wag, but if you've come to say you have our fire starter in jail, we can jump up and down. Well, Tori can. I'll have to settle for waving my cane in the air."

"Sorry, no." He shook his head and gave a tired smile. "I'd probably be jumping with you. One of our officers had to make a trip to Forest hills. I had him pick up sandwiches." He lifted a bag. "And stop by that bakery." He nodded to the box he cradled in his arm. "Cost me extra sandwiches and pastries, but if they're as good as last time, it's worth it."

"The smells coming from that bag have more than Dandy's mouth watering." Tori laughed as she held the door open for her aunt and Derrick. Mindy led the way and Dandy followed, sniffing hopefully at the brown sack.

Derrick put the food on the table.

"Tea or coffee?" Aunt Tilly opened the dishwasher and placed clean glasses on the counter.

"Tea sounds good with the sandwiches but some of your coffee would go great with the pastries later." He stooped down and rubbed both dogs on their heads. When Mindy started sniffing at his pocket, he laughed and gave both dogs a treat. He stood as Tori put three glasses of tea down near the food while Tilly started a pot of coffee. "Ted is going to join us."

She turned from scooping grounds into the filter and raised a brow. "So this isn't just a social call?"

The doorbell chimed before he could answer. Tori went to let Ted in.

"I've been bribed with lunch to come." He grinned as he entered carrying a small kit. "Not that I needed a bribe, but I can always hope Tilly's cookies will be dessert."

"Nope." Tori said as they entered the kitchen. "We are being treated with delicious pastries from Betsy's Bakery in Forest Hills, but I'm sure Aunt Tilly is willing to serve cookies if you prefer."

Dandy's tail wagged his whole back end as he rushed to greet Ted.

"You won't even think about my cookies after eating one of those pastries," Tilly said carrying a fourth glass of tea to the table and taking a seat.

"That's a preposterous statement." Ted took off his uniform jacket and hung it over the back of his chair.

"Well, sit." Tilly waved him into the chair. "Derrick was just about to tell us the real reason for your visit." She eyed the sandwiches Derrick had taken out of the bag. "Soon as he finishes passing around our food."

Derrick handed everyone a sandwich, sauce and order of

fries. He unwrapped his and took several bites. Tilly was evidently willing to wait as she dug in, too. Most of her sandwich was gone when she looked at Derrick and raised a brow.

Derrick reluctantly put down the fry he had started to pop into his mouth and answered. "We believe the pants Dumpster Pete found belonged to the arsonist. There's a smudge of soot and a trace of gasoline around the bottom of the left leg. We were able to retrieve the fabric Ms. Stella cut from the pants when she patched them. We'd like to get a DNA sample from Dandy if you'll agree."

"Of course we'll agree. Well, Tori and I will agree. I'm not sure Dandy will."

Derrick picked up his fry again. "That's why I asked Ted to come along. Dandy might cooperate for him."

Tori glanced at the large brown dog lying beside Mindy. "If he won't, we can give Carl a call." She took a couple of bites of her sandwich and asked, "Did you learn anything about the guy from the pants? Any DNA?"

Derrick shook his head. "Not much. We have a better idea of his size. The pants were men's and high quality, but they are a popular brand so I don't think we can trace where they might have been bought. We're waiting on the DNA report."

"We've checked with doctors and hospitals." Ted added then chuckled. "We are on the lookout for someone who doesn't want to sit down."

"Tilly scoffed, "So nothing again."

"Nothing yet, ma'am, but we're looking at every lead." Ted shook his head as he stirred a fry in ketchup.

It took three tries to convince Dandy the swab Ted was sticking in his mouth was not a treat to chew up. It wasn't a game he was enjoying either. But when Ted finally jerked an unchewed swab from his mouth and gave him several treats and a large chew bone, he forgave the humans of their shenanigans.

***

Aunt Tilly slowly climbed the stairs, tightly gripping the banister and using her cane. Tori followed, ready to catch or assist if she faltered. "Aunt Tilly, I'm sure I can find your safe if you give me directions."

"Time I started using stairs instead of a ramp all the time." She paused and took a deep breath. "Don't remember there being so many of them though."

"You could have started with the steps to the porch."

"Humph," was her aunt's only comment. At the top, she paused again. "I may do a sit and scoot to get back down." She chuckled. "That's how you used to do it." She started down the hall then stopped and turned toward her former bedroom door. "You should be using my old room with the adjoining bath. More convenient than trotting down the hall to use the facilities or get a shower."

"I figured you would be moving back into it as soon as you can manage the stairs."

"Being so close to the kitchen and the television is handy and I've gotten used to my tiny room."

Tori grinned at her comment. The converted bedroom was probably as big as this room if not a little larger.

We'll get someone to move your things in here." She looked at the floor. "We'll get the carpet replaced first."

"There's no need for that." Tori started to argue.

Her aunt turned and gave her a hard stare. "You still plan on staying or you had enough cooking lessons?"

Surprised by the question, Tori stared back at Aunt Tilly. "I'm planning on staying if it's still okay with you."

"Then we'll go looking at carpet samples tomorrow and maybe some paint for the walls," she replied in a no-nonsense tone and continued down the hall to the door leading up to the attic. "Now get your grandmother's jewelry and come on. Can't believe you've been hiding it under your mattress with all the attempts someone has made to break-in. If I hadn't been pushed down my stairs long before you came, I'd be thinking that's what they're after."

Tori trotted obediently down the hall to the bedroom she had been occupying and quickly returned with a small green pouch.

Aunt Tilly opened the door to the attic and leaned over, pressing under the edge of the third step. Tori's eyes widened as her aunt lifted and the top of the step swung up on hinges. "Here hand me that jewelry and I'll close it and show you where to press to open it when you want to get in here." She dropped the bag containing Tori's jewelry into the metal lined space. She started to close the lid and stopped. "What is this?" She lifted a large manilla envelope from the safe.

A frown creased her forehead as she pried open the clasp and pulled out the pages. The top page was a handwritten note. Aunt Tilly's face paled and she wobbled a bit as she recognized Mary's handwriting.

Tori put her hand out to support her aunt. "What is it?"

Tilly started to read aloud, *"I'm sorry about invading your space, Tilly. I saw you with it open one day and crept back downstairs. It took a while, but I finally figured out how to open your secret compartment. If you find this and I'm not alive, take it to the police. My death—"*

An explosion rattled the window at the end of the hall and vibrated the floorboards. The alarm screaming and the dogs barking simultaneously sent a stab of fear through Tori's chest. Aunt Tilly dropped the papers into the compartment and slammed the top shut. Tori grabbed her phone from her pocket and dialed 911.

"Get these dogs back or I'm going to shoot them." The roar of a familiar voice came from the first floor.

Tori held the phone out to her aunt and turned toward the stairs, but her aunt grabbed her sleeve. "No, Tori. I love those dogs but don't go down there."

"What's your emergency?" a female voice enquired through the cellphone.

"A break-in at Tilly Statton's." Tori answered then pushed the phone into her aunt's hand. "Talk to her." She jerked away and rushed downstairs.

Tori froze just inside the kitchen. The backdoor was busted inward. Glass was shattered across the floor. Talbert stood outside on the porch, a gas can by his feet. He jerked the gun in her direction and yelled through the opening. "I'm coming in. Call your dogs off or I'll be stepping over their dead bodies."

Dandy crept forward, the ruff on his neck standing up. Mindy stood her ground and barked.

"Talbert, what are you doing? Are you crazy?" Her voice shook as she yelled over the noise of the alarm.

“Call them off and give me the papers Mary left here.” He shouted. H stepped through the door and pointed his gun toward Dandy who was ready to spring.

A shotgun blast sounded. Talbert screamed. He dropped his pistol and grabbed his thigh as Dandy leaped, flattening Talbert on his back. The dog stood on the man’s chest, teeth bared inches from his throat.

“Guard!” Tori shouted, hoping Dandy wouldn’t finish his attack and sink teeth into the man who had been breaking into their house. She clenched her fists. Tori wanted him to bite Talbert but not on his throat.

Charlie came running up. “Dang. Missed again. Wouldn’t have happened with Pa’s gun.”

“Call that dog off.” Talbert’s voice rose an octave with each word. “He bit my leg. I’m going to sue.”

Tilly arrived as sirens sounded in the distance. She hobbled across the room and snatched Charlie’s gun from his hand. “Looks to me like you got him.”

“Not what I was aiming for.” Charlie muttered, disgruntled.

Tilly headed for the laundry room, gabbing her own gun from its place against the wall as she went.

When she re-entered the kitchen several minutes later, pounding started at the front door as two officers cautiously moved up the steps to the back porch with guns drawn. Tilly gripped the countertop with one hand and leaned on her cane as Tori pivoted and ran to open the front door. She flipped the lock and pulled it open.

Two officers entered with tentative movements and guns drawn.

Tori pointed toward the kitchen. “Talbert Hatchett is on the floor with a large dog guarding him. He blasted in our back door.”

They moved down the hall scanning each room as they went.

Tori wanted to run back to Aunt Tilly, but she slowed and followed the officers. The alarm silenced. Tori breathed a sigh of relief. Aunt Tilly must have turned it off. She could hear Talbert shouting. “Shoot that dog. He bit me.”

When they entered the kitchen, one officer had his gun aimed at Talbert. The other had secured the pistol in an evidence bag and was attempting to call Dandy off Talbert's chest. He straightened and looked at Tori. "Ma-am, if you would call the dog off."

"Dandy, good boy. Come." She started to move closer, but one of the other officers raised his arm to bar her.

"Not too close, Ma-am."

Tori stopped and repeated her command. "Dandy, come! Good dog. Come." Release and guard were the commands Carl had told her. She'd stuck the list of other commands Trudy had given in her purse after giving it a quick scan and hadn't looked at it again. What did she need to say so the dog would relinquish his prisoner to the police? She tried again. "Dandy, come here! Release!" This time the dog at least turned his head toward Tori. "Good boy. Come." She repeated the command, "Release." The dog turned his attention back to his prisoner and growled then hopped off Talbert's stiff body and walked to Tori. She knelt and hugged him as he licked her face. She rubbed the slobber from her cheek and praised him again. "Good dog."

She grabbed hold of Dandy's collar and stood. Charlie was helping her aunt into a chair at the table. Mindy was clutched in her arms. Talbert lay on his back, feet in the doorway, hands cuffed in front of him. Derrick and Ted Morrow had arrived. Derrick squatted beside Talbert examining his thigh as Talbert continued to shout, "That dog bit me."

Derrick stood. "The EMTs are on their way. When he stops screaming, read him his rights." He turned a stern face toward Tilly. "Where is your shotgun?"

Tilly pointed toward the laundry room. "Behind the door."

Derrick retrieved the gun and cocked it open as he moved back into the kitchen. "No bullets?"

"You took 'em."

He pierced Tilly with a look then sniffed the gun. "Doesn't seem to have been fired," he said in a relieved voice.

"Tori and I were upstairs when he blew our door away. By the time I got down here," she pointed at Talbert, "Dandy had ended that crook's shenanigans." Hearing his name, Dandy tugged toward her.

Clinging to Dandy's collar, Tori moved with him to stand by her aunt. "I ran down because he was shouting and threatening to shoot the dogs. When I got here, Dandy was going for him."

Derrick's face paled and his hands tightened around the shotgun when she said she ran down. He opened his mouth but shut it without saying anything. He turned to Charlie.

Charlie threw up his hands. "Hey. I heard a blast and came running. By the time I got through the gate, that guy," he pointed toward Talbert, "was yelling and waving a gun." He narrowed his eyes at Derrick. "I needed my Pa's gun. Dandy is a hero."

The chaos finally ended and Talbert was hauled off to jail via the hospital. Martha was allowed into the house. Bill and Charlie had gathered boards and plywood from various neighbors and secured the back doorway. George, the waiter at Ed's Eating Place, had arrived with food, though no one had eaten much.

"I think you two should stay at the hotel until you get that repaired." Derrick tilted his head toward the boards blocking the back entrance.

Tori shook her head. "We've got two dogs to take care of."

"I can take them home with me." Ted offered.

Both Tori and Tilly shook their heads. Tilly added, "You've got that scallawag in jail." She pointed her finger at Derrick. "You keep him there and we're safe. And we've got Mindy and Dandy to protect us even if you did claim you had to take Hank's grandpa's gun to make sure it hadn't been fired."

"You and Charlie will both get your shotguns back after Talbert's trial." Derrick gave Tilly a lopsided smile that almost looked like a grimace.

Martha pushed her chair back and started clearing plates. "We never did get a chance to aim that gun at Talbert. Guess it's a good thing since he had his own firearm." As she reached to take Tori's half-full plate, she was startled as Tilly straightened and banged a fist on the table.

"Dang. I plumb forgot! Tori," she turned to her niece, "go get those papers of Mary's that we found. Front lefthand corner." She cued Tori in on how to open the hidden compartment.

Chapter Twenty-Five

"Talbert's in jail and charged with breaking and entering, attacks on you two," Derrick nodded toward Tilly and Tori, "arson and property damage. We threw in trespassing for good measure." He held up his hand before they could comment. "But he's claiming he was out front tapping in your phone number to ask if he could come in. When he heard an explosion, he grabbed the gun he keeps in his car and ran to the backdoor where the sound had come from. The big dog attacked him before he had a chance to make sure you were alright."

He raised a brow as his gaze traveled from face to face and settled on Tilly. "A dog bite?"

She returned Derrick's stare. "I was upstairs talking to the 911 operator. Took me a while to get down. I missed the whole shebang. And," she put her hands on her hips. "You checked my gun and said it hadn't been fired."

"Charlie...?"

"Said you haven't given him back his Pa's shotgun," Tilly said with satisfaction.

Derrick turned toward Tori.

If her shotgun had been leaning against the wall, I might have grabbed it. I don't know how to shoot a gun but Talbert was threatening to shoot Mindy and Dandy. With all the commotion, I can't say I saw Dandy bite him, but...if you check other parts of his anatomy," color tinged her cheeks, "Dandy evidently got a good chomp when he tried to burn down Aunt Tilly's house."

Derrick picked up his cup of coffee. "That has been checked out. The pants Dumpster Pete found have Talbert's DNA and the fabric Stella cut away to patch the pants has traces of Dandy's saliva. The partial print he left with the hole in his glove says he was in your house searching through things until Tori arrived and changed the locks."

"What about those papers that Mary left here?"

"We are still investigating before we file charges on that information. He's evidently been stealing from his clients for several years. That yellow sports car he drives is probably what alerted Mary that something was going on. Talbert thought he had charmed Darla Simms into destroying the copy of the new will in Whitmore's office, but she decided to hedge her bets and misfile it. When Mary died in that accident, she got scared and left town with the excuse that her mother was sick. She evidently knew Mary didn't drive when it was raining because she had canceled appointments with Whitmore when the weather was bad. We think Mary must have said something to Talbert about having proof he was embezzling from his clients and that's what he was looking for when he broke into your house." He shrugged. "Seems one of the client's he was stealing from is the grandson of a Chicago mobster who isn't feeling kindly about his grandson losing money. We followed up with Betty and other staff at Ed's Eating Place about those cousins who joined Talbert for lunch. Seems they were sent by granddad to deliver a message. It made him more desperate to find the proof Mary had. He bargained to repay the losses when he inherited Mary's millions, but the gangster granddad wouldn't be understanding with the truth. Stealing from a client is a lot worse than losing their money on bad investments. Talbert needed to make sure Mary's papers didn't fall into the mobster's hands. A life or death matter."

"What about Mary's accident?"

"Darla Simms has denied Talbert's alibi that she was with him, but I'm afraid there's no evidence that says it was anything but an accident."

A woof and a couple of yaps at the replaced backdoor broke the silence that followed his statement. Tori stood and let the two dogs in.

"You still have Dandy?" He rubbed the big dog's head and leaned over to pet Mindy then reached into the pocket Dandy was sniffing and gave each a treat.

Tori nodded. "When Carl heard Dandy had saved our lives a second time," she didn't mention it was with the help of Charlie's grandpa's gun, "he agreed to let us keep him. We'll take him out to the farm every so often and let him run. Aunt Tilly plans to show him a T-bone steak before we make the trip."

Derrick chuckled at that. He rubbed his hand down the back of his head as he turned his face to Tori. "Now that this case is closed or will be as soon as Talbert goes to trial, and your aunt has two dogs to protect her..." he paused a moment looking uncertain. "How about a dinner date?"

Martha gave Tori a wink and exchanged grins with Tilly.

The end.

About the Author

Janie Dean grew up in the south on a family acreage with her brothers and with a large extended family nearby. Even as a child, she read mysteries and played mystery games that let her imagination run wild. After receiving a bachelor's degree, she ventured from the south and pursued a master's degree at a college in the Northeast and then job opportunities out west. Her husband's work took her and her children overseas which led to many new experiences in foreign places.

Recently, she resettled from Florida to Colorado to be near family. Throughout her experiences she has written stories. Still enjoying mystery and intrigue, her passion continues through her cozy mystery stories.

www.ingramcontent.com/pod-product-compliance
Lightning Source LLC
LaVergne TN
LVHW012049160826
845678LV00014B/2759

* 9 7 9 8 8 4 2 6 1 8 3 0 9 *